DEAD
FALL

Books by Nancy Mehl

ROAD TO KINGDOM

Inescapable
Unbreakable
Unforeseeable

FINDING SANCTUARY

Gathering Shadows
Deadly Echoes
Rising Darkness

DEFENDERS OF JUSTICE

Fatal Frost
Dark Deception
Blind Betrayal

KAELY QUINN PROFILER

Mind Games
Fire Storm
Dead End

THE QUANTICO FILES

Night Fall
Dead Fall

DEAD FALL

NANCY MEHL

BETHANYHOUSE

a division of Baker Publishing Group
Minneapolis, Minnesota

Published by Bethany House Publishers
11400 Hampshire Avenue South
Bloomington, Minnesota 55438
www.bethanyhouse.com

Bethany House Publishers is a division of
Baker Publishing Group, Grand Rapids, Michigan

Printed in the United States of America

Library of Congress Cataloging-in-Publication Data
Names: Mehl, Nancy, author.
Title: Dead fall / Nancy Mehl.
Description: Minneapolis, MN : Bethany House Publishers, a division of Baker
    Publishing Group, [2021] | Series: The Quantico files ; 2
Identifiers: LCCN 2021023578 | ISBN 9780764237645 (paperback) | ISBN
    9780764239403 (hardcover) | ISBN 9781493433803 (ebook)
Subjects: GSAFD: Mystery fiction. | Suspense fiction.
Classification: LCC PS3613.E4254 D423 2021 | DDC 813/.6—dc23
LC record available at https://lccn.loc.gov/2021023578

Scripture quotations are from THE HOLY BIBLE, NEW INTERNATIONAL VERSION®, NIV® Copyright © 1973, 1978, 1984, 2011 by Biblica, Inc.® Used by permission. All rights reserved worldwide.

Cover design by Studio Gearbox

Author is represented by The Steve Laube Agency.

Baker Publishing Group publications use paper produced from sustainable forestry practices and post-consumer waste whenever possible.

21 22 23 24 25 26 27   7 6 5 4 3 2 1

To Brandon Brotton,
an exceptional young man who loves God and
promised me he'd try harder in his English classes.
Brandon, I'll make you a character in one of my books when
your parents say you're old enough to read them, okay?
In the meantime, keep giving it your best.
I'm so proud of you!

Those in law enforcement pay a heavy price when they constantly look into the dark minds of evil.

JOHN DAVIS, *DARK MINDS*

1

John Davis turned up the collar on his jacket as he swiftly walked away from the shrill voices bleeding through from the hotel banquet hall behind him. March certainly wasn't going out like a lamb. This last blast of cold weather was intense.

He took a quick look behind him. If he didn't make a fast getaway, he'd be stopped by some convention attendee asking him for advice on how to get their book published. Or even worse, begging for help finding the person who murdered their child, husband, wife, brother, sister, or parent. Over the years, the darkness in the eyes of the grieving had taken a toll on him.

He'd just turned seventy-six. Maybe it was time to stop speaking to groups full of people who thought murder was somehow exciting. Who believed they could learn behavioral analysis during a three-day convention. He'd been at this since his early days at the FBI, when profiling was just an experiment. Now, thanks to television shows and movies that romanticized the process, everyone and their dog thought they could understand the evil that festered in the hearts of certain human beings.

Although statistics and analysis helped to narrow down possibilities so law enforcement had a better chance at find- ing violent criminals, those procedures couldn't explain the kind of malevolence they witnessed. As a Christian, he knew where true evil came from, but that knowledge didn't banish the images that burned in his mind. The ones that showed up in his nightmares.

He took the key card he needed to enter the building that housed the hotel's guest rooms from his pocket. Before he fit it into the card slot, he thought he heard someone behind him. A quick look around showed no one. Just his imagina- tion. Why was he so rattled? He'd been uneasy ever since he'd arrived in Bethesda.

John entered the building and made sure the outer door behind him clicked shut and locked. He hurried to the eleva- tor and more than once punched the button to the third floor as if it would somehow make the elevator move faster. When it finally arrived, he hurried inside and pressed the button to close the door. He didn't want anyone riding up with him.

The elevator had just started to move when his cell phone rang. It was one of the Murder Will Out convention organiz- ers and speakers, a successful suspense author he respected. This guy got it right. Few writers did. Some of the things included in novels made John cringe. In fact, he'd publicly criticized several of them. But not D. J. Harper. John recom- mended his books to those who wanted a real look into the lives of behavioral analysts.

"Hi, D. J.," he said into his phone.

"Hey. You were great tonight. Thanks again for coming."

"You're welcome. You've done a great job with this group. This convention's larger every year."

D. J. laughed. "Sure, because you show up. You're the main event, you know. The FBI's most renowned profiler."

D. J. was being humble. He had a huge readership, and after every convention his book sales rocketed well beyond John's own. Seemed to be a win-win situation for them both.

"What can I do for you?" John asked, hoping there wasn't anything. He was so tired his bones hurt. He just wanted to lie down and close his eyes.

"I thought I'd ask if you'd like a nightcap. We've been working so hard that we haven't had much time to talk."

John couldn't hold back a sigh as he exited the elevator and headed down the hall. "I'd love to, D. J., but I just can't. Not even for you. I'm beat."

"I understand completely. As the years go by, it gets harder and harder to keep up with all these young, eager fans. I'm getting by on fumes as it is. Hey, by the way, a rather odd guy asked to meet you. I told him you weren't available for personal meetings. Just wanted to warn you."

"There's always at least one, isn't there?"

D. J. chuckled. "You're right. Some people get so entrenched in this stuff that it warps them."

"I worry about that."

"I do too, but it sells books. Hard to walk away from that." He paused for a moment. "Ever wonder if we've sold our souls?"

"Every day."

John was almost to his room when a group of people got off

the elevators at the other end of the hall. They were dressed up, so they were probably coming from the semiformal dinner that was the last event of the convention. He hurried to slip into his room before they saw him, but he didn't make it.

"Mr. Davis," a woman in the group called out. "We really enjoyed your lectures this weekend."

John nodded and tossed her a smile before sliding his card into the key slot. He was happy to hear the door unlock. Thankful to be free, he quickly stepped inside and closed the door behind him. The final click caused him to nearly groan with relief.

"Hey, sorry I rushed out after my speech," John said into the phone. "Hope I didn't come off as a snob."

D. J. laughed. "Nah. Just the regular disappointed groupies who wanted a chance to talk to you. They'll get over it."

John sat down on the side of his bed. "I had the strangest feeling after leaving the banquet hall. I . . . I can't really explain it. Almost like someone was watching me. I guess I'm letting my professional life bleed over into my real life."

"Too many meetings, too many serial killers."

"Yeah, you're probably right."

D. J. grunted. "If our fans only knew the truth. But no one wants to hear that. The carnage. The twisted facts that make you want to puke."

"Nothing exciting about looking at photos of young women slaughtered by one of these psychopaths. Most television shows and novels aren't honest. They portray us as heroes and the UNSUBs as inhuman. But the frightening thing is they *are* human. Some can fit neatly into society so that no one knows what they really are. Some of the people here tonight could be working next to a monster and not know it."

"You're thinking of Ted Bundy."

"That's the kind of killer that scares me the most. The ones who can't connect to society? They're easier to find. Sometimes I wonder how many Bundys are out there. Making friends. Gaining trust. Just waiting for an opportunity to . . ." He sighed. "Sorry. I'm babbling. I'm just so tired tonight. Truthfully? I'm too tired every night. It might be time for me to go home and spend what time I have left with my family."

"You do what you need to do, John. You've given enough."

"Thanks. I appreciate that."

Maybe D. J. was right. These things sucked the life out of him. His speeches were whitewashed versions of the truth. People wanted *nice* killers. Stories you could repeat in polite society. Some of the more sordid facts stayed in the minds of law enforcement, lurking in the recesses of their thoughts, sometimes trying to claw their way out, overthrowing the idea of a sane and sensible world. A world where redemption still existed.

"Thanks for the call, D. J., but I've got to hit the hay. I'm out of here first thing in the morning. I have an eight a.m. flight."

"I could meet you for breakfast. You have to eat."

"Maybe. Can I let you know after I get up?"

"Sure. Just call me. No pressure. Hey, thanks again for coming."

"You bet. Talk to you in the morning."

John disconnected the call, D. J.'s words echoing in his head. *"You're the main event, you know."* He'd done thirty of these speaking engagements last year. It was March, and here he was at it again. He was exhausted, inside and out. He had enough money, and his ego didn't need more attention. He'd made his mark. So why keep going?

He took off his jacket and tossed it over a nearby chair. He'd told housekeeping not to clean the room but to leave fresh towels. He checked, and sure enough his used towels were gone and new ones had been left in their place. He noticed that a tray from breakfast was still on the table. He'd assumed they'd take it, but it seemed they took it literally when he said towels only. He thought about putting the tray in the hallway, but he might run into another excited convention fan. He decided to just leave it on the table. The cleaning staff would get it tomorrow after he left.

He grabbed his sweats out of his suitcase. He'd hung up his convention clothes, but everything else stayed packed. Faster and easier when he was ready to check out.

After a quick shower, John grabbed his cell phone. Sometimes Susan wanted to video chat so she could tell him how much she missed him. He needed to hear that now. He just wanted to go home to Houston and sit by her side on the couch with the fireplace crackling in the background as they drank hot cocoa and watched a funny movie. He was at peace then. The demons quieted. The flashes of horror stayed buried.

He called Susan using the new app he'd recently downloaded. He'd been sent an offer for a free three-month trial. If he decided to keep it, the cost was surprisingly low, and it was supposed to be better than Zoom. It not only allowed you to see the person you were talking to but recorded the video in case you wanted to replay it later. He'd accepted the offer only because he missed Susan so much when he was gone.

When she answered, he saw her beautiful face smiling at him. Her warm voice filled his ear.

"I love this new video calling program," she said, "but I'd like to see you too. Isn't it supposed to work both ways?"

"Sorry. I haven't figured out the problem yet. You know I'm useless when it comes to technology. I'll ask Brandt to look at it when I get home. I'm sure he'll take pity on his clueless grandfather and show me how to work this thing."

They chatted for a few minutes before John told her he had to get some sleep. "I can't wait to be home. I love you."

They always ended their calls the same way. He waited for Susan's "I love you more" before hanging up.

He put down his phone, but then he decided to check his email. He found nothing vital, but one message's subject line—in all caps—caught his attention: *John. Read this. Important.* He thought about ignoring it, but curiosity got the better of him. It was probably from a Nigerian prince telling him he would get millions of dollars if he helped the man transfer his billions, but John had to know just what was so important to someone. He opened it and read the message: *Those in law enforcement pay a heavy price when they constantly look into the dark minds of evil.*

It was a quote from his book *Dark Minds.* John shook his head and exited his account. Someone playing games. Probably another serial killer groupie trying to impress him. It had happened many times before.

John got up and made sure the door was locked, then flipped the metal swing bar closed as well. As he turned around he noticed an envelope on the floor. A bill? He picked it up. He wasn't paying for his room. The people in charge of the convention were picking up the tab. He opened it anyway and found a page from a book folded inside. He walked over to the bed and sat down. The lamp on the nightstand was still on, and he held the paper under the light. It was a page from *Dark Minds*. What was going on?

Three sentences were underlined in red. *In those early days, I worked with several great agents. The success we had didn't belong to one person. We were a team, each agent bringing his special skills to our efforts.* He turned the page over and found a numeral scrawled on the back, but he had no idea what it meant.

John frowned. He was getting irritated. Tomorrow he'd talk to the people in charge of the convention as well as the hotel manager. They shouldn't have allowed this to happen. But as he thought about it, he sighed. It wasn't anyone's fault. The hotel was full, and management couldn't watch every single guest. Neither could the organizers watch every attendee. He should be used to it. At least a dozen times he'd had to contact the police for help against people who'd felt compelled to get involved in his life. Who thought they knew him since they'd read his books. He prayed this wasn't another stalker. If anything else unusual happened tonight, he'd call the manager and let him know.

But right now all he wanted was sleep. He was safely locked inside his room. This situation only served to reinforce his new commitment to stay home with Susan and enjoy whatever years they had left together. Maybe God was sending him a message, confirming what he felt in his heart.

He put the envelope with the page inside on the nightstand, then got up and opened the long drapes that covered the large glass windows stretching across the wall on the other side of the room. Good, a full moon was out, and the hotel property had some outdoor lights too. He never slept in the dark. Hadn't for years. Not since he'd learned what can lurk there. He also didn't like feeling closed in. He mentally acknowledged the moon's beauty, but tonight his soul was too deadened to really appreciate it. He turned off every light in his room, then climbed into bed and lay on his back, staring up at the ceiling. He'd decided. This would definitely be his last speaking engagement. He'd cancel the rest.

He was just dozing off when his phone rang. Thinking it might be Susan, he rolled onto his side. When he saw her name on the screen, he answered.

Supervisory Special Agent Alex Donovan was closing out the paperwork on the most recent case she'd worked for the Behavioral Analysis Unit at Quantico. A violent rapist had been caught in Oregon and would be spending the rest of his life in prison. Every time she and her fellow agents helped law enforcement capture criminals by creating profiles that narrowed down the field of suspects, Alex felt great satisfaction. She knew some women would live long, safe lives because of the work the BAU did. She was so thankful to be here. This was all she wanted to do.

She kept glancing toward the hallway that led to their unit chief's office. This morning Jefferson Cole was meeting with a new member of their BAU team, but Alex wasn't the only one distracted by that. Word had spread that Kaely Quinn, an agent once part of the BAU, had returned. Kaely was almost a legend. Her father had been an especially notorious serial killer, and her unusual ways of profiling had caused a previous unit chief to push her out. After spending several years in a field office in St. Louis, she'd recently been approved by the FBI Career Board to rejoin the BAU.

Alex was a big fan of Kaely's. Even though she hadn't been allowed to work officially as a behavioral analyst in St. Louis, Kaely had been instrumental in closing quite a few troublesome cases. Alex was excited to meet her and learn more about her methods.

"You're gonna get a crick in your neck if you don't stop staring toward the boss's office," someone said from behind her. Alex jumped, then looked up to see SSA Logan Hart grinning down at her.

"Funny," she said softly. "Are you telling me you're not a little excited about meeting her?"

"Not really. I know she has a great reputation, but I'd rather get to know her before I fall down and worship at her feet."

"Also funny. But I'm not worshiping her."

"I'm just teasing. But I do wonder if getting so much attention has given her a big ego. We don't need that here. We're a team."

"I doubt Jeff would have championed her return if he didn't think she'd be an asset. Just keep an open mind."

"How about you do the same? Or do you intend to kiss her ring when you meet her?"

"You're a real comedian this morning, aren't you?"

Logan laughed. "Sorry. All I really care about is that she does good work—and isn't a diva."

Alex snorted. "A BAU diva? What does that look like?"

"I have no idea. I'm sure she'll be fine."

He'd started to walk away when Alex's phone rang. When she answered, she heard the voice of Alice Burrows, Jeff's administrative assistant. "Jeff wants you in the conference room ASAP," she said. "Bring Logan and Monty with you, please." Without another word, she hung up. Alice was a friendly person, not usually so abrupt.

"Hey," Alex said, calling Logan back. She lowered her voice. "Jeff wants us and Monty."

He nodded. "I'll get Monty." Monty Wong was a close friend of theirs, and she respected his ability and tenacity. He talked a lot about his grandmother. They were very close. Even though he joked about her quite a bit, bringing up something funny she'd said or done, it was obvious he adored her. She lived in Burke, Virginia, about twenty minutes from Quantico.

Monty had recently joined Alex and Logan at church. Logan had been inviting him for quite a while, and he was really happy when Monty finally accepted. The three of them always ate out after the service, and Alex enjoyed her time with the two men. They were the closest thing she had to a family, although she was careful not to get too close to them. Working as a team meant keeping your personal life out of the equation. It could get in the way.

She followed Logan as he made his way to Monty's desk, and then the three of them walked down the hallway to the conference room. Jeff sat at the head of the table, and next to him was Kaely Quinn. Alex had seen photos of her, but she'd had no idea how petite the woman really was. FBI agents had to pass several tests of strength and agility, so Kaely had to be strong even though at first glance she didn't look it. Her curly red hair was held back by a hair tie, and her hands were folded on top of the table in front of her.

As Alex sat down, she noticed Jeff's expression. Something

was wrong. The last time they'd met like this they'd ended up facing a serial killer who had almost cost Alex her life. She felt her stomach tighten.

Once everyone was seated, Jeff nodded toward Kaely. "This is Kaely Quinn," he said. "She worked here several years ago and was dismissed from our unit for circumstances beyond her control. I'm pleased to welcome her back."

Alex smiled at Kaely and saw her visibly relax. The previous unit chief, Donald Reinhardt, had left the BAU a few years ago and had been teaching training classes at the academy until recently. He was the one who had forced Kaely out. Alex's memory of him was of a rather imperious man who looked down on almost everyone around him. The stories she heard from other agents made it clear his departure was welcomed.

Jeff introduced the other agents sitting at the table.

"I'm happy to meet you all," Kaely said.

Each agent acknowledged her, and then all eyes focused on Jeff, who seemed hesitant to speak. What was going on? Alex glanced at Logan, who slightly shrugged.

"We've been called in on a death that happened in Bethesda," Jeff finally said. "I want you to meet with the local police. Go over the evidence. Help them find the UNSUB who did this."

"All of us?" Logan asked.

Alex was thinking the same thing. Four analysts seemed like overkill, especially for a single murder case. "Who was killed, Jeff?"

His deep sigh made it clear this was personal. "John Davis. He was speaking at one of those murder-mystery conventions. He spoke on Saturday night, the last night of the convention, and then went back to his room. A friend of his, an author named D. J. Harper, asked someone from the hotel to go into Davis's room Sunday morning when he didn't hear from him and he didn't answer his phone. He was supposed to tell Harper whether he wanted to get together for breakfast before he flew home. Davis was found on his bed. Dead. A knife in his chest."

"We heard he'd died," Logan said. "But it was made to sound as if he'd died of natural causes. Maybe something like a heart attack."

Alex had been saddened when the man's death was announced, and like Logan, she'd assumed he died of some kind of physical problem. But murdered?

John Davis was instrumental in forming the BAU. She'd read every book he'd written about the cases he'd worked. Most books several times. He was almost a father figure to behavioral analysts. He really understood the job. Understood the agents who dealt with crimes they couldn't mention to anyone because they were too awful. Too graphic. She'd also read D. J. Harper's books. Great mystery novels that stayed on point with the facts. He did his research, and it showed.

"The police have kept the circumstances under wraps," Jeff said, "although they may not be able to keep them quiet for long."

"So the police have asked for our help," Logan said, stating the obvious. "I take it they have no suspects?"

"Correct. The door to his hotel room was locked from the inside. No fingerprints on the knife except Davis's. The knife was delivered by room service with his breakfast of steak and eggs early Saturday morning."

"Maybe he was trying to pull the knife out," Alex said.

"If he was, he failed. It was plunged deep into his chest up to the handle."

"Are you trying to tell us Davis killed himself?" Monty asked.

"No one could have entered that room," Jeff said. "Not when it was locked from the inside and on the third floor."

"No balcony?" Kaely asked.

"No. Nor did any of the rooms on either side or above or below have one."

The room was silent as the agents looked at each other.

"What's going on, Jeff?" Alex said slowly. "We don't get called in to help with suicides."

Jeff didn't answer, just turned toward a large TV on the wall. He picked up a remote, pointed it at the screen, and turned it on. Alex stared at the TV, where she saw a screenshot from an email message: *Those in law enforcement pay a heavy price when they constantly look into the dark minds of evil.*

"Davis received this email Saturday night after the close of the convention."

"Do we know who sent it?" Monty asked.

"It's being investigated now, but so far no one's been able to track it."

"I'm fairly certain that's a line from one of Davis's books," Alex said. "It was at the beginning. You know, like an introduction." Alex had practically memorized his books.

Jeff frowned at her. "That's right," he said. He clicked the remote, and a photo of John Davis's body appeared on the screen. He was lying on top of a bed. Alex would have thought he was sleeping except for the knife sticking out of his chest.

"If this was murder, it was personal," Kaely said. "Stabbing someone means you have to get close to them. We all know that kind of killer wants to enjoy the experience, wants to look their victim in the eye and make sure they know why they're going to die. But you're telling us no one was in the room except Davis? Yet you don't think this was suicide?"

"Hang on," Jeff said. He clicked the remote again, and another image that looked like a page from a book came on the screen. He enlarged it so it could be easily read. Some of the sentences had been highlighted: *In those early days, I worked with several great agents. The success we had didn't belong to one person. We were a team, each agent bringing his special skills to our efforts.*

"That's also from Davis's book," Alex said. "Where did this come from?"

"It was in an envelope on the nightstand. The police suspect someone shoved it under Davis's door."

Alex shook her head and stared at Jeff. "So the police want us to go to Bethesda and create a profile of someone who can get into locked rooms and kill people? Someone who also likes to quote from Davis's book?" She shook her head. "Are we to consider a ghostly bookworm?"

The sides of Jeff's mouth quirked up. "No, no ghosts. But the police want you to help them find the person responsible. And there's more."

He clicked another button, and a shaky video popped up. Someone was pointing what appeared to be a phone's camera toward a window. Inside the room, a woman sat near a fireplace. She appeared to be reading. Then a deep voice—clearly altered electronically—said, "Thank you for joining me, John. As you can see, I'm here with Susan." Suddenly, the barrel of a gun filled the screen. "I'm a great shot, and if you don't do exactly as I say, your dear wife will die."

The person speaking laughed. It was awful. High-pitched and cold.

"I'm going to count to thirty, and by the time I've finished, you must be dead. Thirty seconds doesn't give you enough time to call your friends at the FBI to help Susan. They'll never make it in time. It just gives you enough time to do what I say. I think by now you realize you're being watched, that I know exactly what you're doing. I want you to die. I want you to know I outsmarted you, so don't try to block my view. Don't try to hide in the bathroom. And don't bother begging for your life. I have no compassion. If you pick up that phone by your bed or do anything except what I've told you to do, Susan dies."

The speaker paused a moment, then began to count. "One . . . two . . . three . . . four . . . five . . . six . . . seven . . ." When the speaker reached the number thirty, the screen went dark.

All four agents sat in stunned silence. Logan had seen some disturbing things in this job, but this was new. It had shaken him to his core. It took everything he had to push back his personal feelings and lean on his training.

"So because of this, we believe Davis found that knife and killed himself?" he asked.

"Any evidence at the scene to suggest otherwise?" Alex added.

"No," Jeff said. "We have to assume John took this threat seriously and ended his own life with the only ready tool he could find—the knife. A knife able to do the job. Our UNSUB might have thought Davis had a gun with him, but Mrs. Davis said he didn't take one when he traveled by air. Too much bother at security checks."

"Davis could see that the UNSUB was outside his house," Monty said slowly. "But how did the UNSUB watch John? Was this like a Zoom call? Could he see John through the phone?"

Jeff shook his head. "No. He couldn't see John on the phone. We have techs looking at it, but it seems this app was set up as a one-way transmission. John could see whoever was on the other end of a call, but they couldn't see him."

"Okay," Kaely said slowly. "I'm guessing the caller spoofed someone's number. . . ."

"Yes," Jeff said. "Davis's wife's."

"So John picks up his phone thinking it's his wife calling. Then he sees this person—probably a man—outside his house with a gun threatening to shoot his wife. The guy gives him thirty seconds to take his own life or his wife dies. Yet the phone isn't set up to show what John's doing." She shook her head. "How in the world could the UNSUB know John obeyed his instructions? That he'd killed himself? He couldn't be in two places at once."

Jeff shrugged. "I can't answer that question. It's possible the UNSUB couldn't see him at all. Maybe that was a lie."

"Do you think John considered that?" Monty asked.

"He'd have to," Kaely said. "But he had only thirty seconds to decide what to do. When you've been given a choice like that, knowing that someone you love could die . . ."

"You don't take any chances," Alex finished for her.

"Right."

"I don't buy it," Logan said. "John Davis was smart. I think he'd have to be convinced he was actually being monitored."

"The police went through the room with a fine-tooth comb," Jeff said. "Couldn't find any cameras. Nothing that could have recorded Davis's last moments."

"What about prints on the envelope or the book page?" Alex asked.

"Nothing, and we're not sure the envelope was shoved

under his door. Maybe someone at the convention gave it to him. The hotel has security cameras, but the two in the hallway outside Davis's room point toward each elevator. No one who didn't belong there is on the tapes. If they used the stairs, a camera wouldn't have picked them up."

"Again," Alex said, "it's not possible this man was at Davis's house and at the hotel at the same time."

"Maybe he had help," Monty said.

Jeff held up his hand. "We don't know how he watched Davis, assuming he really was, but what Davis saw wasn't a live feed. It was a video recorded earlier. So our UNSUB might not have been in Houston when Davis got the call."

When Logan realized what this meant, he almost couldn't grasp it. "You're saying his wife wasn't at risk? That Davis killed himself for nothing?"

"I'm not saying that. She probably wasn't in danger when John saw her life being threatened, but the UNSUB could have gone after her later and made good on his threat."

"But if Davis had realized the truth," Kaely said in almost a whisper, "he could have called the police to go to his home and secure his wife before that could happen. And he wouldn't have had to die."

Jeff was silent as the reality sank into everyone's mind. Finally, he said, "I'm afraid that's true. Mrs. Davis said he wasn't proficient with his phone. If he had been, he might have been able to tell he wasn't watching a live feed." He sighed. "If he hadn't answered the call . . ."

"The UNSUB wasn't taking chances. That's why he spoofed Mrs. Davis's number."

"To ensure John would pick up the phone," Monty said.

"Exactly."

Monty cursed softly.

Logan was having a hard time processing what they were hearing from Jeff. The way Davis died was diabolical and incredibly clever. "So you want all four of us to go to Bethesda to profile this guy?" he asked.

Jeff sighed. "Yeah. I need all of you. The police chief is convinced there will be more deaths. Unfortunately, I agree with him." He nodded at Logan. "You're lead agent on this one."

"You think we have a serial?" Alex asked. Logan could hear the doubt in her voice. Frankly, he felt the same way. The UNSUB appeared to be focused on John Davis, and he was dead. Why would this guy continue killing?

Jeff nodded toward the screen and clicked the remote again. "This is the other side of the book page." Someone had written a large number one.

No one said a word. Jeff was right. This might be only the beginning.

After the meeting, Alex called her neighbor Shirley Stewart. Shirley and her two children took care of Alex's dog when she was called out of town. Krypto, a large, white pit bull, was her closest friend. She'd rescued him after he was dumped at a local shelter. It had taken a lot of love, but his sweet nature was stronger than the sadness that had overwhelmed him for so long. He no longer showed any signs of abuse. Krypto was a happy dog who loved everyone. If this were a long-term assignment, she could have taken him with her. But she could be home by tonight. And she didn't worry about him when he went to the Stewarts' house. They loved him, and he was great with their kids.

Alex hated not being able to say good-bye to Krypto, but she couldn't do anything about that. The Stewarts had a key to her place so they could pick him up when necessary, and her go bag was in the back of her car. It went everywhere with her. That way, if she had to leave on a moment's notice, she was ready without having to run home. Inside she'd packed personal clothes, essentials, her vest and FBI jacket, handcuffs, and ammunition for the gun she wore.

As usual, Shirley was more than happy to keep the big dog. "Of course he can stay here," she gushed. "Maizie has missed him, and so have the kids." She laughed. "Okay, we've all missed him. We all need some Krypto time."

Maizie was the Stewarts' cat. Not long after Alex moved to Quantico, Maizie had escaped from the family's house. They found her later in the day, curled up next to Krypto, who had designated himself her protector. The two were now the best of friends.

"Thanks, Shirley. I might be back tonight, but I'm not sure. I'll call and let you know."

Alex looked at her watch. The kids wouldn't be home from school for a while, but she was certain going straight for Krypto was the first thing they'd do. Alex smiled to herself despite the ache she felt inside every time she left him. He was her only family. She'd felt alone most of her life, but with Logan's help, she'd recently given her life to Christ. She was still learning what that meant. Finding out God was real and that He actually knew her name and loved her was a revelation she was adjusting to. Thanks to church and a weekly Bible study she'd been going to with Logan when they weren't working, she was learning how to trust God little by little.

She still had problems with people, though. She'd never had anyone she could count on. She wanted to let others in, but her instinct was to protect herself. She was grateful that Logan understood why she struggled so much in this area. He knew some of her past, and he was patient with her.

She walked outside with Logan, Kaely, and Monty to the government-owned SUV they'd drive to Bethesda. Black, of course. Logan had once joked that if their vehicles had to be SUVs, at least they should be bright yellow. It was a happier color. She laughed softly at his silly joke. The longer she knew Logan, the more she liked him. He was a great agent as well as a good man.

Her mind drifted to Kaely Quinn. She was excited to be assigned to a case with her. Although Alex shouldn't be intimidated by Kaely, she was. Alex was a good analyst, but Kaely was legendary. Maybe some of the woman's genius would rub off on her.

She hurried to her car and grabbed her bag. Her little blue Volkswagen bug was dwarfed by the huge SUV, and it reminded her of the story of David and Goliath. She had a company vehicle, but she drove her Volkswagen whenever she could. She really loved it.

She joined the others at the SUV. Everyone was there except Monty.

"He's driving himself," Logan said when Alex asked where he was. "He wanted to go by his grandmother's place before meeting us. She hasn't been feeling well, and her house is on the way. Jeff said it was okay as long as he didn't run late to the meeting in Bethesda."

Alex nodded and tossed her bag into the back of the SUV.

"Still can't believe we're working on a case that involves

John Davis," Kaely said. "He was one of my heroes." She frowned. "We can start thinking we're immortal, you know? Smarter than everyone else because we study the behaviors of criminals. But it's the UNSUBs who don't stick to the script that can get to you."

A chill ran up Alex's back. What Kaely said was true. They were first trained as FBI agents. Behavioral analysis was part of the basic training, but those who went on to work for the BAU received more intensive training. It could leave you feeling that you were smarter than the unknown subjects you profiled. But getting lulled into a false sense of security could cost lives.

"The email bothers me," Logan said. "I would have seen it as a threat. Taken it seriously. I would have found some way to arm myself."

"Me too." Kaely shrugged. "We won't know until we hear what the police have, but I agree with you. It seems strange that Davis didn't do that."

"He retired from the FBI a long time ago. Maybe his age and lack of agility cost him."

"That's possible," Alex responded. "Or maybe it was his surroundings. He was probably approached regularly by people who think what we do is exciting. He may have chalked the email up to some fan."

"I agree," Kaely said. "He was in a hotel full of people who found him fascinating. I don't think he would have automatically assumed the person who sent the email was dangerous. And the page in the envelope was simply from one of his books. Not threatening in itself."

Alex sighed. Davis might have been able to figure a way out if he'd acted sooner, but once he was down to thirty seconds, there wasn't anything he could do. Especially with the life of a loved one at stake.

"I'll drive unless someone else wants to," Logan said.

Alex shook her head. "That's fine with me."

"Me too," Kaely said. She smiled at Alex. "You take shotgun. I'll get in the back."

"Sure." Alex climbed into the front with Logan.

Once they were inside, Logan said, "Is everyone ready? No stopping along the way. If anyone needs to go . . ."

The women laughed as he drove out of the parking lot and headed toward the highway.

Alex couldn't help but think about what Logan said. Could age have contributed to John Davis's death? Would she someday find herself outwitted by an UNSUB who wanted to prove his mental superiority? As if the weather were in sync with her mood, the sun slipped behind gray clouds and rain began to make patterns on the tinted windows.

Alex shuddered even though the car was warm. She felt like she was getting ready to face an old adversary but had no idea who it was.

4

When Logan, Alex, and Kaely arrived at the Montgomery County police station, they were led to a conference room toward the back of a busy squad room. Although this would be a joint task force, the police chief wasn't setting up a command post in a separate location. At this time, no other special units would join them. The BAU was just there to provide a profile to help the police track down their unknown subject.

Most of the looks they got as they passed through were friendly, but Logan noticed that a few officers didn't seem too pleased to see them. They had no reason for resentment. Their chief had asked for the FBI's help. In a high-profile case like this, the FBI had to be invited to assist. Only when it was a matter of national security, involved interstate travel or interstate communication, or was some other kind of federal case would the FBI step in. Only those circumstances made the situation their purview.

Most law enforcement officers tracking a violent unknown subject actually wanted their help. But there were always some who didn't like the implication that they couldn't find the UNSUB without the FBI's help. In Logan's mind, finding criminals before they hurt innocent people was the only important motivation. Of course, it worked both ways. He had little respect for agents who looked down on local law enforcement. Those agents didn't seem to last long.

After escorting them to the conference room, the officer who'd shown them the way closed the door and left. They were alone. Logan glanced at his watch.

"Are you wondering about Monty?" Alex asked.

"Yeah." He reached into his pocket and pulled out his cell phone. After selecting Monty's number, he listened to the phone ring over and over. When Monty's voice mail finally kicked in, Logan left a quick message. "Hey, where are you? I know you're afraid of your grandmother, but maybe you should be a little more concerned about Jeff." He disconnected the call and shook his head. "Hope everything's okay."

"He'll be here," Alex said as they all sat down at a large table. "He's been late before."

Logan was certain Monty had taken his personal car instead of the vehicle supplied by the Bureau. He often drove the unreliable 1999 Volvo his grandmother had given him. Logan had advised him more than once to get rid of it, but Monty refused. He didn't want to hurt his grandmother's feelings. Maybe today he'd finally face reality.

The door to the room swung open, and three people walked in. They sat down at the table before saying anything. The man at the head was obviously the Montgomery County police chief. A tall, thin man with a hawk-like nose, he carried himself as if he expected deference. Logan was pretty sure he got it.

The man on his left was short and stocky and looked to be in his thirties. He seemed tense. The woman who sat on the chief's right was also tall. Almost as tall as Logan. Her blond hair was pulled back and worn in a bun. She was older. Maybe early forties. She had a friendly face, and her hazel eyes had an intense quality. She wore black slacks with a white blouse and matching black jacket. She was also the only one who smiled at the group.

"Thanks for coming," the police chief said. "I'm Chief Joshua Gorman." He looked to his left. "This is Detective Ben Cooper." Then he looked to his right. "And this is Detective Julie Palmer. She's the lead detective assigned to this case."

"Please call me Julie," she said.

Cooper stayed silent. Detective Cooper it was.

Logan, Alex, and Kaely introduced themselves. Then Kaely said, "You're concerned that you might have a serial?"

Chief Gorman shrugged. "Not sure. But whoever gave Davis that envelope wrote a number one on the back of a page from his book. Is he trying to tell us there's a number two and three? I don't know, but I think we need to make that assumption just in case, don't you?"

Logan wasn't so sure this was a serial killer, but he agreed with the chief. They didn't want to wait around for a second death to find out.

"We're looking at people who might have had a problem with Mr. Davis," Gorman said. "With all the books he's written about his cases, the list seems long. He helped put away a lot of criminals."

"I'm not sure that will prove helpful," Alex said.

Gorman frowned. "Why do you say that?"

"Because the people he profiled are either dead or in prison," Kaely interjected. "These were very violent criminals. Not the kind to be paroled."

"That's true," Logan added. "It doesn't hurt to check, though. I also recommend you look into Davis's personal life. We can provide you with a copy of our Victimology Checklist. It will help you when interviewing friends, family, neighbors, and people he's worked with down through the years. I'd offer the list to the police in Houston too, so they can assist from that end. If you work together, you can gather information faster."

"Sure. Thanks."

"But Davis retired years ago, right?" Kaely said, looking at Logan.

"How long ago?" Julie added. "Isn't retirement from the FBI mandatory at fifty-five?"

"It's fifty-seven now, or after twenty years of service," Logan said. "Davis was seventy-six when he died. He retired at fifty-five. It would be unusual for someone to wait more than twenty years to seek revenge, but all this time he's kept his hand in by writing quite a few books and speaking at events around the country. He may have even consulted privately. Probably need to check for files at his residence or an office if he has one. Who knows who he may have angered over the years?"

"We thought of that," Gorman said. "His wife says no to consulting. Just writing and speaking."

"We're already investigating," Julie said, "but where do you think we should concentrate our efforts?"

"Look at Davis's life in the last couple of years," Logan

said. "Ask those same family members, friends, neighbors, and associates if he's had run-ins with anyone."

Julie was writing notes in a small spiral notebook while Cooper used his phone. Logan liked Julie's style. He was old school too. With a notebook, he could quickly flip through pages of notes. He'd tried using a program on his phone but eventually stopped for two reasons. First, invariably someone would call, throwing him off. The second reason should be clear to everyone in the room. Phones could be hacked, but anyone wanting his notebook would have to go through him first. He had faith he could defend himself— and his notes.

"We need to figure out what the number one on the back of the page means," Alex said.

"I agree," Logan said. "Maybe it doesn't indicate other victims. But at this point, I think we should assume it has significance to our UNSUB or it wouldn't be there."

"As terrible as this sounds," Alex said, "another death would help us figure out what's going on. But right now our job is to help you find a way to get out in front of this guy. A second death just isn't acceptable."

"If you want information about the early days, you could contact Evan Bayne," Kaely said. "He worked with John Davis in the beginning, when the BAU began. Of course, back then it was called the Behavioral Science Unit. Davis was the one who coined the term *serial killer*."

"I understand the two had a falling out in the early nineties—thirty years ago," Alex said. "Davis stayed with the FBI, but Bayne left after only ten years of service as an analyst. He started writing books before Davis, although Davis's books were more popular. Sold a lot more than Bayne's."

"Do you know what happened between them?" Gorman asked.

Logan shook his head. "They never talked about what their disagreement was about publicly. Eventually, they appeared to put the past behind them. Both showed up at some of the same crime conventions, like the one Davis was attending here. I don't think they were ever friends again, though."

He frowned and looked over at Alex. "Wait. Wasn't there some kind of lawsuit a few years ago?"

"Yeah, I'd forgotten about that," Alex said. "Davis said Bayne wrote about a case in one of his books, giving himself credit for helping find an UNSUB because his profile was so accurate. But the case was really Davis's. If I remember right, the suit was settled out of court."

"Actually, Bayne would make a good suspect," Kaely said with a smile. "But he's in his seventies too, and he has his own life. I'm sure his books were profitable enough to make the lawsuit not much more than a bump in the road."

"You could talk to some people who worked with Bayne," Logan said. "We'll give you a list. Again, not sure you'll find anything helpful there, but it won't hurt to rule him out. I just think your UNSUB will be someone more contemporary."

"So we should look for someone in his past or someone in his life now?" Julie said. "You're casting a pretty wide net." There wasn't any irritation in her tone. She was simply stating a fact.

"You're right," Logan said. "We can't tell you much yet. Let us go over the information you've compiled. We'll work the profile and do the best we can to narrow your search."

"If you dig up anything else that might help us, please let us know," Kaely said. "Is the Davis autopsy completed?"

"Yes," Gorman said. "We're expecting the report this afternoon."

"We need that," Logan said, "along with all your crime-scene notes. What you've gathered from witnesses. From family . . . Basically, everything you know, we want to know."

"Of course. We're at your disposal, and so are our resources," Gorman said. "We appreciate you being available to help us. I thought because of Mr. Davis's profession, you would be the best people to give us what we need to find this guy." He raised an eyebrow. "I assume it's a guy?"

"Probably," Alex said. "But again, we need time to work the profile."

"Can you send a copy of that video to our Cyber Crimes Unit?" Logan asked. "I'd like to see if they can remove the voice distortion. Maybe they can produce the actual voice. You may need to match it against any suspects."

"Sure," the chief said.

"One thing to keep in mind," Logan added, "is that the numeral one on the back of the page might not mean anything. The UNSUB may have put it there just to elicit a response. To frighten you."

"Trust me," Gorman said. "If this is the perp's only victim, no one will be happier than me. But that number bothers me. A lot."

"We may have figured out how our UNSUB was able to watch Mr. Davis," Julie said.

Everyone waited expectantly. Thinking that Davis wasn't actually being watched had made his death seem even more tragic and unnecessary.

"Someone at the convention noticed a drone outside the

hotel the night Mr. Davis died. We're wondering if it was there to surveil him."

"I don't know," Cooper said. Logan had been wondering why he hadn't spoken yet. He was happy to know the man could talk. "Drones are getting pretty popular. Everyone and their dog has one. It might have had nothing to do with Davis."

"Drone or not, since the video of Mrs. Davis was pre-recorded in Houston, the perp could have been in Bethesda Saturday night," Gorman said. "The phone is at your lab in Quantico. Maybe they can also figure out when the video was recorded."

"That won't be hard," Logan said. "My guess is it wasn't too old. It had to look recent enough to fool Davis."

The door to the room opened slowly, and Monty stepped inside. When everyone at the table looked his way, he gave them a sheepish grin. "I'm really sorry. I stopped off to see my grandmother, but when I got ready to leave, my car wouldn't start. She called a friend of hers, who came over and got it going. Cleaned the contacts on my battery. It's running like a charm now."

"We've barely started," Julie said with a welcoming smile.

That was hardly true, but Logan appreciated the grace extended toward Monty. It was obvious he was babbling a bit out of nervousness. Although the three law enforcement officers didn't seem offended, Logan was still a little perturbed with him. Being a member of the BAU was a privilege. Showing up on time to important meetings seemed like a small thing to expect. He'd said something about it more than once, but here Monty was, late again. Logan worried about his friend. He didn't want him to risk his job with the BAU.

As Monty slid into a chair next to Kaely, Chief Gorman took his cell phone from his pocket and called someone, asking them to bring everything they had on the John Davis case so far.

"What can we get you?" he asked as he put his phone back into his pocket. "I assume you've already had lunch?"

The three of them nodded.

"What about coffee? Or something cold?"

All four of them asked for coffee. Again the chief took out his phone. He told someone on the other end to bring coffee, along with cream and sugar. "Do you need anything else?"

Logan looked at the other agents, who all shook their heads. "We're good," he said.

Gorman stood, and Julie and Cooper followed suit.

"If you need me, just ask anyone in the squad room to locate me. And like I said, whatever resources we have are at your disposal." He started toward the door but then stopped and turned around. "Thanks for coming. It's not that we couldn't handle this alone, but I strongly feel we have to cover every base. I don't get this feeling very often, but when I do, I'm always right."

"What kind of feeling do you mean?" Alex asked.

He shook his head. "It's an instinct in my gut. I'm sure you've had it. Comes from spending time in law enforcement. My gut's telling me this case won't be easy. In spades."

Without another word, he opened the door and walked out. His detectives followed.

He carefully pored through the pages of *Dark Minds*, looking for just the right sentences. The words he needed to display his superiority to Davis. It should be easier, but Davis droned on and on about his accomplishments, making it challenging to find just what he wanted. But with effort, he finally uncovered what he was looking for.

After laying out two photocopied pages in front of him, with his choices highlighted, he turned them over and wrote the numeral 3 on one and 4 on the other. The numeral 2 was already where it needed to be—of course. He smiled. He'd outwit every single one of his victims—all six of them—and the members of the FBI's elite BAU too. He'd prove that no one was capable of stopping him. No one.

⸻

"I hope Chief Gorman doesn't really plan to run this case by his gut," Monty said when the door closed behind the detectives.

Kaely shrugged. "I know what he's talking about. An almost sixth sense we develop after a while. I think he's right. This case is certainly troubling."

"What do you mean?" Alex asked.

"If Davis was killed for retribution, what could he have done lately that would cause someone to create such an elaborate way to murder him? He doesn't work cases anymore. Like we said, anyone he helped put away is either dead or still in prison. This has to be something more recent. How ridiculous is it that he spends years working to put violent, sadistic criminals away and stays safe, but he speaks at some conventions, writes some books, and now he's killed in this weird way?"

Everyone was silent. Alex turned Kaely's comment over in her mind. "Maybe this is a family member of someone he helped send to prison? I can't answer your question about why someone like that would wait so long, but maybe for some reason our UNSUB had no choice."

"I think someone with a relative in prison should be considered," Monty said.

"Look, it's not our job to be investigators," Logan said, his tone rather sharp. "We have to concentrate on what we're here to do. Let the police search for suspects. We need to go through all the files, look at the crime-scene photos and ME's report, and study the victimology before we draw any conclusions."

Alex had noticed a slight change in Logan. Was it because he was the lead agent? Yet she'd been on other missions when he was lead, and he'd never acted this way. She watched as his jaw tightened when he looked at Kaely. Was he intimidated by her? If so, Alex was surprised. She'd never seen him affected by anyone like this. He was usually a model of professionalism.

"You're right," Alex said, "but there's nothing wrong with bouncing possibilities off each other before we do that."

Logan frowned at her, but she decided to ignore him.

Monty looked back and forth between Alex and Logan before saying, "I'm just trying to understand what the UNSUB wants. Any ideas?"

"John Davis wrote a lot of books," Kaely said. "Maybe someone he mentioned, even briefly, holds a grudge. Feels slighted. The UNSUB could be angry that he wasn't more than a side note. Not as important as the killers who commanded more attention."

"Wouldn't hurt to check out spouses or children of people mentioned in *Dark Minds*," Monty said.

"But again, everything in those books happened a long time ago," Logan said. "This doesn't seem like something associated with the past."

Kaely shrugged. "Maybe. I'm with the chief, though. This will be a tough one. Davis was well-known, knew a lot of people, and helped send a lot of criminals to prison. This may be akin to finding that proverbial needle in a haystack."

Alex could see Logan was irritated. He was the agent in charge, but Kaely seemed to be taking over.

"I see a problem with your premise about someone mentioned in his books," Logan said, directing his remark to Kaely.

"Oh?" she said.

"Davis was careful not to write about anyone who might get out of prison someday," he said. "He knew his family could be in danger if he did."

"You're right, Logan," Alex said. "He mentioned that several times in his books. Nor did he give the real names of people who were accessories to crimes—criminals connected to the violent killers he wrote about. Sometimes he simply called them suspects. But even though he didn't name everyone, it wouldn't be hard for people to figure out who he was writing about. His friends and family would also know about it. Then there are public records, trial transcripts, and news articles."

The door opened, and an officer walked in, holding several files under her arm and a tray with coffee cups. Logan stood and took the tray. He put it in the middle of the table and turned back to take the files, but the officer had already handed them to Kaely. "A lot of this is in our data files," she said, "but I read that you like to look at hard copies of reports, so we copied everything. I think you'll find what you need here." She was obviously starstruck with Kaely Quinn.

Kaely's cheeks reddened as she took the files. To her credit, she just smiled at the officer and thanked her. The officer offered everyone at the table a quick smile before leaving the room.

"I'm so sorry," Kaely said after the door closed. "That was inappropriate. If you'd rather, I'll ask for access to the data files."

"Don't worry about it," Alex said. "Personally, I like hard copies better myself. And don't feel bad about the officer's reaction. We realize you're somewhat of a celebrity."

"I'm not," she said quickly. "A celebrity is someone who's tried to acquire fame. I never wanted it. Being known as the daughter of a serial killer isn't something anyone chases after. It's thrust upon you."

"Regardless," Alex said, "this will be better. Especially with the four of us working together."

Alex glanced at Monty, who didn't seem to care one way or the other. Logan just nodded and said, "It doesn't matter to me. I'll bring Monty up-to-date while you two start going through the files. Now, let's get started, okay?"

While Alex and Kaely began working through the case notes and reports, Alex noticed Logan seemed more relaxed. He was a fair man who would give Kaely a chance. They needed to forget egos and help stop a dangerous killer before he struck again.

After they'd worked through the files for a couple of hours, an officer brought them a copy of the autopsy report. It didn't offer any surprises. John Davis had died from the knife plunged into his heart.

They snacked on what they could find in a vending machine and kept working.

It was close to midnight when the chief returned. When he opened the door to the conference room, Alex noticed his surprised expression.

"I thought you'd be gone by now," he said.

"I notice you're still here too," Logan said with a smile.

Gorman sighed. "We're still at it. We started checking family and friends of prisoners Davis helped to incarcerate. The list isn't long. Like you said, most of the prisoners are dead. The few still alive have been shunned by their families." He looked at Kaely. "I know you understand. They don't want to be associated with famous felons. They've built new lives and didn't appreciate it when we contacted them. We were still poring through Davis's books, looking for someone he might have slighted. But when you let me know he was careful not to mention people like that, we stopped.

We also contacted the author who coordinated the convention where Davis spoke last week, D. J. Harper. He's coming in tomorrow so we can question him. Except for his wife, Harper is the last person Davis spoke to—as far as we know."

"And you're also looking closely at his friends, associates . . . anyone who might have a reason to want him dead?" Logan asked.

"Of course, but Davis had a long career. He knew a lot of people." Gorman sighed deeply. "His wife gave us a few names that didn't check out. She put Evan Bayne at the top of the list. Problem is he lives out of the country now. Australia. That makes him an unlikely suspect, but we're trying to contact him anyway." He paused. "We really need you to point us in the right direction. So far, you're not giving us anything we couldn't have come up with on our own." Gorman's words were spoken sharply, his frustration evident. "When will you be able to give us your profile?"

Alex gazed around the table at the assembled group of analysts. They'd been going back and forth all day. She was convinced too many cooks were making the soup. "We should have something by noon tomorrow," Alex said since everyone else stayed silent.

"Look, why don't you all get some sleep, then come back bright and early?" Gorman said. "There's a nice motel about four blocks from here. I'll call and see if we can get you some rooms."

"That's a good idea," Logan said, yawning. "Thanks."

"Don't worry about me," Monty said. "I'll stay with my grandmother."

Alex smiled, but her germaphobia made it challenging to stay in motels and hotels. Still, she always packed her usual can of disinfectant just in case. Hopefully, the place wouldn't be too bad.

"I think we're pretty close to nailing this down," Logan said after Gorman left the room. "But we need to stop worrying about *how* the UNSUB pulled this off and more about *who* he is."

"I agree," Alex said. "But it's hard not to think about how this was planned and carried out. It's so different. How an UNSUB carries out his crime is important. Part of his MO. It tells us a lot about him."

"Yeah, I know," Logan said. "I feel like we have pieces of it but not enough to understand it yet."

"You're right," Alex said. "We need to stay focused on what we can understand."

No one disagreed with her. They began to gather papers and photos taken from the files and dispose of their trash. By the time they were done, the chief was back.

"Got you some rooms," he said, "but they only had one double room with two beds and one single with a connecting door. Can agents Quinn and Donovan share a room?"

"It's fine with me," Kaely said. "Is it all right with you, Alex?"

Although Alex was thrilled to spend some time with Kaely, she couldn't help but wonder if Kaely would think she was weird if she wanted to disinfect the room. Unfortunately, it looked as if she had no choice.

"Sure. Sounds good."

"I saw the vending machine wrappers scattered around the table," Gorman said. "Not much of a dinner. So I called a local pizza place too. They're going to deliver to the motel. Should be there not long after you check in."

Frankly, Alex wasn't sure she wanted to eat just before going to bed. Although her nightmares weren't as frequent as they'd once been, she still had them. She silently prayed that God would keep them away tonight.

"Thanks, Chief," Logan said.

Gorman gave them the address of the motel, and they got up to leave.

"Do you mind if I copy some of this before we go?" Kaely asked.

"No need," Gorman said. "These are copies. I gave them to you in case you wanted to work on this outside of the station." He looked at Logan. "And I'll give you a digital file to send to the FBI." Then he gestured toward the hard copies on the table. "I'm sure I don't need to remind you that no one else is to see this information."

"We understand," Kaely said.

Alex instinctively exchanged quick looks with Logan and Monty. They'd all heard of Kaely's unique way of profiling, using files to "see" an UNSUB. A tingle of excitement ran up and down Alex's spine. Would she get to see her process in action?

When they got out to the parking lot, they said good-bye to Monty before climbing into the SUV. No one spoke on the way to the motel. Alex was tired, but she was also turning the case over in her mind. She was convinced they were looking for someone with a grudge related to Davis's work, but so far the police hadn't found a suspect—someone who knew Davis was at that hotel.

She wondered about the people who attended the kinds of conventions where Davis spoke. Could the UNSUB be one of them? Someone trying to show they were smarter than Davis? She was glad they were bringing in thriller writer D. J. Harper. He could provide important information since he was at the same hotel where Davis died and may have been the last person to speak to him. Alex couldn't help but wonder about the man. He lived in the area and had told the police he'd gone home after the convention ended on Saturday night. The police knew Mr. Harper and respected him. Still, she felt they needed to keep him on the list of suspects. Gorman's files said he was the person who'd made Davis's reservation, and he knew what room he was in.

Of course, right now Evan Bayne was at the top of the suspect list, although he seemed pretty unlikely. He was fairly old, and his feud with Davis had been a long time ago. The lawsuit still bothered her, though. Could something like that have set him off enough to kill? She didn't know. She'd never run across a case like this before. Most behavioral analysts would draw the conclusion that whoever killed Davis was angry. Stabbing a human being was so up close and personal. Hard to do. Messy. Shooting someone from a distance was easier. No blood on your clothes. But the UNSUB hadn't stabbed him. Davis had stabbed himself. How do you profile that?

She sighed loudly without realizing it . . . until Logan looked at her.

"Tired?" he asked.

"Yeah. And a little confused. Are we working a murder or a suicide?"

"Good question. I keep wondering about Davis's life insurance company. What will they do?" He was quiet for a moment. "If they determine his death was suicide, will they refuse to pay out?"

"I'm not an expert," Alex said, "but my policy pays on a suicide after I've had the policy for two years."

Logan shook his head. "Kind of morbid, isn't it?"

Alex wasn't so sure the question of suicide was just for the insurance company. Wasn't it part of the profile? How could the UNSUB know Davis would be *able* to commit suicide? Even if you loved your spouse more than life itself, the act of killing yourself wasn't easy. But as she thought about it, she realized she knew the answer. Just like her, Davis had lived a life saturated in death and destruction. After viewing the horror that human beings visited on each other, the act of murder began to lose its shock. Whoever backed Davis into a corner knew that. Knew he would be able to fulfill the act he'd been encouraged to carry out.

Logan slowed the SUV. "Here we are," he said. He pulled into the parking lot of a small but attractive motel. *The Foxfire Inn.* Maybe this would be all right after all.

Logan jumped out and went inside. He came back a few minutes later. "We're on the other side," he said.

He drove around to the back of the structure. There was good lighting. The doors were metal. Also good. More secure. FBI agents noticed these things without really thinking about it.

"You're in 110, and I'm in 111," he said. "Right next door."

Logan had just opened his door when a beat-up car pulled

up next to them. The name of a local pizza place was displayed on a lighted sign on the roof, and the fresh-faced teen driver lowered his window. "Chief Gorman ordered some pizza for folks stayin' here. Is that you?"

"Yeah," Logan said. He got out of the SUV and stepped up to the car window, where the kid handed him two large pizza boxes and a bag.

"There's paper plates, napkins, and plastic forks in there," the kid said. He reached over and lifted a six-pack of cola from the seat next to him. "I'm supposed to give these to you too."

Alex got out of the car and hurried to Logan's side. She took the ice-cold cola since his arms were already full.

Logan set the pizza boxes on the hood of the kid's car and started to reach into his pocket, but the boy waved him off. "I've already been tipped. I was told you weren't supposed to pay anything."

Logan picked up the boxes and thanked him. The kid nodded, then backed up the car and left the parking lot.

"Kinda late for a pizza place to be open on a weeknight," Alex said. "It's gotta be almost one in the morning."

"You're right. We better check it out before we eat this. I'll call the restaurant and confirm."

Kaely had come up behind them. "It's sad, isn't it? I mean, that we're always on guard, suspicious of everything?"

Logan nodded. "It might be sad, but it's a good way to stay alive. Too many people hate law enforcement these days." He asked Kaely to hold the pizzas while he unlocked the doors to their rooms. "Let's eat in your room," he said. "It's bigger. Probably has a larger table."

"Sure," Alex said. The pizza smelled awesome, and her thought about going straight to bed vanished when her stomach growled. It was so cold outside that the idea of chowing down on nice hot pizza sounded heavenly.

Logan switched on the room lights and took the pizzas from Kaely. Alex glanced around the room before heading back to the SUV, where she opened the back and began grabbing their bags. The room looked updated and cheerful, and a light scent of lavender made it seem as if it had been recently cleaned. Still, although she should feel relieved by the condition of the motel, she'd disinfect the room herself. Check under the sheets on her bed. Things she had to do before she could sleep.

She really liked Kaely Quinn. But would her roommate take her seriously once she brought out her can of disinfectant?

7

Logan called the pizza place and confirmed that the order had come from them. Then they all devoured pizza while sitting at the table in the double room. It had only two chairs, though, so Logan had opened the connecting door and grabbed one from his room. Although Alex felt uncomfortable sitting in a chair she hadn't sanitized, she tried to ignore it. At least they had clean paper plates, and the utensils and napkins the restaurant sent had been sealed in plastic wrap.

Before they'd started eating, Kaely had asked if she could say a prayer over the food. She'd heard Kaely was a Christian, but Alex noticed Logan looked surprised. He must not have known. Maybe that would help him feel better about Kaely.

No one brought up the case as they ate, probably because their brains needed a rest. Instead, they exchanged light banter, which helped Alex relax. After eating too much, they put the remaining pizza into one box, and Logan carried it out to the SUV. Since the temperature outside was below freezing, it would stay safe.

After they'd decided to head back to the station at eight in the morning, Logan left for his room. Alex told Kaely she was welcome to take the first shower. While Kaely was in the bathroom, Alex sprayed the telephone, the TV remote, the light switches on the walls and lamps, the door handles, and the bedspread on the bed she'd claimed as hers. She pulled the covers down and checked under the sheets. No bugs. With the water still running in the bathroom, she opened the window, hoping the smell of her disinfectant would dissipate.

She heard the shower turn off and quickly closed the window. By now the room was cold, so she cranked up the heat and sat down at the table.

Alex had turned on the TV and was flipping through channels when the bathroom door opened and Kaely came out wearing an FBI T-shirt and sweats. Her red hair was wrapped up in a white towel as she walked to her bed and sat down on the edge.

"What is that smell?" she asked. "It's a little overpowering."

Alex felt her face flush. "I . . . I'm sorry. I always disinfect hotel rooms. Especially since COVID-19. It's just safer, I think."

Kaely frowned. "Wow. It's just really strong. Can we crack the window for a bit?"

Alex got up and opened the window again. She was embarrassed by Kaely's reaction, although she couldn't blame her.

"I'm sorry if I offended you," Kaely said. "That wasn't my intention. What you're doing is really smart. You can never be too careful."

"I'm not offended," Alex said. She just wanted to move on.

Did Kaely see her as some kind of nut now? No matter what she'd just said?

"You have a problem with germs, don't you?" Kaely asked gently. "As I'm sure you know, that's usually a side effect of trauma. An effort to control your surroundings."

"Yes, I know, thanks." Alex realized she sounded a little snippy, but Kaely wasn't the only behavioral analyst in the room. She knew exactly why she had a fear of germs. Since becoming a Christian, she'd been getting better, but she still dealt with some of the side effects of her troubled up-bringing.

"I'm sure you do," Kaely said, her tone still gentle. "I seem to be putting my foot in my mouth this evening. Sorry." She sighed. "This case is baffling. I think it's because we've wandered off course, trying to solve the crime rather than simply deliver a profile." She took the towel off her head and rubbed her hair until it was almost dry.

"I agree. It's just so . . . interesting."

Kaely grinned. "I thought you were going to say confusing. But you're right."

Alex saw an opening and took it. Although they'd see each other at work, it might be a while before she'd have another chance like this. She took a deep breath. "Kaely, can I ask you something?"

"Sure. Anything."

"I . . . I wonder if you'd tell me about the way you profile."

Kaely frowned at her. "I write profiles the same way you do."

"I . . . I know. I don't mean to put you on the spot, but most of us have heard about your technique. I would love to see it in operation."

Kaely looked away for a moment, then cleared her throat.

"There are a lot of things in this world we can't see, Alex. But they're real. Even more real than what we can see."

"I don't understand."

"I still use my . . . method, but I'm very careful with it. Evil is out there. We both know it. We've seen it. Our minds, our imaginations, can sometimes create an opening for something dark. It happened to me, and I don't want it to happen to you."

Alex frowned at her. "I'm not sure what you mean."

Kaely stared at her for a moment before saying, "I'm sorry. I'm sure you don't. There's really nothing wrong with my technique. Just because I had a bad experience doesn't mean you will." She shook her head. "I'm transferring my own experience to you, and that's not fair."

Alex didn't know what to say. She still wanted to learn Kaely's unique way of profiling. Her goal was to be the best analyst she could be, and she needed every weapon in her arsenal. "I . . . I've seen evil," she said. "We see it all the time. Not something you ever get used to."

"I don't think we should get used to it. If we do, we've lost a piece of our humanity."

Alex just stared at her. She'd seen the worst of the worst as the field coordinator for the National Center for the Analysis of Violent Crime in Kansas City before joining the BAU. Things you couldn't get out of your mind no matter how hard you tried. They still haunted her dreams, along with the nightmares she'd carried with her for years. Logan told her God would deliver her, but that it didn't always happen right away. She wasn't sure what God was waiting for, but at least now she wasn't afraid to go to sleep at night. The awful dreams occurred less and less often, and the fear associated with them was lessening too. The past few times, she'd found herself sitting up in bed after a really bad nightmare, whispering, *Jesus, Jesus, Jesus.*

"Look," Kaely said, "I'm talking about the evil behind our nightmares. The darkness we can't see."

Alex choked back a gasp. How had Kaely known she was thinking about her dreams? She swallowed before saying, "You mean . . . the devil?"

"Yeah. The devil. A spiritual war is waging behind the evil we see on earth. Satan is real, and we need to know how to stand against him."

"I don't know much about him," Alex said. "But his existence would explain a lot of the awful things we deal with. Even before I became a Christian, I was aware that there was . . . something. Something beyond what I could explain."

"The important thing is to learn that we have authority over him. Jesus put him under our feet."

Alex had heard this before. At church and from Logan. She knew it was true, but she didn't really understand how it worked. She was still learning how to keep her mouth shut when she needed to and how to forgive people who upset her. She was a work in progress.

"Look, like I said, there's nothing wrong with my technique," Kaely told her. "Of course I'll teach it to you. Sorry if I frightened you. I'm just a little sensitive about it because of what happened to me. But you're not me."

"It's okay. I'm an adult. Not so easily upset." Even as she said the words, Alex wondered why Kaely Quinn made her feel like a child. She wasn't used to feeling like that, and she didn't like it.

Kaely stared at her for a moment. "Okay." She walked

over to the table, and Alex followed her. When she sat down across from Kaely, it reminded her of a séance. She knew it wasn't, but it still sent a shiver through her.

"Okay, let's do this," Kaely said. "You say you've heard about my process?"

Alex nodded. "Sorry. It's not a secret."

"I know. But just to make sure I'm clear, I use the information we've collected about the UNSUB and then try to picture him—or her—as if the person is real and sitting across from me. If we've decided the UNSUB is white and in his forties, I start with that. Then I take any other evidence and build on it." She smiled. "It helps me see them. I can weed through all the extraneous material and narrow it down in my mind." She shrugged. "It doesn't work for everyone. It might not work for you."

Alex didn't say anything. She just nodded.

Kaely picked up the folder the police had given her, then said, "Would you move over to your bed?"

"Sure." Alex got up and sat on the edge of the bed, leaving the chair across from Kaely empty. Logan had taken the third chair back to his room.

"Okay," Kaely said, "I need you to be quiet. Just let me talk, okay?"

Alex nodded. She was excited to see this work—but also just a little bit nervous. She chastised herself for being so ridiculous.

Kaely opened the file and began to read through the notes and peruse the photos. Then she looked at the chair Alex had vacated. "You're a white male. You consider yourself highly intelligent. Smarter than everyone around you. You don't like to kill close up . . ." Kaely frowned at the chair.

"No, that's not right." She was quiet for a moment. "It isn't that you're unwilling to get your hands dirty. You killed John Davis in a way that proves you're superior to him. You chose this method to make it clear that with all his knowledge and experience, you're smarter." She stopped again, then looked away for a moment before staring at the chair once more. "You knew John Davis. Not just from what you read about him. That makes you at least in your fifties? Sixties? And you were willing to take a chance that he loved his wife enough to kill himself. How could you be sure?"

Alex was a little disappointed. All this had already been discussed with Logan and Monty. Hardly anything new.

"You have no compassion for people like Davis. Or even his family members." Kaely shook her head slowly. "Wait a minute. No. It isn't his family members you hate. You hated him. But why?"

She still stared at the chair, and Alex found herself looking at it too, as if someone were actually sitting there. The hair on the back of her neck stood up.

Kaely sat back, a look of surprise on her face. "You don't despise John Davis. You despise what he did. You hate him because he could do something you can't."

Alex turned her head to stare at Kaely. At almost that same moment, out of the corner of her eye, Alex thought she saw someone sitting in what had been an empty chair.

On their way to the station, Alex, Logan, and Kaely stopped by a donut shop they'd noticed the night before. They bought a dozen donuts and coffee. Although Alex wanted to make a joke about the shop being so close to the police station, she wasn't really in a humorous mood.

Of course, there hadn't been anyone sitting in that chair last night. That was just her imagination. Kaely had stopped right after Alex's hallucination. Alex had wanted to ask her questions about what she'd said, but Kaely told her it was late and they needed sleep. It was obvious Kaely was bothered about something too.

When they entered the station, they saw Chief Gorman on the phone in his office, so they just carried the donuts and coffee back to the empty conference room. Logan offered to get napkins and plates. When he returned, his expression was tight, his forehead creased.

"What's wrong?" Alex asked.

"I don't know, but something's going on. Chief Gorman looks upset."

"This is a police station," Kaely said. "It could be anything."

Logan nodded. "True, but when he saw me, he put down the phone and stepped out his door. He wanted to make sure we were all here. Said he'd meet with us as soon as possible."

Alex shrugged. "He probably wants to ask us about our profile. We need to wrap this up."

"Maybe," Logan said slowly, "but I get the feeling he's getting ready to tell us something we don't want to hear."

Alex took a chocolate donut from the box and grabbed a paper plate from the stack on the table.

"Alex is right," Kaely said. "We need to get our profile ready this morning."

"I agree," Logan said. "We'll start work after we meet with the chief. But first, let's finish breakfast." He took a bite of his donut and washed it down with coffee.

Kaely took a cake donut with cherry frosting and nibbled at it. Alex found that amusing. Logan's donut was gone in three bites, but Kaely might be working on hers for a while.

Alex had just taken another bite of her donut when the door opened and Monty walked in. "Sorry," he said. "Grandmother still wasn't feeling well this morning. I had to run to the drugstore for her."

"Is it anything serious?" Alex asked.

He sat down next to Logan and shook his head. "No, I don't think so. To be honest, I don't think she wanted me to leave. She seemed worried. I . . ." His eyes grew moist. "Sorry," he said, his voice shaking a little. "My grandmother raised me. She . . . Well, she's my only real family."

Logan frowned. "Didn't you mention your parents to me once?"

Monty nodded. "We're not close. When I was young, they went back to China. I was in school and didn't want to leave my friends, so Grandmother Wong offered to take me in. My parents moved to California a few years ago, but they don't have much to do with either of us. It's not that we're really estranged. It's just that they have their lives, and we have ours. And if my grandmother can't care for herself, my father will probably want to put her in a nursing home." He took a sip of the coffee he'd brought with him. "I won't let that happen. I'll take care of her if she needs assistance." He chuckled. "She's pretty stubborn, though. And strong. She's eighty years old and determined to be independent."

"She's blessed to have someone like you in her life, Monty," Kaely said.

He smiled at her. "Thanks. It goes both ways."

The door swung open so suddenly it made Alex jump. Chief Gorman walked in without saying a word, then grabbed a chair at the head of the table and sat down.

"Something's happened," he said. "I think it might affect your profile."

"Tell us," Logan said, setting his cup on the table.

"Evan Bayne's dead."

"That's terrible," Kaely said slowly, "but he was getting kind of old, wasn't he?"

"Seventy-one. But his death wasn't due to natural causes."

Suddenly Alex's donut didn't look so appetizing. "How did he die?" she asked.

"Like I told you, he and his wife live in Australia. On Monday, around noon, they were taking a walk at a location near Sydney called the Gap. They were vacationing there. It's a beautiful place where high cliffs look out onto the sea. His wife, Gloria, said he got a phone call, and then his face turned white. He told her he loved her, put his phone on the ground, and jumped off the cliff. Gloria got to the edge just in time to see his body wash out to sea. By the time other people got there, he was gone. His body hasn't been recovered."

No one spoke. The chief opened a laptop on the table, then pressed a button on the large-screen TV that sat on a pedestal in the corner of the room. He brought up a grainy film that filled the screen. Although it was dark, a nearby streetlight showed a woman who looked to be in her mid-to-late twenties walking down a sidewalk, holding a little girl's hand. It was obvious they were being filmed from the interior of a car.

"Evan Bayne, you have thirty seconds to take your life," the same low voice they'd heard on John Davis's video said, again obviously altered, "or I will drive this car straight into your granddaughter and great-granddaughter. If they don't die the first time I run over them, I will back up and make sure the job is done. I will also kill them if you ask your wife for help or exit this app. This isn't a joke. I've already killed John Davis. Now, put the phone where I'll be able to see you end your life. Here we go, Evan." Then he began to count. "One . . . two . . . three . . . four . . ."

As the count continued, the picture suddenly jiggled and then turned sideways. They heard Bayne tell his wife he loved her. Then they watched as he ran toward the edge of what appeared to be a cliff while his wife screamed, "Evan! Evan, stop! Evan!" But Bayne jumped. A woman ran toward the edge of the cliff, and when she got there, she looked down, then screamed again and fell to the ground. The screen went black.

"Gloria Bayne told the Sydney police her husband was fine until that call, so his phone was turned over to them. When we tried to locate Bayne for our investigation, one of his neighbors told us he and his wife were in Sydney, but they had no contact information to give us. That's when we called the Sydney station for help locating him. By the way, they immediately contacted Bayne's daughter and her family. They're okay. No threats of any kind."

Alex couldn't seem to find any words. What they'd watched was horrible. A man so distraught that he could only think of jumping off a cliff in front of his wife. What a terrible way to die.

"He had only thirty seconds to decide what to do," Kaely said. "Not enough time to think of anything else." She looked at Gorman. "No drone?"

"No. Not that any witnesses saw. The Sydney police techs were investigating Bayne's phone when we called. He had an app like Zoom. It's called Chatter. The killer spoofed his granddaughter's telephone number. Bayne wouldn't have thought anything about answering the call since he and his granddaughter used Chatter all the time. And he made sure all Bayne could see was the video, not who was showing it. But unlike Davis's call, both sides of this one were recorded. We can both hear and see what happened on Bayne's end."

"I . . . I have that app," Monty said. "My grandmother and I use it. I'm so busy working I don't get to see her as often as I'd like."

"So the UNSUB hacked Bayne's phone," Alex said. "He knew about the app and that Bayne and his granddaughter used it. He didn't have to be in Australia. Where does the granddaughter live?"

"In Maryland. Frederick."

"He didn't have to travel far from Bethesda to pull this off, then," Kaely said.

"Was the video he showed Bayne recorded?" Logan asked.

Gorman nodded. "Yes. Like Davis, Bayne didn't have the time or probably the technical knowledge to realize it wasn't happening at that moment. You know, even if these videos were recorded at another time, it doesn't mean this guy won't go after the families."

"Right," Logan said. "Our unit chief said that too. This UNSUB is evil but a genius. Thirty seconds isn't enough time to do anything but die."

"You said Bayne died Monday around noon," Monty said, "and we can see the sun shining on this video. But the video he was shown looks like it was taken at night. Or was it early morning?"

"The video of the mother was recorded around six a.m. She's single and an early-shift nurse. Every weekday plus Sunday she takes her little girl to a babysitter who lives a few doors down. That made it easy for our perp to film her. But Sydney is fourteen hours ahead of us. Bayne died early Sunday morning our time but Monday around noon Sydney time."

"Davis died around ten p.m. here, so that means the UNSUB orchestrated two suicides within about eight hours," Alex said. "How long does it take to fly from here to Australia?"

"Over twenty hours," Logan said. He smiled. "Church conference."

"So the UNSUB probably wasn't in Australia," Monty said. "Looks like he got Bayne to kill himself from here." He shook his head. "Murder by phone. This certainly is a new one."

Alex was quiet for a moment before opening the file she'd brought with her. "The first message the UNSUB sent was an email to Davis. 'Those in law enforcement pay a heavy price when they constantly look into the dark minds of evil.' This was a general threat to those in law enforcement. Then came the page from Davis's book. 'In those early days, I worked with several great agents. The success we had didn't belong to one person. We were a team, each agent bringing his special skills to our efforts.'"

Her gaze swept around to the people sitting at the table and then settled on Chief Gorman. "This was a clue. He was telling us who he was going to target next. We didn't interpret it that way because we were focusing on Davis. We weren't sure there would be other deaths although we suspected it."

"If we'd realized it soon enough, maybe we could have stopped Bayne's suicide," the chief said.

Alex shook her head. "No. Davis worked with a lot of people. Bayne hadn't been involved with him for years. I wouldn't have guessed Bayne was the next target. None of us would have."

"So was a page left at Bayne's crime scene?" Monty asked.

Gorman nodded and picked up a piece of paper. He held it out to Alex. "This was mailed to their hotel and arrived two days before the phone call, but his wife said they hadn't bothered opening it since they were on vacation. Mailed from here, by the way. From Bethesda. And the numeral two is on the back."

Alex took the copy and read, "'Down through the years,

I've found that most people on the side of good or of evil have one thing in common. They were shaped and fashioned by their families.'"

The room was quiet. Alex was certain everyone was trying to figure out what the message meant.

"Is he threatening families more directly now?" Monty asked.

Gorman shrugged. "Maybe, but his anger seems to rest not on who Davis and Bayne were but on what they did."

Alex remembered Kaely saying almost the same thing when she was profiling the UNSUB in their motel room.

"Does this make it harder to write a profile?" Gorman asked.

"Not harder," Logan said. "Just . . . different." He looked at his colleagues sitting around the table, then addressed Gorman. "We need some time to work. I know you need this profile as soon as possible."

Gorman nodded just as Monty's cell phone rang. He took it out of his pocket. "Sorry, I need to take this. It's my grandmother."

Sitting next to him, Alex suddenly recalled Monty saying he and his grandmother used the same app Bayne had. She had a sudden sense of danger and reached out in an attempt to keep him from answering his phone. But she was too late.

As soon as he answered the phone, Monty's face went slack. He stared at Alex, who wrestled the phone from his grasp and clicked the speaker button. A voice said, "I've got your grandmother here, Monty." Alex held the phone out so everyone could see. They all watched as a large man in a dark leather jacket, wearing a ski mask and gloves, stood next to an elderly Asian woman, a gun held to her head. His voice was high and unnatural. He was obviously trying to disguise it.

Alex gently set the phone in the middle of the table, resting it against a pile of files. Everyone moved to one side of the table so they could see the unthinkable. Gorman grabbed a nearby notebook, wrote something down, then slid it to Monty, who picked up a pen and quickly scribbled something beneath Gorman's message.

Gorman grabbed the notebook and hurried out of the room, handing it to a nearby officer. Alex was pretty sure it was Mrs. Wong's address. Although Gorman had to try, there was no way anyone could get there in time.

"I guess you know what comes next, don't you?" the man said. "And by the way, say hello to your friends for me. Let's see. There's Kaely Quinn. Pretty famous, huh? Or should I say infamous? Alex Donovan. Made quite a name for herself, saving the world from a possible contagion. And Logan Hart. Right by Alex's side again, huh, Logan? Got feelings for the pretty lady? I'd bet anything you do. Kind of like Kaely Quinn and Noah Hunter? But I digress. We were talking about Monty, weren't we? This is his moment to shine." He laughed, but it was dark and merciless.

Alex shivered at the coldness that seeped through the phone. "What do you want?" she asked. "Tell us. Maybe we can help you."

"Don't try to handle me," the man said, his tone changing to one full of anger. "You have nothing I want. But Monty does. I want to hear the panic in his voice. And I want to hear him beg. Sadly, I didn't get to enjoy that with Davis. Not that it will do any good. So it's your turn, Monty. One . . . two . . ."

Monty's grandmother suddenly spoke loudly but firmly into the phone. "Bae," she said. "You will not give this man what he wants. Do you hear me?" Then she spoke in Chinese before the man hit her in the face with his free hand.

Monty stood and yelled, "No!"

The man took up the count again. "Three . . . four . . . five . . . six . . ."

Monty's grandmother yelled something else in Chinese, and the man hit her again.

As Monty reached for his gun, Logan and Gorman grabbed

him. Gorman held him in a tight grip, and Logan took his weapon away.

"Give it to me!" he yelled, tears streaming down his cheeks. "Please. You don't understand—"

"I understand that your grandmother doesn't want you to do this," Logan said, his voice firm. "That's what she just told you, Monty. Do you really think she'll want to live without you? Besides, we have no idea if this guy will keep his word."

In the background, the macabre counting continued. Monty fought hard to get away from Gorman. After securing Monty's gun, Logan helped to hold him back.

"Twenty-one . . . twenty-two . . . twenty-three . . ."

Monty's screams alerted officers in the outer room, and they threw the door open, their guns drawn.

"Get out," Gorman yelled at them. "We're okay. Close the door."

At first the officers didn't move. But when Gorman yelled at them again, they finally left. Alex couldn't think about them. All she could do was watch the phone and pray quietly.

"Twenty-seven, twenty-eight, twenty-nine . . ." The man stopped counting and stared at them through the screen. "You should have been faster, Monty. You and your friends are making me do this."

Alex jumped, and a small scream escaped her mouth as simultaneously the screen went dark and a shot rang out.

"No. No." Monty's body went limp, and he fell back into his chair. "How could you do this?" he asked through the sobs that racked his body. "You had no right . . ."

Kaely got up and walked over to him. "Monty, what did your grandmother say to you?"

"She . . . she said she was ready to go home to be with her

ancestors." He had trouble getting the words out. "That this was what she wanted. And that I still had a life to live."

"If you love her, then you have to honor her wishes," Alex said. She couldn't stop the tears that slipped down her cheeks. She was devastated for her friend. "She didn't want you to die, Monty. If you'd killed yourself, that pain would have been worse than death to her. Do you understand?"

For a moment, Monty just stared into Alex's eyes. As tears still streamed down his face, he finally nodded. "Yes. I know you're right, but—"

"You don't have to finish that," Logan said. "We all understand." He slipped into the chair next to Monty and put his hand on the distraught man's arm.

"We didn't see him shoot your grandmother, Monty," Gorman said. "I have officers on their way to her house. Maybe it was just a threat. Remember, the other messages were prerecorded."

Alex knew he was trying to give Monty some hope, but she was certain the elderly woman was dead. This video was different. The UNSUB wasn't fooling around. He was responsible for three deaths, but this was the first time he'd directly taken a life. A complete departure from his previous MO.

"I need to go to her house," Monty said. "She shouldn't be alone."

"Not a good idea," Logan said. "He was trying to kill you, Monty. We don't know where he is. He could be watching you." His eyes swept the room. "We need to stay together. No one goes anywhere alone."

Monty stood. "I understand what you're saying, but you can't force me to stay here. I have to be with my grandmother. I don't want a lot of strangers with her now."

"Monty," Alex said, "Logan's right. You'd be telling us the same thing. Besides, we need to talk about this. I'm sorry. I realize this is the worst time possible to bring this up, but . . ."

"But everything's changed," Kaely finished for her.

Alex nodded.

Monty slowly sat down again.

"What do you mean?" Gorman asked.

Alex took a deep breath. "The first two, John Davis and Evan Bayne, could have worked together on a case, but Monty's never been involved with them. They both retired years ago."

"Then why—" Monty's eyes suddenly got big. "You're right. He's not going after people who were involved with him or his family, he's . . ."

"Pursuing us," Logan said, his expression solemn. "I think his targets are behavioral analysts."

He drove slowly away from the old lady's house, the ski mask thrown onto the seat beside him, angry that he'd been forced to kill her. He hadn't wanted to pull the trigger, but it certainly wasn't his fault. If her grandson had really cared for her, he wouldn't have put him in a position like that.

He looked down at his jacket, spattered with blood. He liked this jacket, and now he'd have to get rid of it. That made him even angrier. Monty Wong was selfish. He was almost glad Monty would have to live with the guilt of causing his grandmother's death.

It took him almost an hour to reach the out-of-the-way motel where he'd been staying. He parked the car and walked quickly to his door, unlocking it and stepping into the cheap room that barely took care of his needs. This was the kind of place where you could pay cash without anyone caring who you were. Where the guy in the office didn't even look at you. Even if he did, he'd only see what he was supposed to see—an overweight bald guy with a big nose and dark mustache.

He carefully removed his jacket and put it into a plastic trash bag. He'd toss it into the dumpster out back when he left. Then he took off the padding underneath the jacket and hung it in the closet. After that, he removed his colored contacts and put them in their case.

Then he undressed completely and got into the shower. Even though no blood had touched his skin, he felt the need to cleanse himself. As the hot water washed over him, he smiled. Three down, three to go.

The chief stepped out of the room when one of his officers knocked on the door. Monty had calmed down, but his sadness was so strong Logan could almost feel it.

"Now what?" Monty asked. "Alex is right. This changes everything. We need to start over on the profile."

"Monty, you need to go home," Alex said gently. "You need time. Time to grieve. And you have to call your parents."

Odd that Alex's mind would go there. A woman without a family. Of course, maybe that's why it occurred to her. She valued something she'd never had.

"I'll call them later," Monty said. "They barely paid any attention to my grandmother. The rest of my family is in China. I lost touch with them a long time ago."

"Well, we're here for you," Kaely said. "We may not be your idea of family, but we all care about you."

"She's right," Logan said. "Please, Monty. Go home. I

insist. We'll send someone with you, just until we're sure what's going on."

"I will, but first I need to go to my grandmother's. And they won't let me in yet. Please don't make me leave." His eyes filled with tears, and he quickly wiped them away.

The door opened, and Gorman walked in. "Monty," he said, "please come with me. We have a counselor on call who wants to talk to you. Make sure you're okay."

"I don't want to leave—"

"Monty, go with him," Logan said. "I mean it."

It looked as if all the air suddenly left Monty's body. When he stood, he almost collapsed. Gorman put his arm around him and led him out of the room. Logan got up and quietly closed the door behind them.

"We've got to do everything we can to help catch this guy," he said. He wanted to sound professional since he was in charge of this team, but he was incensed. The first two deaths were bad enough, but this time the UNSUB had hurt his friend. That made it personal to him and his team.

"We'll do our best," Kaely said. "But this is something I've never seen before."

"None of us have," Logan said. "Where do we start? He's willing to change his MO to suit his endgame."

"At least we understand his motive," Alex said. "He hates behavioral analysts. But why?" She sighed deeply, as if trying to calm herself, then frowned. "Let's start over. I think we're pretty sure now this is a male. We thought he might be older, but maybe we should add a few more years to him. This took a lot of planning. Younger men are usually more spontaneous and don't have the patience to pull off something so detailed. Also, I believe he thought Monty would shoot himself before we had time to stop him. I think he wanted us to watch Monty die, a way to punish all three of us. Frankly, it's diabolical."

"He has a real need to be in control," Kaely said. "He's the puppet master who expects his puppets to act out his play perfectly. But Monty didn't do that."

"That's right," Alex said. She paused for a moment. Logan could tell she was thinking. "Okay, his move today was theatrical. Hateful. But I don't think it was personal. I know it was personal to Monty, but what I'm trying to say is that he was angry with Davis and Bayne. Those deaths were personal. They were first because they were the most important. Both men were in their seventies. I think he knew them."

"You're right," Kaely said. "I also noticed that the UNSUB was overweight and of medium height. His eyes looked dark, but he could have been wearing contacts. At least we have a partial physical description."

"Good," Logan said, writing down Kaely's observations.

"So what else can we deduce about him?" Alex asked.

"Well, we thought he was someone who didn't like to get his hands dirty," Logan said slowly. "But he proved us wrong."

"I still don't think he likes killing close up," Kaely said. "I believe he really thought Monty would shoot himself. And that we would stand by and allow it. I don't think he's a man who understands friendship or loyalty. Or even the love of a grandmother who would tell her grandson to let her die. He doesn't comprehend love. Something else . . . My gut tells me that now that Davis and Bayne are gone, his most important goals accomplished, he's even more focused on his plan. How to execute it. His anger has been satisfied. Now he just wants to prove that he's smarter than us."

Alex nodded slowly. "It's going to be difficult to guess what his next move will be. We don't know what his plan is, and we can't trust him not to change his MO again. But whatever is coming, it's already been set up."

"Okay, so he wants to kill profilers," Kaely said matter-of-factly. "Which means no one in the BAU or who's retired from the BAU is safe."

"Isn't that jumping the gun a bit?" Logan asked.

The door swung open, and Gorman walked in with Monty. "Can we have the room?" he asked.

They all got up and headed for the door. Another man was standing behind Gorman. He was in plainclothes, but he had a detective badge from Fairfax County, Virginia. His expression was serious, and his manner was focused. He barely acknowledged the three of them. Logan was certain he knew what Gorman was getting ready to do. He wondered if he should stay. He and Monty were friends and had spent time together outside of work. He was closer to Logan than to anyone else in the BAU. But the look on Gorman's face made it clear he wasn't looking for an argument, so Logan followed the women out the door.

"Might as well go into the community room and get some coffee," Kaely said. "Ours is cold."

When they entered the break room, they found a couple of officers and two or three other staff members sitting at tables. After getting coffee, the three sat down at an empty table in the corner.

"I feel awful for Monty," Alex said. "He's such a good guy. I can't believe this happened to him."

"I didn't see this coming," Kaely said. "Pretty bad thing for a behavioral analyst to admit."

Alex took a sip of her coffee and then set the cup down. "I

didn't either. I was certain this had to do with someone who felt wronged. Who was going after the people he thought caused him some kind of injustice. But Monty never worked with Davis or Bayne. Except for their profession, there's nothing else tying them together. Still, I don't believe the UNSUB is just picking random analysts. He has a reason for each target, but we have no idea who's on his list."

Kaely stared at her for a moment before saying, "Maybe you're right about injustice. But different from what we originally thought."

"What do you mean?" Logan asked.

"What if he wanted to be accepted into the BAU but was rejected? If he's someone who wants to prove he shouldn't have been turned away?"

Logan considered what she said. It made some sense. "I guess so."

"Or maybe he was rejected because he didn't have the kind of experience necessary to make it in," Kaely said. "Perhaps his perception of himself is so inflated that he thinks he should be accepted without the proper credentials. Psychopaths and sociopaths think the world revolves around them. Maybe he blames the fathers of behavioral analysis for his failure. Could he see them as people who were chosen when he wasn't?"

"That's interesting," Alex said. "His high opinion of himself certainly wouldn't carry him through the FBI's training program. Takes some real humility and guts to get through to the end."

"So investigators need to look for men who were rejected for the BAU or the FBI?" Logan asked. "That might be a pretty long list."

Kaely nodded. "Yeah, it is, but all we can do is work the

profile and then let the police search for the UNSUB. We just need to come up with a profile that won't leave them with too many possibilities."

"I understand what you're saying," Alex said slowly.

"But?" Logan said. He could tell she had a problem with the idea.

"What about agents who were kicked out of the BAU?"

"That's a much shorter list," he said.

"We can suggest that, but not without bringing up the other possibility." Alex sighed. "This could be tough."

"We can only do our best," Logan said. "Once we release our profile, we have to let it go, even when the case has touched someone we care about."

The staff sitting at the other tables began to whisper and look at something behind them. Logan turned his head to see D. J. Harper standing at the door, looking a little lost. Logan got up and went over to him.

He stuck out his hand. "Mr. Harper? I'm SSA Logan Hart. We're with the BAU, and we're working your friend's case."

Harper shook his hand. "I'm here to talk to Chief Gorman, but I was told he's busy."

Logan gestured toward their table. "I don't think you'll have long to wait. Please sit with us. Can I get you a cup of coffee or maybe a soda?"

"Coffee sounds great, thanks." Harper walked to the table and sat down next to Alex.

Logan poured a cup of coffee, then brought it to him. "I'm sorry. I should have asked if you need sugar or creamer."

"Nope. Black and strong, otherwise what's the point?" he said with a smile.

Harper was tall with a high forehead and blond hair mixed

with gray. He had bushy eyebrows and bright eyes that conveyed intelligence.

Logan started to introduce Alex and Kaely, but Harper held up his hand, signaling him to stop.

"The lady with the long dark hair is Alex Donovan," he said. "My sources tell me you took down a very dangerous man. Someone who wanted to kill thousands of people." He shook hands with Alex.

"Well, actually, not that many people were at risk," she said with a smile.

"But you didn't know that. Well done."

"Thank you."

"And this young lady is Kaely Quinn. A legend. In fact, if you want to know the truth, I fashioned my protagonist Anastasia Bouderoux after you."

He held out his hand, and Kaely took it. "I guessed that," she said. "Especially since Annie's father was a serial killer."

"I hope I did you justice."

"I only wish I was as smart as Annie," Kaely said with a smile.

"I don't think you need to worry about that." Harper took a sip of coffee. When he put his cup down, he said, "I'm here to talk to the chief about Saturday night. He's hoping I saw something that might help find the person who killed John. I've been briefed about the way he died." He shook his head. "He also told me about Evan Bayne. It's hard to believe they're both gone."

"Yes, it is," Logan said. "And as far as Saturday night, it's possible you didn't see the UNSUB. He might not have even been on the property."

"I heard about the drone," Harper said. "The longest range consumer drone operates under a mile away. They're not allowed to go higher than five hundred feet due to FAA guidelines. And most fly only about ten minutes. I think your UNSUB was pretty close. He couldn't risk pushing the drone past its limits. Besides, there's no way he could have gotten the results he needed if he was too far away."

"What do you mean?" Logan asked.

"Since he had no more than ten minutes to interact with John, he must have been watching John's window to see when his lights went out. Then he sent the drone up and made his phone call." He smiled. "Had to research drones for a novel. I know more about them than anyone should."

Logan frowned. "But how did he know the drapes would be open?"

"It was no secret that John hated the dark and was slightly claustrophobic. He always opened the drapes at night. He actually mentioned that in *Dark Minds*. A result from years of seeing what men do in the darkness. Whoever was out there with that drone knew that." He sighed before picking up his cup.

"I remember that," Alex said. "I should have thought of it."

"So you're telling us the UNSUB was right outside Mr. Davis's hotel room," Kaely said. "That means someone may have seen him."

"John's room was on the side of the building that faced a copse of trees. I think that's where the killer hid. But you're right. Someone probably saw him. They just don't know they saw something important."

"The chief didn't mention any outdoor security cameras," Logan said.

Harper shrugged. "I don't know anything about that. But I do know the police need to find this guy pronto. I have a bad feeling this isn't over. Not by a long shot."

hief Gorman came into the community room and greeted Harper. "I'm sorry to keep you waiting. It's been a rough day. If you'll follow me, we'll go to my office and talk."

Harper said good-bye and left with Gorman.

"Where's Monty?" Logan asked.

"I hope he went home," Alex said. "I'm really worried about him." She sighed and shook her head. "Well, I guess we need to get to work." She threw away her cup, then headed back to the conference room. Kaely and Logan were right behind her, but before they reached the room, Chief Gorman stopped them.

"I wanted to let you know Monty's grandmother is definitely deceased. Our crime-scene techs are going over her house now." He hesitated a moment. "I've spoken to your unit chief. He's ordered Monty back to Quantico. He said he'd feel better if you all came back and worked there. Until we know for certain who this UNSUB is targeting, he thinks you need to be under protection."

"We want to be here," Kaely said. "Two of the victims were killed in this area. We'd rather stay close to the crime scenes. We also need to see whatever you get from the grandmother's house. It might help us. Besides, I'm certain we're safe for now."

"What makes you say that?" Gorman asked, frowning. "Because you're in a police station?"

"Not only that, but it's a sure thing none of us will be answering our phones," Logan said. "In fact, let's all turn them off now."

Each agent took out their phone and switched it off.

"Your boss said you could work here today if you insisted, but tonight you're all going to the FBI Academy at Quantico. We have no indication that any of you are in immediate danger, but we need to be especially careful. Monty's being driven to Quantico. He needs some time to decompress. He's not happy about it, but he's under orders."

"I'm glad," Alex said. "He's angry, and he wants to help find the person who did this. But he needs some time to deal with what's happened. Sweeping it under the rug will only cause more problems down the road."

"Was a page from Davis's book at the scene?" Alex asked.

Gorman nodded. "With a three drawn on the back."

Although she expected it, Gorman's response sent a chill through her.

"Your chief is sending FBI police officers to pick you up later."

"What about our SUV?" Logan asked.

"Leave it here for now," the chief said. "Monty's car is outside too. If the UNSUB is watching, it might be better if he thinks you're all still here."

"All right," Logan said. "We'll need to pick up our things from the motel."

"Your boss is taking care of that too," Gorman said. "He has agents in plainclothes packing up your stuff. They'll have everything ready for you when you reach Quantico." He handed Logan a file he had in his hand. "This is the information we have from Sydney. Right now they're working the case as if it's a single incident. We're in communication with them. I'm sure they'll realize these deaths are all connected, but it might not happen immediately. At least they're willing to hear what we come up with. They want to solve their case as much as we want to solve ours. I also put a copy of the book page found at Monty's grandmother's house in there. One of the cops took a photo on their phone and sent it to us."

Even the mention of a cell phone creeped Alex out a bit.

"Thanks," Logan said.

"What else do you need?"

"How about some lunch?" Alex asked. "And a lot of coffee?"

"You got it," Gorman said. "I'll send one of my officers in to take your food order. And we'll put on a fresh pot. I need to get back to Mr. Harper. Hopefully, he'll have something helpful for us." He frowned. "I want Cooper and Palmer to join you if they get back before you leave. They're out following up on another case."

Alex hoped Harper could help, but he couldn't create information he didn't have. She was certain the UNSUB would have done anything he could to stay away from the author's sharp eyes.

They returned to the conference room and sat down. Alex was torn between the case and being concerned about what her friend was going through.

"I hurt for Monty," Kaely said when the door closed.

Alex sighed. "I was just thinking the same thing. I'm not sure Jeff should allow him to work this case at all. I know he said he wants to be involved, but I think this is going to hit him hard when he's alone."

"I agree," Logan said. "I'm glad we'll all be close by if he needs us." He opened the file Gorman had given him and took out the sheet of paper on the top. "Here's the copy of the page left at Mrs. Wong's." He held it up and began to read.

"'After we proved that the Behavioral Science Unit could help law enforcement find UNSUBs faster, agents began to ask if they could join our unit. Evan Bayne and I, along with a couple of other agents working alongside us, developed a list of requirements to join the unit. Over the years, the FBI refined the prerequisites needed to apply. Although the list is strict, it stresses experience over education, which is good. Very few people make it.'"

He pushed the paper toward Alex. "What's he trying to say? Remember, each note has hinted at the next killing. It seems he might be hinting about someone who didn't make it into the BAU. You may be on the right track, Kaely."

Kaely nodded. "If I am, this guy has a grudge against the BAU and is trying to prove the Bureau was wrong to reject him. I agree this could include a lot of people."

"Let's just get started and see where we end up," Logan said. "Maybe we'll be able to narrow it down further than we think."

"I hope so," Alex said.

As he looked through the pages, Logan handed each one to Alex, who read them before pushing them toward Kaely. Alex couldn't find anything different from what they'd already been told. Again, Gloria Bayne had been interviewed and said everything was fine until her husband took that call. Then he put down his phone where his actions could be viewed and ran toward the cliff.

As Alex read through the report, she couldn't help but feel bad for Bayne's wife. Gloria testified that she'd seen her husband's body wash out to sea. There was a strong undertow in that area. Bayne wasn't the first person who'd died in those waters, and none of the bodies were ever recovered. A note in the file mentioned that the area was closed to swimming because it's shark infested, which might explain the other reason the bodies never showed up again.

Alex shivered. She loved the ocean, but the idea that man-eating creatures lurked beneath its surface was too close to the reality of her profession. Evil dwelt in the shadows, not only in the ocean but above it. She prayed that God would help them stop this particular predator before he claimed another victim.

Jeff sat in his office, his chair turned around so he could look out the window. He felt distinctly uncomfortable. Three deaths, each one connected to the Bureau. Behavioral analysts targeted. He didn't believe in coincidences. This situation bothered him. He wanted his agents back here. He wanted to believe they were out of harm's way, but he wasn't so sure. He wouldn't relax until they were all back under his watch.

Protecting people against themselves was another story, though. Each of the three threats had targeted someone the victim cared for, and two of the analysts had taken their own lives as a result. One had tried but had been prevented by fellow agents. Jeff had been with the Bureau a long time, but he'd never seen anything like this.

He checked the time. Monty should be here soon. Jeff prayed he would find the right words to comfort him. He wasn't good at this kind of thing.

He'd decided to let Logan, Alex, and Kaely stay at the police station today because they wanted to be close to any evidence that came in. It was hard to predict just what piece of information would provide the key that would help them develop an accurate profile. But tonight they were going to the academy. Monty would be driven there after they finished talking. Quantico had great security, but the academy's was better. And besides, it not only had rooms for them to stay in but there was also a food court. This was much better than trying to safely put them up at a hotel. The academy even had a shop where they could buy clothes if they hadn't brought enough. And most importantly, it would be almost impossible for anyone to get close to them. The place had two security stations. People wanting to get through to the academy first had to pass the security gate at the marine base. Next came the guard gate stationed at the entrance to the academy. Jeff had called the academy and talked to the assistant director for training. She understood the situation and had given Jeff permission to send his people there. They had a new recruit training group on site now, but they were leaving Saturday morning.

Jeff wanted to put his people in the Jefferson building

since it was closer to other staff. Easier to guard. The assistant director told him they were doing some maintenance and renovations and the second floor was the only one with available rooms, but she was happy to let them stay. Although it would be a tight fit. Only five rooms were finished, so they'd have to double up. That worked out fine since his unit consisted of four women and four men. Jeff decided to keep one room a single in case Monty wanted to be alone. He felt bad locking him down after his grandmother's death, but he'd had no choice. Jeff had to keep him safe. His other agents' close family members were being guarded too, some of them moved into safe houses.

It was hard to believe what had happened—and harder still to accept that the UNSUB could be targeting all the analysts working for the FBI. After being notified as to what was happening, other field offices were also keeping a watch on any retired analysts in their area. The Bureau couldn't be too safe.

The other BAU unit chiefs were putting guards up at the homes of their team members as well. Jeff reviewed all the units in his mind. BAU 1 addressed international and domestic terrorism threats, arsons, and bombings. BAU 2 was the Cyber Unit. BAU 3 worked with crimes against children. His unit, BAU 4, dealt with crimes against adults. They also had ViCAP, the Violent Criminal Apprehension Program, at their disposal, which consisted of a database and web-based tools made available to law enforcement agencies to connect homicides, sexual assaults, missing persons, and unidentified human remains. More than five thousand law enforcement agencies were able to participate in ViCAP, contributing to more than eighty-five thousand cases in the system.

BAU 5 was the training and research unit. All in all, almost sixty agents were in the BAU. Several other agencies were also represented at the BAU. They included Alcohol, Tobacco and Firearms; the US Capital Police; the State Department; and Homeland Security. Each of these units had a couple of behavioral analysts, and they'd been notified too.

Yet something made him feel as if his unit was the primary target. He had no proof, but his gut told him he was right. All the other BAU unit chiefs agreed but still went along with his suggestion of providing additional security. He'd also suggested they not use their phones, just in case.

Although his people would have no access to cell phones until they could set up something safe, Jeff still felt uneasy. So far this UNSUB had been incredibly clever. Surely he knew the BAU would protect its agents. So what was his next move? The possibilities flooded Jeff's mind like a tsunami. But right now he had to take care of necessities. He had FBI police officers picking up Logan's team's belongings at the motel in Bethesda and inspecting Mrs. Wong's home. His other four agents had been told to quickly pack, make arrangements with family if they needed to, and wait for transport to the academy.

There was still a lot to do to make this work. He picked up his phone and called Alice. "Bring a notebook in here," he told her. "This is gonna be a tough one."

12

After consuming mediocre sandwiches from a nearby deli and finishing three cups of too-strong coffee from the station's kitchen, Alex was hopeful they were making some progress. This was such a different profile. Some serial killers didn't like to get up close and personal with their victims, such as David Berkowitz, known as the Son of Sam. He shot his victims. Others wanted to experience their murders firsthand, such as Dennis Rader, whose nickname, BTK, stood for bind, torture, and kill. Sometimes killers used a combination of methods. Richard Ramirez, the Night Stalker, employed both styles.

Alex sat back in her chair and went over what they thought they knew so far. This UNSUB had profiled as someone who wanted to keep a distance from his victims until he shot Monty's grandmother. Logan believed he'd made that change to add drama to his threat. If they hadn't been able to see him live, he wouldn't have been as threatening. Alex agreed. It explained why the UNSUB had changed his MO.

She could only hope this would backfire on him. Maybe he'd left something behind—some kind of evidence that would lead to his capture.

They'd also decided he was older because it seemed as if he may have known Davis and Bayne, and the murders were so well planned. That had taken time and patience. This indicated he probably wasn't holding a full-time job, yet he had enough money to travel and buy a drone. He was probably retired, giving him the time to carry out his detailed plan. A younger UNSUB would probably be rushed because he worked somewhere.

Even though they wondered if he'd had some personal contact with Davis and Bayne, they wouldn't have been involved with his rejection by the BAU. They may have developed the behavioral analyst program, but they probably wouldn't have been directly involved with hiring and firing. So why go after them?

So far the crime-scene techs hadn't discovered any evidence pointing to the UNSUB at the grandmother's house. But they were continuing to work the scene, and hopefully they'd uncover something. Mrs. Wong's closest neighbors had been questioned, but no one had been able to provide any information. Her house was set back from the road, so it was unlikely anyone would notice a visitor. BAU agents were developing a neighborhood-canvass questionnaire so they could interview everyone who lived nearby. The police were checking surveillance videos from homes and businesses in the area, but it didn't look promising.

Alex was convinced their UNSUB wasn't finished. If for no other reason than the page left at Monty's grandmother's, which was surely another clue.

"I still wonder if one of the reasons our UNSUB wanted his targets to commit suicide was because he didn't want their families to be able to profit from any life insurance policies," Logan said. "Maybe this was another way to hurt them."

"Could be," Alex said. "I had to deal with a few murders in Kansas City fueled by spouses wanting to cash in on large policies. A couple of the deaths were staged to look like suicides—but only after the suicide clause was no longer valid. Like the one in my policy."

"Well, I hope Davis and Bayne had good policies and their widows are able to receive those benefits," Logan said. "It certainly won't make up for their loss, but at least they'll be taken care of financially."

Alex was looking at a copy of the page from Davis's book sent to Bayne, the one investigators said had arrived at his hotel two days before his death. The UNSUB had caused the deaths of two other people near Bethesda, so it seemed clear that this was his comfort zone. He'd taken chances with Bayne's killing. So many things could have gone wrong without him actually on site. But his plan had been constructed perfectly, and everything had gone the way he'd wanted.

Of course, there was the video taken in Frederick. Either the UNSUB had gone there himself to film Bayne's granddaughter and great-granddaughter, or he'd hired someone to do it.

The crime-scene techs hadn't found anything on the Davis envelope or book-page copy that would help them find the UNSUB. No fingerprints. No DNA. That didn't surprise Alex. She didn't expect him to be sloppy.

Alex sat forward again and picked up yet another page from their files.

After several hours of back and forth, Logan said, "Let's talk about the messages the UNSUB has sent so far. What's he trying to say?"

"I think Davis is his main focus," Alex said. "I mean, Bayne wrote books too. So why isn't he quoting him? Everything revolves around Davis. I still think our UNSUB knew him. Had a reason to resent him."

"Most of the time a serial killer is triggered by a person or event in his life," Logan said. "I think you're right. Something happened between him and Davis."

"I agree," Kaely said. Her words came slowly, and her forehead was furrowed.

"What are you thinking?" Alex asked.

Kaely began flipping through the information from Australia. "I realize it's not our job to solve the case, but what the UNSUB knew keeps nagging at me. It wouldn't be too hard to find out where Davis was going to be. I'm sure his presence at the convention was promoted. But how did the UNSUB know his room number, let alone which window was right? And Bayne? For crying out loud, the man was in another country. How did he know Bayne would have such a convenient way to kill himself? And Monty? It's not like he has a public profile. How could our UNSUB know about his grandmother? And when Monty would arrive at the police station this morning? It seems to me that he wanted us around to watch Monty kill himself. This guy certainly has access to a lot of information. That makes me nervous."

"Maybe he gained some of it from their phones?" Logan asked.

Alex cleared her throat. "It could be, but I still feel like he knows a lot more than he should." She shook her head. "We should at least let the chief know this needs to be looked at closely."

"You believe he has someone on the inside?" Logan said.

"Don't you?" Kaely asked. "Someone is giving him information. I can imagine someone coming after me. I've had some unfortunate press coverage." She looked at Alex. "But why pick Monty? Can you guys think of any reason he would become a target after Davis and Bayne and not one of us?"

Alex shook her head. "Monty's never been in the public eye that I know of. Most of what we do is done in the shadows."

Logan let out a long sigh. "Look, I think we're getting off track here a bit. We need to address our UNSUB's interest in targeting behavioral analysts. If we dig any deeper, we'll be trying to do the job of investigators. Right?"

"Not necessarily," Kaely said. "Aren't we talking about his MO? He broke his pattern for Monty. Why? What's the UNSUB's final goal?"

"We can't apply the same standards we use in other cases to this guy," Alex said. She was confused too, but a few things were clear in her mind. "We know most serial killers have poor childhoods. They have a negative relationship with their mothers. Or perhaps their mother died. But I don't think this applies here. Our guy wants to kill profilers because . . ."

A thought formed in her mind. She looked back and forth from Kaely to Logan. "He killed Davis and Bayne because they were the cream of the crop. Maybe he went after Monty to let us know he could get to us. He wants us to know he's in control. That he can get to us anytime he wants to."

Although her suggestion made sense, the reality of it made her suddenly feel cold inside.

13

Gorman scanned the first page of the extensive profile they'd given him. "So this man is older, probably in his late fifties or sixties. He may be connected somehow to the FBI. We need to look for someone who may not have made it into the FBI, or obtained his real goal, which was the BAU. Or he could have been an analyst but was asked to leave. He wants us to know that he's better than all other behavioral analysts. He's knowledgeable about technology. He was able to hack into the victims' apps and cell phones and manipulate them."

He sighed. "Actually, most people don't realize how easy it is to hack into a cell phone." He frowned and looked up from the report. "But aren't your phones protected by the FBI?"

"Yes," Logan said. Alex noticed that he ran his hand through his thick dark-blond hair, something he did when he was worried. "That's why we decided he had more than a basic knowledge of the technology needed to break into our phones. However, we do use them for personal calls sometimes. If he hacks into phones, he'd know how to spoof the numbers of our families and friends and call us, making us think it was one of them." He shrugged. "I'm not an expert on this. We talked to someone in the Cyber Crimes Unit. He says our UNSUB certainly has enough knowledge to be dangerous."

"Which reminds me," Gorman said. "Cyber Crimes couldn't find anything helpful from the voice on any of the videos. No matches. Harper couldn't tell me much either, but he did mention someone odd at the convention who particularly wanted to meet Davis. He sat with our sketch artist and came up with this."

Gorman handed each team member a drawing of an over-weight man with a large nose and a long chin. "He wore a cap," Gorman said, "but Harper thinks he may have been bald. He talked to so many people he can't remember all the details. Frankly, I'm shocked he came up with this much information. He also warned me that this guy might not have anything to do with what's happened. Davis was approached by fans quite frequently."

"The man at Monty's grandmother's was overweight too," Alex said, "but he was wearing a ski mask so we couldn't see his face."

"So it could be the same man," Gorman said. "Harper said the odd guy was of medium height and so was the man with Mrs. Wong."

"It's possible," Logan said, "but that's a real leap. A lot of people are overweight."

Gorman sighed and pointed at them. "I know you turned off your phones, but I need to take them. Agent Cole said if he has to speak to you before you get back, he'll call me and I can relay the message. I'll send your phones with the agents who pick you up."

"Will we get new phones when we get to Quantico?" Logan asked.

"Yes. Your tech guys will meet you and give you phones with numbers on a very limited distribution list. This should help keep you safe."

"Okay," Alex said slowly. "But what about you?"

Gorman held out the report. "You said he's after FBI profilers. I'm not one. Why would he come after me? How would he even know who I am?"

"You're connected to us now," Kaely said. "I think that puts you in his line of sight. Just be careful. And use your landline phones. Try to stay off your cell phones. At least while we're still here."

Gorman frowned. "We'll try, but if this guy is after analysts, we don't qualify."

"It's your call," Logan said, "but I agree with Kaely. I know it will be a little difficult, but it will be safer. It's just temporary."

"All right, but I doubt that will work for me all the time." Gorman went back to the report. "So this guy's anger is focused on John Davis." The chief sat down in one of the chairs at the table. "Then why didn't he stop after he caused Davis's death?"

Alex handed him a paper from one of their files. "Look at this," she said. "First our UNSUB sends him an email that reads, 'Those in law enforcement pay a heavy price when they constantly look into the dark minds of evil.'"

Gorman gazed at the information she'd put in front of him. "That's a quote from Davis's book *Dark Minds*, right?"

"Yeah. You've read it?"

He nodded. "I think I've read every book he's written. *Dark Minds* was one of the reasons I went into law enforcement." He laughed. "Actually, a lot of your profile fits me. I tried to get into the FBI, but I didn't make it. Several of my officers tried too and weren't chosen. I took rejection as a sign that I was where I was supposed to be. In the end, I'm glad I did. Not sure I'd be comfortable with some of the things you people have to deal with."

"My point is that he's talking about those in law enforcement. If he was just targeting John Davis, why would he refer to them?"

"Then there's the mention of a heavy price," Logan added. "We think he feels called to visit this heavy price on anyone who fits that description. But especially those who work with the BAU."

"Okay. So what about the pages sent to or left with the victims?" Gorman asked.

Alex took another piece of paper from the file. "Here's the page from the first killing." Gorman picked it up and read the highlighted words aloud. "'In those early days, I worked with several great agents. The success we had didn't belong to one person. We were a team, each agent bringing his special skills to our efforts.'"

He shook his head. "Was he talking about Davis? Or was he hinting at his next victim?"

"The second death was Davis's ex-friend, Evan Bayne," Logan said. "I think this was directed toward him."

"Sounds like Bayne would have made a great suspect," Gorman said. "Too bad he's a victim."

"Except our UNSUB doesn't seem to care about the feud

between Davis and Bayne," Logan said. "Going after Monty's grandmother proves that."

"Let's look at the book page left at her house," Alex said. "On the back of the page, he wrote the numeral three." She picked up the copy of the page and read, "'After we proved that the Behavioral Science Unit could help law enforcement find UNSUBs faster, agents began to ask if they could join our unit. Evan Bayne and I, along with a couple of other agents working alongside us, developed a list of requirements to join the unit. Over the years, the FBI refined the prerequisites needed to apply. Although the list is strict, it stresses experience over education, which is good. Very few people make it.'"

"I've read this several times," Gorman said. "I don't understand what he's saying."

"We're not sure either," Kaely said, "but mentioning the requirements needed to join the BAU might confirm our earlier suspicion that he's angry about being rejected from the BAU. I think he's mentioning the prerequisites because he thinks they're too stringent." She frowned. "But this can't be what triggered him. If we're right about his age, he couldn't have recently been rejected from the BAU. Most people who ask to join the BAU are younger. Agents who've spent several years in the field. In their late twenties or early thirties."

"So you don't know what triggered him?"

"No," Alex said. "Having that knowledge would help a lot, but so far we haven't been able to find it."

"But we still think he was rejected by the BAU in some fashion," Logan added.

"You know, the number of people rejected for the BAU has to be rather large."

"We know," Alex said.

Gorman sighed and put the report he'd been holding on the table. "I'll go through all of this carefully. Thank you for your hard work."

"Wait a minute," Kaely said. She reached for the paper with the message left at Mrs. Wong's house. She read it slowly, then looked at Logan. "I just realized something." She pointed at the paper. "This sentence? 'Evan Bayne and I, along with a couple of other agents working alongside us, developed a list of requirements to join the unit.'"

"So?" Logan asked.

"I'm an idiot. I totally missed something important. When the BAU was in its infancy, Davis not only worked with Bayne but was assisted by another agent. I know him. He was in his early twenties back then. In his late sixties now. He was teaching some classes at the academy for a while, but he left not long ago."

"Who are you talking about?" Gorman asked.

"Donald Reinhardt. The man who kicked me out of the BAU three years ago."

14

The chief called Jeff with his concerns about Donald Reinhardt, and Jeff promised to track him down and bring him in. At this point, Alex didn't know whether Reinhardt was a target or their UNSUB, but either way, Jeff needed to find him.

Jeff was sending FBI police officers to take them back to Quantico, where the Bureau could keep an eye on them. They would establish a task force on site. Since agents were involved and two deaths had happened outside of Gorman's jurisdiction, the FBI was now able to step into the case without being asked by local law enforcement. Gorman offered to send Detectives Cooper and Palmer to a motel nearby so they could assist the team when necessary. The offer was accepted with gratitude.

Along with Logan and Kaely, Alex was ready when the officers arrived. No one talked much in the car. She felt odd that they were the only unit being housed at the academy, but according to Gorman, Jeff was taking extra precautions with them. Because of Monty, he felt the threat was directed toward them more than any other BAU unit.

Alex was certain Kaely and Logan were both doing exactly what she was—turning the details of the case over and over in their minds. They'd done their job, and she stood by their profile, but she still felt unsettled. As if they'd missed something. Something important. Profiling an UNSUB who might actually be targeting you was a strange feeling. Maybe that's why she couldn't relax.

They were dropped off in front of the Jefferson dormitory, where they would be staying. The other four members of their unit were also being housed there. Members of the other BAU units who lived in base housing were allowed to remain but were ordered to stay watchful. Special agents from other locations were shipped in and assigned to patrol the streets to help the FBI police officers and make sure all BAU agents stayed safe.

By the time they'd had some dinner in the food court and Alex and Kaely had checked into their room, Alex was balancing exhaustion against a desire to talk to Kaely. She wanted to discuss their profile. Was Kaely feeling the same uneasiness Alex couldn't shake? She was quiet as they unpacked, but when they were done, Alex decided to take a chance.

"So what do you think?" she asked Kaely. "Are you happy with our profile?"

Kaely shrugged as she sat down at the small table on one side of the room. "I'd certainly like to narrow it down more. So far we've identified the UNSUB as possibly someone who was rejected by the FBI or, more specifically, the BAU. It's so broad. That doesn't make me feel like we've succeeded at our job."

Alex sat down on one of the twin beds. "But how can we narrow it down any more? Frankly, I've got a headache from thinking about this UNSUB. I get the feeling he knows how much he's confused us."

Kaely looked up at her, a strange expression on her face. "Why did you become a behavioral analyst?"

The sudden question caught Alex unawares, but she tried to answer honestly. "When I was a kid in school, we had these days when the fathers or mothers came in and talked about their jobs. One of the students brought an uncle who'd retired from the BAU. I could hardly breathe as he talked about what he'd done. I knew then I wanted to be part of the FBI. And I never wavered."

"Did your parents support your decision?" Kaely asked. "You don't have to answer that if it makes you uncomfortable."

Knowing some of Kaely's background made Alex feel it was only fair that she should share her own. She didn't usually talk about her past. Logan knew because of an assignment they'd had together that intersected with her childhood.

"I never knew my father, and my mother died when I was young," she said. "I lived with my aunt. I don't think she understood my decision."

Kaely frowned. "You said you lived with your aunt. Usually people say they were raised by someone. And you looked away and clasped your hands when you said it. That means answering the question upset you." She stared at Alex as if expecting her to explain.

"I know how to read body language too," Alex said, her tone

sharp. She instantly regretted her reaction. Kaely had been
treated unfairly because of her background, and Alex knew
what it felt like to be judged by a past you had no control
over. She decided to take a leap of faith and be honest with
Kaely. Her instinct told her she could trust her.

Alex took a deep breath. "As I said, I never knew my father.
My mother actually committed suicide when I was twelve.
My aunt wasn't stable, and I was the adult in the family. I
had to clean the house, pay the bills, take care of everything."

"Do your nightmares come from living with your aunt?"

This time Alex felt a real flash of irritation. "How do you
know about the nightmares? Did you get that by profiling
me? You asked a question. I answered it. Isn't that enough?"

To her surprise, Kaely smiled. "I'm sorry, Alex. I know
what it's like to have people insert themselves into your life.
You had a nightmare last night. It didn't last that long, but it
concerned me."

Alex had no memory of the dream. "I . . . I'm sorry. Why
didn't you wake me up?"

"I've had my share of nightmares. I'm sure you have an
idea why I was plagued with them. But what about you? You
don't have to talk about it if you don't want to. You can just
tell me to mind my own business."

Alex's annoyance dissipated like a cloud being blown away
by a gentle wind. Kaely wasn't being nosy. She was just asking because she cared. Alex took another deep breath. "My
aunt's house was a disaster area when I moved in. She was
. . . Well, she was an adult with the maturity of a child. She
honestly didn't see anything wrong with the mess she lived
in. I had to spend the first few nights in a filthy room, and
in the dark, cockroaches came out. The house was full of

them. They climbed on me. I ended up spending the night on a chair. With the lights on. I . . . I've had a fear of roaches and being in the dark ever since. I'm doing better now that I understand why the nightmares came."

Kaely's eyebrow arched. "And why is that?"

Alex frowned at her. "I'm sure you have an opinion."

"Please don't take this so personally," Kaely said gently. "It's just that you and I are a lot alike. We both came from dysfunctional homes, and we've both dealt with nightmares. I guess it makes me feel as if I can understand you. Regardless, I can see you have an affinity for this job. You're a great analyst."

She peered at Alex as if trying to see into her thoughts. Alex found herself looking away in discomfort. Who was Kaely Quinn? She'd never met anyone quite like her. She was starting to get a little freaked out.

"That's where your problem with germs started," Kaely said.

"Yes, I know." She gave Kaely a wry smile. "I have the same training you do."

"Getting any better?"

Alex nodded. "Getting free seems to be a process, though. And it's very early in my journey."

"Logan's a Christian too, isn't he?"

"Yes, he's the one who told me about God. We were on an assignment, and I thought we were dying. I figured it was time. I wanted to know where I'd end up if I didn't make it. Wasn't willing to risk eternity, I guess." She leaned forward. "I keep praying the nightmares will stop. They've certainly decreased. But I still don't like being in the dark, and the germ thing has remained with me." She grinned. "Of course, after the COVID pandemic, I look like a genius."

Kaely laughed. "Good point. Don't worry about the night-mares. Sometimes deliverance is instantaneous, but most of the time it's gradual. Just be honest with yourself and God. Don't try to hide your painful past. It has to be dealt with. Give it to God, and He'll bring you through. Trying to forget about past hurts never works. They'll continue to haunt you until they're confronted and dealt with."

"Are your nightmares gone?"

Kaely nodded. "But I still have dreams. God speaks to me through them. Thankfully, I haven't had a nightmare in a long time. After my father died, things improved."

"I can imagine. Having someone like that for a father—"

"You don't understand," Kaely said. "Not long after he died, I received a letter from a man who was in the cell next to my father's. Before my father was murdered, this man heard him burst into sobs." She cleared her throat, and her eyes grew shiny. "He heard him cry out, 'Oh, God, forgive me!' And the inmate swears a strange light was emanating from my father's cell."

She wiped away a tear that rolled down her cheek. "I know God visited him that night. Hours before he was killed, he was forgiven and redeemed. I'll see him again, but I'll meet the man he should have been. Before the abuse and pain he endured. Before the evil deeds he committed."

"So you think God will actually forgive someone like your father?" Logan had told her about God's forgiveness, but how could God welcome someone like Ed Oliphant into heaven on the last day of his life? It seemed impossible.

"God forgives anyone who accepts Christ's sacrifice," Kaely said. "Jesus didn't attach stipulations to His atonement on the cross with the names of people forbidden to receive His free gift of salvation. Even those who call on Him at the last minute." She grinned. "Or believe they're dying."

"I guess I deserve that," Alex said, smiling. "I go to church with Logan and to a Bible study too, but it's all a little hard to understand."

Kaely grinned. "I don't know if any of us can completely understand the love of God, but it's important that we accept it. It took me a while. Like you, I wasn't sure what a loving Father looked like. But I'm learning. You will too."

Alex nodded. Kaely's words really resonated with her. "Thanks, Kaely."

"Why don't you take the first shower?" Kaely gestured toward the file on the table. "I'd like to go over the notes and see if I can come up with anything else that might help us narrow the search."

"You're going to use your technique again, aren't you?"

"Yes."

"I'd like to stay, if it's okay with you."

Kaely hesitated. "I'm not sure. You seemed a little upset last time. Can you explain why?"

Alex thought about telling her the truth, that she'd had a glimpse of someone sitting in that chair. But she was afraid Kaely wouldn't let her learn more about her method of profiling—and she couldn't let that happen.

After Alex told Kaely she'd just been excited to see her process, which was true except for the word *just*, Kaely agreed to let her watch again. Then Kaely suggested she help Alex clean before they unpacked. At first she was embarrassed, but Kaely put her at ease. Together it took them only a few minutes to disinfect the room and the bathroom to Alex's satisfaction.

"This was a good idea," Kaely said. "A lot of trainees have been through here and a little cleanup never hurts." She sat down at the table again and picked up the file she'd brought with her. "Before I do this, let's talk for a moment," she said. "Maybe you can help me see our UNSUB more clearly. He's coloring outside the lines. His plan to make people kill themselves is detailed, perfectly planned, and expertly executed. He's clearly the kind of serial killer who uses his brain over his brawn. He not only doesn't want to get his hands dirty, but he goes to great lengths not to do the deed himself."

"And then there was Monty," Alex interjected from her spot on one of the beds.

Kaely stared at her for a moment before slowly repeating, "And then there was Monty. The UNSUB not only shows up in person but has a gun. Again, he's distancing a little—it's not a knife. I get the feeling pulling the trigger was distasteful to him."

"So why do it that way?" Alex asked. "Why did he change his MO? Show himself. Didn't he force himself into a corner?"

Kaely leaned back in her chair and crossed her arms. She was quiet for several seconds. "I'm not sure. Monty had that app, the one that's supposed to show both sides of a conversation. Why not hack it too? Force Mrs. Wong into killing herself? And again, why pick Monty anyway? I have family. A mother in Nebraska and a brother in Colorado. A fiancé right here at Quantico. Why not choose me? Monty hasn't been in the news. I doubt anyone outside of the Bureau—and I guess the Montgomery County police—know he's working this case."

She frowned. "Or why not you? Besides the Train Man case, you made a name for yourself in Kansas City. Your work on the Overland Park Rapist case was exceptional. You were mentioned in the papers and interviewed on local television." She smiled. "Well done, by the way."

"Thanks, but it would be hard to threaten me. I have no one," Alex said. "Well, a dog. But I doubt the UNSUB cares about Krypto."

"Krypto? Like Superman's dog?"

Alex nodded.

"Interesting."

Alex sighed. "Please don't profile me again. Let's get back to the case."

"Okay," Kaely said slowly. "But we might want to talk about your choice of names sometime. As friends, Alex."

Alex couldn't help but smile hearing Kaely Quinn call her a friend. "Okay."

"You know, it's possible that Monty's grandmother was just easy to get to," Kaely said. "Her house was isolated. He didn't have to go through a lot of preparation. The choice could have been that simple."

Alex nodded. "I wonder if he let us see him because it made him feel more powerful. You know, you can see me, but you can't catch me?"

"It's a possibility. Or like Logan suggested, just to be more dramatic."

Alex frowned at her. "You mentioned your mother and brother. Have you notified them about what's happening?"

"Oh, they know something's going on," Kaely said. "Before we left the police station, Gorman told me the FBI started watching them twenty-four-seven after they learned Bayne died. They were alerted of a possible danger but not given details. Jeff told the chief I could be the next person on this guy's list. As soon as I have clearance, I'll explain what I can to my family. For now, they just know they need to stay safe." She shook her head. "This kind of thing isn't new to them, unfortunately."

"I'm sorry. Families shouldn't have to pay the price for the job we do."

Alex couldn't help but think about something that happened when she was the coordinator for NCAVC while stationed in Kansas City. A lead detective from the local KCPD lost his wife to a drug kingpin who'd wanted to teach the detective a lesson. His fellow officers took the assassination personally and hunted the guy down. They committed all the department's resources to finding the lowlife, who would be spending his golden years in prison.

Many of the detective's fellow officers had wanted to end the kingpin's life, but they played it by the book. The lead detective decided if they killed the scumbag without cause and the truth was uncovered, losing their careers would actually be a win for him—even if he never knew about it. Arresting him gave the detective some closure, but it didn't bring his wife back. He tried to work for a while, but he ended up taking early retirement because he'd lost his passion for the job.

"No, they shouldn't, but it happens." Kaely shrugged. "Like I said, I'm used to it. And I know they're safe, including my brother's family, so I'm not worried. I hate that their lives get disrupted because of me, but they're supportive. They're proud of what I do."

Alex felt a twinge of jealousy. She had no one who really cared about her—except Krypto. He might not be human, but she honestly didn't know what she'd do without him. Someone was glad to see her when she got home. She was important to someone. She needed that assurance. That kind of love.

Kaely opened the file and began to look through it slowly, methodically. For quite a while, she didn't say a word. Alex watched as Kaely stared at the empty chair across from her as if someone were there.

She jumped when Kaely suddenly said, "You want us to know you're smarter than anyone in the BAU. Certainly smarter than John Davis. But why?" Kaely was quiet for a moment. Then she pursed her lips. Finally, she took a deep breath. "I'm certain you were rejected in some way by the FBI. Most likely the BAU. Was it Davis who rejected you? Or was it someone else? Bayne? Did you know them? They're both obviously important to you."

Kaely was quiet, as if she were listening to someone. Alex clasped her hands tightly.

"You came up with a clever way to kill people so you could impress us and because you like to keep your hands clean. But then you killed Monty's grandmother yourself. Why change your MO?"

Again, Kaely stopped as if someone were talking. After a pause, she said, "You wanted to shock us. Show us that you were capable of doing whatever you needed to do. You were hoping Monty would take his own life, but you knew that might not happen. Did you know he was with us when you called him? Did his grandmother tell you he would be?"

Kaely's forehead wrinkled as she continued to stare at the chair. "Did you work for the FBI? If you're in your late fifties or sixties, you had to retire. Is that why you're angry? Was that your trigger?" Again, she was quiet for a while. The seconds ticked by, but Kaely didn't say anything else. Finally, she said, "Or were you fired? That would make you feel as if you had something to prove."

For the first time, she looked at Alex, but she didn't say anything. Then her gaze swung back to the chair. "Are you finished? Or do you plan to keep going?" Another long pause, then she nodded. Alex realized Kaely really was seeing something. Or someone. It was unsettling. Thankfully, this time Alex didn't see anything.

"How did you know John Davis's room number? And

where Evan Bayne was when you called him with that video? And what about Monty?" Kaely's eyes widened. She blinked several times, a look of surprise on her face.

She directed her gaze at Alex again. "We were right about someone on the inside. He's close by. In fact, I believe he's watching us."

―――

"They think hiding at the academy will keep them safe?" He laughed. "It only makes this more exciting. I anticipated the possibility that they would be moved somewhere."

"But the FBI Academy?" his associate said. "The security there is extremely tight. It will be difficult."

He choked back the rage that boiled inside him. He needed their help. At least for now. "It's not too much for me. All I have to do is adjust the plan some. You still need to do exactly as I say. Do you understand?"

A pause. "Yes, I understand."

"If you don't follow my instructions, you know what's at stake, right?"

"Yes, I know."

"Good. You're my eyes and ears. Keep me apprised of their every move. Now, let's go on to our next target. This one will be so . . . exciting. We'll rock those twits in the BAU to their foundation."

A lex's breath caught in her throat. "What . . . How can you know that?" she asked Kaely.

"This UNSUB knows too much, Alex, and we concluded that he likes to show his superiority to us. Getting next to us, having a minion watch us . . . It fits his profile."

She tried to process what that meant. "So he . . . he could be someone in the Bureau? I guess we'd decided he could be getting information from someone on the inside, but you think it's more than that? That he's . . . physically close by?"

Kaely nodded, then dropped her gaze to the folder again. "And we're right about thinking our UNSUB is specifically targeting people who work for the BAU."

They'd already decided that. This information wasn't new. "The BAU has five different units," Alex said. "Is he going after all of them? Or just ours?"

Kaely stared quietly at the empty chair across from her. After a long pause, she said, "I believe he's got a specific target in mind. An endgame, if you will. He's already chosen each victim." She sighed and looked at Alex. "He chose Monty because he wanted us to see him. To watch him work. Honestly, I think it's because someone in our unit is next. That's just a guess, but I can't think of any other reason for him to target Monty. Jeff must have suspected this same thing, or he wouldn't have moved our unit here." Kaely yawned. "Look, it's late. We need some sleep. Maybe this will seem clearer tomorrow. My brain's too tired to do much good tonight."

Alex was tired too, so sleep sounded good. But she was turning everything Kaely said over in her mind, trying to digest it.

"Like I said before, go ahead and shower first," Kaely said.

"No, you go." Alex pulled her laptop out of her bag and put it on the table. "I want to contact Logan."

"I wouldn't do that, Alex," Kaely said sharply, making Alex jump. "We can't be sure our email accounts are safe."

Of course. What was she thinking? "You're right. Guess I'm sleepier than I realized." She put the laptop back. Better safe than sorry. "Before you take a shower, though, one thing is bothering me."

Kaely smiled. "Just one thing? This whole case bothers me."

Alex nodded in agreement. "You mentioned our UNSUB wanted to make sure we saw him when he called Monty. He wanted our personal attention. Why? Why not do something that would attract the attention of everyone in BAU 4?"

Kaely stared at her, her eyes wide. "You're right. I should have seen it. He's figured out every step methodically. He went after Monty because he knew we would all be together." She shook her head slowly. "It's us. Logan, Monty, you, and me."

"But what if Jeff had assigned a different team?" Alex said.

"How could he know the four of us would be assigned to this?"

"Are you saying Jeff had something to do with it?"

Alex shook her head. "Absolutely not. It was probably the luck of the draw. This could have happened to any team he put together."

"He went after Monty because he needed someone quickly, and Monty was the most vulnerable," Kaely said thoughtfully. "If the team had been a different group, he would have chosen someone else easy to get to." She sighed. "Monty's grandmother was what stuck out. An easy kill. I still believe he wanted to show us he could get to us, and that's why his MO changed. It finally makes sense." She looked at Alex. "And now he has us. He knows who I am. And he knows who you are. That only leaves Logan."

"Should we call him now?" Alex asked.

"I don't know. It's late, and I'm sure he's tired." She lightly slapped her forehead. "I just remembered I promised Noah I'd contact him when I got here." She shoved her hand into the pocket of her jeans, then quickly drew it out, her hand empty. "Shoot. I don't have a phone."

"They have landlines downstairs. They should be safe. Check with someone first, though."

"Right. I'd forgotten." Kaely sighed again. "I'd better call him, or he'll start to worry."

"Where does he work?"

"He's an instructor in the Practical Applications Unit."

"Wow. He's got to be proficient in several areas to teach that class." That unit offered training exercises, firearms expertise, interviewing and investigative techniques, and arrest training.

"He is." Kaely smiled. "I worked with him in St. Louis

before we both came here. I did everything wrong, but somehow he fell in love with me anyway." She stood. "You know what? I'll go ahead and stop by Logan and Monty's room after I talk to Noah. I don't want to upset Logan by keeping this until tomorrow. I think I've offended him a time or two, and I'd rather not do it again. I'll tell him what we suspect. I'll be back in a bit."

She hurried out into the hallway, closing the door behind her.

Alex was left to ponder what they'd discussed. Was it true? Was the UNSUB planning to go after one of them? Why? Was it Kaely? She and Logan weren't important or well-known. Yes, she got some attention a couple of times, but those stories had faded. The Bureau didn't like their agents to be in the spotlight, so no more occasions for the press to talk to her had been provided after the most recent article. She was angry to realize that Monty was just a convenience. The easiest one to get to. No wonder the UNSUB changed his MO. She should have seen it. He always seemed to be one step ahead of them.

She waited a couple of minutes, making sure Kaely didn't come back right away. Then she got up from the bed and sat down at the table. She opened the file Kaely brought with her. She'd seen Kaely do this twice now. Could she do it herself? She wanted to find out.

She read the notes Kaely had written on some of the pages. Then she took a deep breath and looked at the empty chair across from her. She felt a little ridiculous, but she decided to try it anyway. If it worked for Kaely, maybe it would work for her.

"Okay," she said in a low voice, hoping no one next door or walking down the hall would hear her, "you found a way to get two of the most famous profilers in this country to kill themselves. You think you're clever. You spent time setting up your scenario. You're organized, and in fact, you have your next moves already figured out."

Alex sighed. She felt stupid. But she took another deep breath and continued. "You went after Monty because you could easily get to him. You didn't have time to set up a complicated scenario, so you did what was most convenient. You also wanted us to see that you had power over us. What you did was for all of us, not just Monty. Unfortunately for you, we stopped him from killing himself. I don't think you really wanted to pull that trigger. I'm sure you're rather put out with us. Good." Alex could feel resentment burning inside her like a fire she couldn't quench. "You're a coward. That's why you plan your killings from a distance when possible."

She took yet another deep breath. She needed to get her anger under control. It wouldn't help. She needed to use her training. Her instincts. "How long did it take you to come up with your thirty-second scenario? Quite a while, I think."

Alex shuffled through some of the papers again, looking for something, anything else that might move them one step closer to the UNSUB. Although she was trying to stay detached from him and his dark deeds, watching a friend suffer had put a personal aspect to this case. She was angry. She wanted this guy. She'd felt the same way about the creep who'd killed the detective's wife in Kansas City. She'd almost spiraled out of control in her desire to catch him. The rage had consumed her, and she didn't want to go through that again.

Alex breathed slowly, in and out, until her breathing was controlled and steady. Then she began again. She looked at the chair across from her several times but saw no one. Wasn't she supposed to see the UNSUB sitting there?

A story about a case in Nashville the authorities couldn't solve had circulated through the KCPD. Kaely had used her unusual process as a favor for an FBI special agent in charge. He got something more than a profile. Kaely had looked through the file and solved the crime. Just by using this unusual method, she'd actually given them the name of their UNSUB.

Alex sighed. She was pretty sure she wasn't going to come up with a name, but at least she believed they now knew why Monty's situation had been different from the other killings. She glanced at the clock on the wall. Kaely could be back anytime. She needed to wrap this up.

Once again she stared at the chair. She tried to imagine the UNSUB. Older. Sixties, maybe? Probably white since most serial killers are. No one responded. No one sat in the chair. But at least she wasn't seeing the figure she thought she'd seen last time. That had clearly been her imagination.

"Why are you targeting us?" she asked. "Who's next? Kaely?"

Nothing.

"That has to be it. Whatever you want from her won't happen. Her family is protected. She's protected. You can't possibly be after me. I'm not important."

Suddenly, something dark entered the room—like black smoke. It swirled around and then settled into the chair across from her.

Alex heard a low voice that seemed to whisper, "You're not Kaely Quinn. You're no match for me. You will die."

17

Alex had just closed the file and moved to her bed when the door suddenly opened. She jumped when she heard a scream and only realized at the last moment that it came from her own mouth. Kaely stood in front of her, her eyes wide, a look of surprise on her face.

"Alex, what is it? Are you okay?"

Alex struggled to harness her emotions. "I'm sorry. I guess I nodded off for a few minutes. Bad dream."

"Another one?"

Kaely put her hand on Alex's shoulder. Her touch made Alex flinch.

"Wow. Let's get you settled down." Kaely led her over to the chair at the table, the last place she wanted to be. She looked toward the chair where the image had appeared. Nothing was there. The room felt normal again. The only thing that wasn't right was the way her heart was pounding. She was having a hard time catching her breath.

"How about something to drink?" Kaely asked. "I picked up some bottled water from the vending machine."

Alex took the bottle gratefully and forced the cold water down. It actually helped a little. She realized that she'd just lied. As a Christian, she wasn't supposed to do that, and she felt bad about it, but she couldn't tell Kaely the truth.

"Do you want to talk about it?" Kaely asked as she sat down in the other chair.

Alex shook her head. "No. But thanks anyway." She took another sip of water and tried to stop her hands from shaking. "What did Logan say?"

"Monty said he was in the shower, so I didn't get to talk to him. But I'm confident Logan is making sure there's plenty of security in place. Agents are watching all the roads into the complex and all the entrances into this building. With no way for the UNSUB to contact us, I believe he feels fairly confident that we're safe."

"Unless he's already here somewhere," Alex said. "Or maybe he has someone working with him who's watching us."

"Could be. But remember, that's just conjecture at this point. It makes sense to me, but that doesn't make it true."

"I realize that, but the idea that we're being stalked doesn't make me feel very secure."

"Me either."

"Did you talk to Noah?"

Kaely smiled. "Yeah. Hopefully, I'll see him tomorrow. He just completed a new-agents training class. He taught them how to investigate a kidnapping, make entry, handle arrests, and process crime scenes." She sighed. "I think he had a lot more fun than we're having."

"Well, that wouldn't take much."

"No kidding." Her expression became serious. "Hey, I was thinking about something on my way back here. Since the UNSUB got to Monty because it was his easiest move, if he goes after the rest of us, I believe he'll pick us off as he's able."

"I don't think the question is if he'll try again," Alex said. "It's when. And that makes him even more dangerous. He's willing to change his MO to accomplish his goals. We can't figure out his next move if we can't rely on an MO."

Kaely drew up her knees and wrapped her arms around them. "You're right. That's unsettling." She was quiet for a moment, probably trying to digest what Alex had said. "Something about Bayne bothers me. I'm sure the UNSUB wanted him to die. But he wasn't in the same country, and so many things could have gone wrong. Like we said, what if Bayne hadn't answered his phone until later in the day? There's a fourteen-hour time difference between here and Sydney. The timing was . . . well, unbelievable."

"You're right. Anything could have thrown off his timing. Maybe Bayne wasn't supposed to be second," Alex said slowly. "Maybe he was supposed to be first, but the UNSUB had to wait until everything was timed perfectly."

"Yeah, maybe. I don't know. I feel like we're missing something, but I'm too tired to see it clearly. All I know is something about Bayne is different." She rubbed the sides of her head. "This case is giving me a headache."

"Me too."

"He needs to be caught," Kaely said with a sigh. "I'd like to go home someday."

Alex couldn't help but think about Krypto. She missed him so much. Was he missing her too? Or was he having more fun with the Stewart kids? She quickly wiped away a tear that snaked down her cheek.

She was also worried about what she'd seen earlier. Should she tell Kaely what happened? She really didn't want to. She was afraid she would alienate her, yet Alex was really frightened. Maybe Kaely could help.

"I hate just sitting around," Kaely said. "We've got to outthink him. Figure out his next move . . . or at least some idea of what he might do." She yawned. "But not tonight. Jeff wants us all in one of the training rooms in the morning."

"Why?"

"He just wants to touch base, and—" She hesitated a moment before saying, "Donald Reinhardt could be there."

"I guess that makes sense. He's still a suspect, isn't he?"

Kaely shrugged. "To be honest, it's hard for me to believe he's our UNSUB. I may not like the man, and he may not like me, but I don't see him as the kind of person who could do something like this. He just doesn't fit our profile. He's a stickler for the rules. He lives and dies by the FBI code of conduct. We can't take him off the list, but I've spent a lot of time studying people, and he doesn't fit the mold. And he definitely didn't shoot Monty's grandmother."

"What makes you say that?"

"He's tall and thin," Kaely said. "Of course, he could have had someone else kill her for him, but I still can't see it."

"Will it be hard to face him?"

Kaely crossed her arms, a defensive gesture. "No. I mean, maybe. I don't know. He kicked me out of the BAU, but if I hadn't gone to St. Louis, I wouldn't have met Noah." The corners of her mouth turned up. "So no. I guess I don't really care anymore. Besides, he's the outsider. Like I said, he was teaching classes here for a while, but I hear he was forced to leave. He's got a rather unpleasant attitude."

"Sure sounds like a reason to want to seek revenge," Alex said.

"Yeah, but not on profilers. If he wanted payback, wouldn't he target the administration that let him go?"

"You have a point." She'd just opened her mouth to say more when someone knocked on their door. This time they both jumped.

"Now you're making me nervous," Kaely said with a smile.

Alex got up and went to the door. Before she opened it, she looked through the peephole. Logan. She swung the door open.

"Sorry to bother you so late," he said. "But I couldn't sleep. Wondered if you'd like to join me in the food court for some chamomile tea."

"It's open this late?" Alex asked in surprise.

Logan grinned. "No, but they left hot water on for coffee, tea, or hot chocolate. I guess they're used to dealing with FBI agents who don't sleep much."

"Yeah, I'd love that. Just a minute."

Before she had a chance to say anything to Kaely, her roommate called out, "Go ahead. I'm going to get a shower and go to bed. I'm beat. And feel free to tell Logan about our earlier conversation."

"Okay." She started to close the door behind her but then stuck her head back inside. "Is it really all right if I leave you alone?"

Kaely shook her head. "Not a problem. We're being closely watched. Besides, I'm packing heat."

Logan and Alex laughed as she closed the door. Even

though Kaely felt protected, Alex couldn't dismiss a small voice in her head. It seemed to whisper that none of them were really safe.

Nor could she forget the voice that had whispered she would die.

After making them both a cup of chamomile tea, Logan sat down at a table with Alex. "So how's it going?" he asked. "Rooming with a legend."

He expected her to laugh, but she didn't. Instead, her lips thinned, and her jaw tightened.

"That bad?"

Her eyes widened. "No, I don't mean to make it sound . . . I mean . . ." When she took a sip of her tea, Logan noticed her hands shaking.

"Alex, what's wrong?"

She studied him for a moment. "Look, you're the one who led me to God. If I talk to you about . . . spiritual things, will you keep it between us?"

"Sure."

"What do you know about Kaely's method of profiling?"

Logan shrugged. "I was told she looks over the facts of a case and then tries to see the UNSUB. Talks to him as if he were sitting in the room with her. Seems to work for her. I don't have a problem with it."

"I . . . I watched her do it. Once at the motel and again tonight, just before she left to talk to you and Noah. When she was gone, I tried it myself."

Logan could tell Alex was upset, but he wasn't sure why. "Did it work?"

She nodded. "Maybe too well."

Trying not to sound frustrated, Logan said, "I'm sorry. I just don't understand. What are you trying to tell me?"

She sighed deeply. "Look, I know you'll say this was my imagination, but I . . . saw something at the motel. And then tonight, I heard something."

"Like what?"

"I saw someone sitting in the chair at the motel when Kaely did her thing. And then, a little while ago, I tried it when I was by myself and heard a voice."

"What did the voice say?"

She blinked several times before saying, "It told me I'm not Kaely Quinn. That I'm no match for . . . whoever it was. And that . . ."

"That what?" Logan asked gently. He wasn't certain what had spooked Alex, but he knew she hadn't been the same since Kaely Quinn showed up. Alex had battled demons most people would never face. But now she seemed a little weaker and unsure of herself.

"That I was going to die."

She watched for his reaction. Although what she'd said frightened him, he tried not to show it.

"Is this . . . demonic?" she asked.

"Probably."

"So what do I do?"

He leaned closer to her. "Alex, I can't tell you what to do, but my first question is why are you using Kaely's technique? You're a fantastic behavioral analyst. The best I've ever worked with. Why do you feel you have to do things the way someone else does them?"

Her eyes narrowed, and she frowned at him. "There's nothing wrong with learning. If Kaely successfully uses something I don't, why wouldn't I want to try it?"

He was quiet for a moment, weighing his words. He didn't want to offend her. "You're right. We should all want to grow. We need to increase our knowledge about patterns and behaviors that help us to more clearly understand aberrant personalities. But we're all different. What works for one person won't necessarily work for someone else."

"Do you find Kaely's technique strange?"

"Well, yes. For me. Maybe for you too. Look, if it works for her, fine. I'm not knocking her. She's a great analyst. But you need to use the techniques that work for you. And you need to learn more about spiritual warfare. You may have a gift that allows you to see things in the Spirit. A Scripture in Second Corinthians tells us not to compare ourselves with others." He sighed. "Just find out who *you* are, Alex. God will show you. Develop your own gifts and ways of using them."

She hesitated a moment, then said, "I hear what you're saying, but I really respect her. I . . . I'd really like to be more like her."

Logan shook his head. "You have an incredible reputation from your time with Kansas City, and I've watched your work since you got here. You're so talented. Why can't you see that?"

She looked away from him. "I don't know. Maybe you're right." She swung her eyes back to meet his. "I have no one to model myself after, Logan. No father. A mother who checked out on me and eventually killed herself. A mentally ill aunt I had to take care of when I was only twelve. I guess my only identity has been based on my career. But the truth is, I've been playing a role for a long time, acting the way I thought someone like me is supposed to act."

She took a deep, shaky breath. "I know what you're going to say. That now I belong to God, and He has a plan for me. That I need to be like Him. I understand, and I totally agree with you. But I have no idea what a father is. I have nothing to refer to. I've admired Kaely Quinn for a long time. Can you blame me if I see her as a role model?"

"Ever since we started working together, you've battled your demons with strength and determination. And then Kaely Quinn comes along and your insecurities find a target. A person who seems to embody everything you want to be. I don't want you to lose yourself by trying to be like someone else."

Alex took another sip of tea and then leaned back in her chair. She gazed up at the ceiling for a moment. "You could be right. Maybe I'm trying too hard to pattern myself after Kaely. I just want to be the best I can be."

"And you will be. But not by trying to imitate someone else. Listen, Alex, please don't try Kaely's method again. And tell her what happened, okay?"

"No," she said quickly, her voice raised. "I don't want her to know. She'll think I'm pathetic."

"I'm pretty sure she won't. I believe she needs to know. Really."

"I'll think about it." Her eyes narrowed. "So what about the voice? My imagination? Or something else?"

"Did Kaely mention having the same kind of experiences?" Alex nodded.

"Then it could be either one. The story was in your head. Your imagination may have kicked in."

"But you think it might have been . . ."

"Demonic? Yeah, it's possible. But if you don't do it again—"

"Then it won't happen."

"Yes. But again, Kaely knows more about this than I do. I'm sure she wouldn't have shown you her way of profiling if she'd known you were susceptible to this kind of thing. Most people wouldn't have had the same experience you had. I really think she can help you."

"I'll think about it." She gave him a quick smile. "Thanks. I really appreciate being able to talk to you about this." She sighed. "When I was a kid, I saw *The Exorcist*. I just want to make sure my head won't start spinning around, and that I'm not going to suddenly spew pea soup everywhere."

"Well, if you think the pea soup thing is going to happen, could you warn me first?"

For the first time since they'd sat down, Alex laughed. "You'll be the first to know."

"Good. I feel much better. I kind of like this sweater."

She laughed again.

"You heard that Donald Reinhardt may be coming in tomorrow?" Logan said.

"Yeah, I think that's wise since he's indirectly mentioned in the message left at Mrs. Wong's place." She frowned. "So Monty's rooming with you? I've been worried about him."

"Yeah. He could have a room to himself, but he didn't want to be alone. He's a mess. Especially since he's having to handle arrangements for his grandmother over the phone."

"Well, surely he'll be able to attend her funeral."

Logan nodded. "Jeff told him he'll have to be escorted there and back, but they'll make sure he gets a chance to say good-bye. I'd like to go, but it might not be possible."

"Poor guy. I'd like to attend too."

"He called his parents, but it sounds like they aren't interested enough to show up. I don't get it."

"I don't either, but maybe they just can't make it."

Logan shrugged. "Maybe. I'm not going to judge them since I don't know them, but if my kids needed me, I hope I'd move heaven and earth to make sure I was there for them." He took a sip of tea before saying, "So have you and Kaely come to any new revelations? Is that what she said you could tell me? The reason she stopped by?"

"Actually, yes." She filled him in on what they'd been talking about, about who the UNSUB could be targeting next.

"You think he's after us? Kaely, you, and me?" He shook his head. "I can't be a target. Even my mother forgets my name sometimes."

"Very funny. I'm sure that's not true."

"That's a little unnerving. Why you and me? Could it be related to a case we all worked together?"

"Maybe. Or maybe it's just because he sees us as the opposition. The people looking for him. Tomorrow we talk to Jeff. We've been looking at the victims, how they might have triggered the UNSUB, but now we need to concentrate on the four of us." She stopped for a moment.

"What?"

"It's just a big shift in my thinking." She frowned at Logan. "We've helped on . . . what? About a dozen cases together? The biggest one involved Adam Walker. But he's dead. His family is dead. So it couldn't have anything to do with him."

Even the mention of their work on the infamous Train Man case made Logan nervous. "Someone from the Circle?" He shook his head slowly. "This doesn't feel like them. Besides, most of them are peaceful. Just duped."

"We certainly met some who weren't peaceful," Alex said.

"But they were outcasts. Besides, why would they kill John Davis and Evan Bayne? They had nothing to do with what happened with Walker."

Alex drew a circle on the table with her finger. Logan wondered if she realized it. The Circle, a secretive society that believed the world was inhabited by angels and demons, had impacted both of them. But Logan had moved on. Had Alex?

"You're right. Davis and Bayne had nothing to do with the Circle." She offered him a small smile. "Sorry."

"Don't worry about it. Believe me, I think about them too. Wondering what they're up to now."

"Probably nothing. Just waiting for the world to end."

Although she hadn't meant it to be funny, it was, and Logan laughed.

Alex's lip quivered before she laughed too. "Sorry. That was the strangest case I've been involved in."

"Before this one?"

She studied him for a moment. "Yes. The way he's set this up? It's diabolical."

"I agree."

"Kaely also thinks our UNSUB could be here. Watching us. Or maybe someone working for him."

"That's not possible. Everyone here is law enforcement—except for the support staff, and I'm sure they've been thoroughly checked out."

"What about Bradley Summers?"

Summers was an FBI agent who turned out to be an operative for the Chinese, yet the agents who served with him in BAU 1 never suspected him—not for a moment. Washington sent in someone from Homeland Security pretending to be a supervisory special agent, and he was planted into the unit. It took four months, but Summers was finally outed and indicted for treason.

"Summers was an anomaly," Logan said, his tone a little brusque. Several people in DC had also been involved in the scandal. It was a black eye for the Bureau. The men and women who worked in the FBI were proud of the work they did, and a traitor like Summers was hard to accept.

"I know," Alex said. "I'm sorry. That was tough on all of us."

"No, I'm sorry. We all have to get past that. Hopefully, we'll be able to earn back the public's trust." He took another sip of his tea. "Let's forget Summers and look at this situation clearly. Kaely thinks the UNSUB may have some kind of access to us?"

"We both wonder about it. It's just a theory, but the UNSUB knows too much." She pursed her lips for a moment before asking, "Could Reinhardt be a target?"

"I'm sure Jeff's thought about that. He'll be brought in safely."

Alex sighed. "I still feel like we're the next targets. We all have to be careful."

"Okay," Logan said slowly. He paused a moment, then added, "We just need to keep our heads on a swivel."

"I agree. Maybe tomorrow Jeff will have something encouraging to tell us. Who knows, the UNSUB might have already been caught."

Logan nodded, but in his gut he knew that wasn't true. And by looking at Alex, he knew she didn't believe it either.

His agents were safely tucked into the dormitory rooms at the academy, and now Jefferson Cole was in his car, headed to pick up his oldest daughter, Stephanie—no matter what she said.

He'd sent his wife, Lisa, and his younger kids out of town to stay with friends. Ronnie Jameson was a retired SWAT team member who had promised to keep them safe. But Stephanie was still here. She lived alone in a small apartment in Georgetown and had a job nearby at Miller's Boat House. He'd called her this morning and said he was coming to pick her up when the shop closed, insisting she move in with him until the UNSUB was caught. He'd also told her he didn't want her going to work for a while. But she'd ignored him on both counts. Stephanie wanted to be independent, and it was clear that desire battled against any concern for personal safety. Still, he intended to talk her into either staying with him or letting him drive her to Ronnie's.

Jeff realized he was probably being overly cautious. The UNSUB was targeting profilers, and as a unit chief, he didn't actually work cases. His job was to oversee those who did. However, his friend Della Williams, chief over BAU 2, was worried about his well-being. Tomorrow, after meeting with his team, he'd talk with his section chief. If he decided Jeff should hunker down in the dorms at the academy too, he'd have no choice. And if by then he'd convinced Stephanie to stay with him, he'd have a better chance to convince her to go to Ronnie's, which he preferred. He was pretty sure the last thing she wanted was to stay at the academy.

When Stephanie was little, all she wanted was to grow up and work for the "BFI." When she was four, she finally got it right. It saddened him and Lisa a little. They'd found her mistake cute. When Steph turned sixteen, she informed her parents that the last thing she wanted was to be a part of law enforcement. She had a crush on some boy who'd convinced her those who protected America weren't worthy of respect. The way she used to look at her dad with admiration slowly faded. They got along all right. It wasn't as if they couldn't spend time together. It was just . . . different, and it hurt him. More than he could say.

He'd texted her several times that afternoon to tell her he would be there at eight, but she hadn't responded. He was tired. Hopefully, she would be waiting for him.

He'd reached the road that led to the boat shop and started to turn, but then his phone buzzed. He'd turned off his old phone and bought this one so he could text with his family. The UNSUB had no way of obtaining this number.

The screen told him it was Stephanie, so he pulled over, then picked up the phone. Maybe she'd gone home early.

Alex lay on her bed, staring at the ceiling. She was saved from asking Kaely to keep a light on because the light poles outside the dorms gave enough illumination to make her feel safe. Thankfully, Kaely didn't try to close the curtains. Alex couldn't help but remember John Davis had left the curtains open at his hotel and had played right into the killer's hands. The academy was much safer, but still, she wondered if it would be better to close the drapes and leave the bathroom light on. She pushed the thought from her mind. Guards were posted everywhere. No one was outside the window.

So should she quit using Kaely's method of profiling? She found it intriguing. Logan wanted her to stop, but that confused her. Why could Kaely do it and she couldn't? No matter what Logan said, Kaely was a great role model. She was smart and the best profiler Alex had ever encountered. But something Logan once told her echoed in her thoughts: "*God has a plan for your life, Alex. You're unique. Find the path He has for you.*" Tonight he'd said basically the same thing. Although it sounded right, she wasn't sure how to find her own path. Like she'd told Logan, she'd never had a role model. Was it really so wrong of her to choose Kaely as someone to emulate? His protestations bothered her. She was grateful for his friendship and that he'd led her to God, but it was still her life. She had to make the final decision. Besides, the image she saw and the voice she heard had probably been just her imagination.

Her jumbled thoughts fought against the weariness in her body. As she began to drift off to sleep, she admitted to herself that she wasn't sure what to do. She wanted to follow God's plan, but why hadn't He shown it to her? Did He really know her personally? Was she important to Him?

Almost immediately, she saw herself standing in a garden, at the entrance to a maze. As soon as she stepped inside, she noticed a woman's figure ahead of her. Alex began to run after her, calling for her to stop. The woman appeared almost ghostly. Her features were shadowy, and she was surrounded by mist. Every time Alex caught sight of her, she disappeared around another corner of the maze.

Alex began to cry out to the woman, begging her to stop. To wait for her to catch up. She was afraid of getting lost, unable to find her way out. As she ran, she realized the sun was going down. She would be abandoned in this place. Lost and in the dark. The thought terrified her.

Her legs began to burn with the effort of trying to keep up with the wraithlike woman. The air became heavy, and Alex could barely breathe. She was falling behind. Where had the woman gone? Suddenly, she couldn't see anything. She reached out to touch the bushes that made up the maze, but it seemed as if they went on and on in a straight line. How could she find the exit in the dark? Her heart felt like it would beat out of her chest from fear.

Alex finally stopped, and the blackness began to envelope her. She took a deep gulp of air, causing her chest to ache in the process. With what she knew was her last breath, she choked out the words, "Save me, God!"

Almost immediately, a small beam of light caught her eye. She fell to her knees and began to crawl toward it. Little by little the air grew lighter, and she could finally breathe freely. She struggled to get to her feet as strength began to flow through her body. She heard a voice saying, "When you turn to the right or to the left, you will hear a voice in your ears telling you to walk this way."

Alex began to repeat the words over and over as she ran toward the light. She suddenly found herself outside the maze, with the sun shining down on her. She began to thank God over and over for rescuing her, but the next voice she heard wasn't God's. It was a woman's voice.

"Alex," she said. "Alex, wake up."

Alex opened her eyes to find Kaely standing over her, a look of concern on her face. Alex forced herself to sit up.

"What . . . what's wrong? Did I wake you up?"

Kaely sat down on the side of the narrow bed. She chuckled lightly. "You were thanking God for saving you. I kind of hated to wake you up, but you were getting pretty loud. These walls are thin. I was afraid you'd wake someone up."

"I was having a really strange dream. I'm sorry. I had no idea I was having it out loud."

Kaely smiled. "Do you want to talk about it?"

"I don't want to keep you up."

Kaely shook her head. "Nonsense. I wasn't sleeping anyway. I'm just lying in bed, thinking about the case."

"Okay, if you're sure."

Kaely got up. "I think they have hot chocolate in the food court. It's just a powder, but I'm game if you are. Want some?"

"Yeah. That sounds good."

"I'll be right back."

When Kaely walked out the door, leaving it slightly ajar, Alex wondered if she was doing the right thing sharing her dream. Should she keep it to herself? She swung her legs over the side of the bed. Of course, it was too late to ask herself that question now. She'd committed to discussing it with Kaely. She didn't like the way she'd felt lately. Small and childish. Maybe Logan was right. Maybe she just needed to get her act together.

Alex sighed and pushed herself off the bed. She checked the thermostat on the wall. It was chilly in the room. She turned the heat up a little, then sat down at the table. A few minutes later, Kaely pushed the door open, two Styrofoam cups in her hands.

"Doesn't look too bad for a mix," she said as she leaned against the door with her shoulder. After it clicked shut, she sat down at the table with Alex, handing her one of the cups.

Alex took a sip. It was hot and surprisingly tasty. "Thanks."

Kaely nodded. "Look, I don't want you to feel as if you have to tell me about your dream if you'd rather not. It just always helped me to talk about mine."

"Who did you talk to?"

"Mostly Noah. He was always available to listen, but he didn't feel like he had to figure out what they meant. I think down deep we know what our dreams are trying to tell us. We just can't admit it to ourselves."

"Maybe. I've been reading the Bible. Daniel and Joseph interpreted dreams, and I'm certain I couldn't have figured those out. Pretty weird."

"Daniel had a gift, and God used it to bring him to a place of prominence. He was able to bless many people because of it."

Alex grunted. "Not sure this dream measures up to anything that lofty."

Kaely grinned. "That's okay. I once dreamt I created the

perfect profile for a prolific serial killer. Everyone thought I was wonderful."

"Was the killer caught?"

She nodded. "Yeah, a SWAT team broke down the front door of a house and found"—she grinned—"Elmer Fudd."

"The cartoon character?"

Kaely nodded.

Alex laughed. "So we're really looking for cartoon characters?"

"I guess so. It would make all this more fun, wouldn't it?"

"Absolutely. I'm afraid there weren't any cartoon characters in my dream, though."

Kaely took a sip of her hot chocolate before saying, "Tell me."

Alex took a deep breath and told her everything she could remember.

"Wow," Kaely said. "That's really interesting. So who do you think the woman represents?"

Alex had an idea, but she wasn't sure. "I . . . I'm not certain."

Kaely yawned. "Sorry. I don't know either. Ask God what it means." She smiled. "If it's important, He'll tell you. If not, it might have been the aftereffects of something you ate in the food court."

"You're right." She was disappointed. She really wanted to understand the dream and had hoped Kaely would have some insight. But she couldn't expect her to know everything. Besides, she was getting sleepy too.

Kaely reached across the table and extended her hand. Alex reached out for it, and when Kaely bowed her head, Alex did the same.

"Lord," Kaely prayed, "if this dream was from You, please reveal its meaning to Alex. And thanks for loving us and meeting our every need. In Jesus's name we pray, Amen."

Alex mumbled, "Amen," and then she got up from the table and went to her bed. As she slipped under the covers, she thought about the easy relationship Kaely seemed to have with God. She wanted that too. Would it ever happen?

Alex and Kaely got up at six thirty and joined Monty and Logan for a quick breakfast in the food court, where the other four analysts from their unit—Robin Wallace, Bethany Hostetler, Todd Hunter, and Nathan Sampson—all greeted them. They'd been told everyone was to meet in one of the classrooms.

"Which room are we going to?" Alex asked them.

"We have no idea," Robin said. "I guess we just head that way and hope we find the right one."

They walked through the glass-enclosed hallway toward the classrooms. Every building around the dorms was connected by these glass hallways. Recruits referred to them as gerbil tubes. The hallways provided protection from the elements, though. They almost never had to step outside.

As they neared the classrooms, Alex was surprised to see Terry Burnett from BAU 3 headed their way. "We're in here," he said simply, pointing to a classroom on their right.

"What's he doing here?" Alex whispered to Logan. "Where's Jeff?"

They all sat down and waited. The door to the room opened, and Chief Gorman walked in. Ben Cooper and Julie Palmer were with him. Another officer followed. He didn't look like a Montgomery County officer. Alex wondered why he was here. They all sat down on the front row without saying anything.

"Where's Jeff?" Monty whispered.

Alex shrugged. "I was wondering the same thing."

That voice in her head that liked to whisper things she didn't want to hear was trying to get her attention, but she blocked it. Everything was all right.

"Something's going on," Logan said in a low voice.

When the side door opened and a man stepped into the room, Kaely's quick intake of breath made it clear she'd noticed him too.

"Reinhardt," she whispered. "He seems so much older."

He looked the way Alex remembered him, though. Tall, with thick silver hair. He wore black-framed glasses and was neatly dressed. He'd always reminded her of a successful businessman rather than an FBI agent. However, his face was lined, and his gait was slower.

"Are you still convinced he's not our UNSUB?" Alex whispered. "He fits the profile."

Kaely was quiet for a moment. "I don't know, but I still can't see it. The code of ethics we agreed to when we joined the Bureau is sacred to him. His reasons for cutting me loose were based on his honest belief that I would make the FBI look bad."

"That's ridiculous. You're probably the best profiler the BAU has ever had."

Kaely turned to look at her, a slight frown on her face. "Thanks, but I think we need to take things on a case-by-case basis. I haven't hit the target every time. Nobody does."

Alex shrugged. Kaely was just being modest. She'd helped to locate more UNSUBs than anyone else in the room. Alex caught Logan looking at her. She knew he was still concerned about her attempt to use Kaely's profiling method. She couldn't help but think about what he'd said about not losing herself by trying to act like someone else. Was she really losing her identity? Did she even have one? She pushed the troubled thoughts out of her mind. She needed to concentrate on the UNSUB. She wasn't convinced their profile was completely accurate, and it left her feeling disconcerted.

Reinhardt sat down on the front row with Gorman and his detectives. Terry stood and walked to the front of the room.

The voice Alex was trying to quiet began to shout at her. Logan was right. Something was wrong. She wanted to get up and leave the room before Terry said a word. She didn't care what anyone thought of her. But she felt glued to her seat. She couldn't move. She heard Logan whisper something under his breath, but she couldn't understand it.

"It's my sad duty to tell you that last night . . ." Terry's voice shook with obvious emotion. He took a deep breath and tried again. "Last night, Unit Chief Jefferson Cole was on his way to see his daughter Stephanie at her place of work, Miller's Boat House near Georgetown. According to her, he was determined to get her somewhere safe until our UNSUB was arrested, but she'd been refusing to follow his advice. He was going there to insist that she leave with him. When he was a block away from Miller's, instead of his car turning right toward the shop, it went off the nearest pier and into the Potomac."

He took another breath as Alex held hers. "A couple of brave civilians tried to get to him, but the weight of the water against the car doors made it impossible to remove him from his vehicle. Professionals were called in immediately, but by the time they pulled Jeff out, it was too late. The EMTs could do nothing for him."

Gasps rippled through the people seated in the room like small explosions. Alex could only stare at Terry. It couldn't be true. Was this some kind of sick joke?

"We don't think this was an accident or that Jeff suffered some kind of physical problem, although an autopsy will have to confirm that. We don't have much more information at this time, and we don't want to jump to conclusions. When the police have something solid, they'll share it with us. The Georgetown force has been graciously working with us."

Alex looked toward the police officer who'd come in with Gorman. He had to be from Georgetown.

"Chief Gorman is here to tell you what he knows. He's willing to take questions, but as I said, there's not much he can tell us yet."

The chief got up and took Terry's place as he sat down. Alex was certain the agent was suffering. Terry and Jeff had been friends.

"As Chief Burnett shared, we have very little information right now," Gorman said. "The Georgetown police are doing a great job and will update us as soon as they can. I do want to say how sorry I am this happened. I know Agent Cole was greatly respected by his colleagues."

"Chief, was a page from Davis's book left behind?" Logan asked. "Like with the other cases?"

"If so, we haven't found it yet. If it was in the car, I doubt it would have survived in the water."

"Did he have a phone with him?" Kaely asked.

"We did find one in the car." He cleared his throat. "It was inside an evidence bag. It appears Agent Cole had the presence of mind to protect it before the car sank. That tells us he knew what he was doing. We just don't know what caused him to drive into the river. Detective Palmer interviewed Agent Cole's daughter, but she was too distraught by the news to really talk to us. Her mother is on the way here. We'll talk to Stephanie more before she leaves town to be with her family."

Knowing Jeff was aware he was going to die and yet was thinking he needed to preserve evidence was too much for Alex. As she fought back tears, she managed to choke out, "If a copy of a page from John Davis's book was in Jeff's possession, he would have added it to the evidence bag. I think it will show up in the mail."

"I agree," Kaely said.

"Wasn't Jeff advised not to use an unsecured phone?" Monty asked. Alex could see he was visibly shaken. He'd worked with Jeff for several years now. Everyone who'd ever been in Jeff's unit admired him. He was great at his job. He had the ability to chastise his people if they needed it, but he also praised them when they deserved it, making them feel as if they were part of something special. Anyone who'd worked with him was hurting.

"We don't know yet," Gorman said. "When we asked for Stephanie's phone, she told us it had gone missing that morning. We searched her workplace but couldn't find it. She did manage to say something about her father insisting she contact him only by text, but until we look at Cole's phone, we won't know what caused him to drive off that pier."

"The UNSUB was there," Alex said. "He took Stephanie's phone. That was the only way he could pull off this plan. He didn't have any other way to get to Jeff. It's just like the other cases." She frowned at Gorman. "Were there security cameras? Could we have gotten him on video?"

"Yes. A bait-and-tackle business sits right next to the pier where Jeff's car went into the water. We're getting the tapes now." He paused for a moment. "I have a hard time understanding this. Agent Cole wasn't that far from the boat shop where his daughter worked. And he was armed. If he received one of these calls, why didn't he just drive to the shop? He could have protected his daughter without committing suicide."

"He no doubt had only seconds to decide what to do," Alex said. "A block away was too far. And maybe he wasn't sure his daughter was even there. It was too risky. He wouldn't take a chance with her life. No parent would. He wouldn't have done what he did unless he was convinced he had no other option." Her voice broke. "We need everything you can give us, Chief. Please bring us any new information as soon as you get it. Every time this UNSUB makes a move, he gives us more to go on. We've got to stop this guy. Now."

Terry got up and joined the chief. "We've lost one of our own," he said. "We'll keep you updated on our investigation. We know Jeff meant a lot to you. He was our friend too. Logan Hart will be acting unit chief until we have a permanent replacement." He nodded toward Logan. "I'll need to meet with you. Please stay behind." He swung his gaze over the people sitting in front of him. "The rest of you are dismissed."

As others left, Alex stayed seated with Kaely, Monty, and Logan, aware that Reinhardt was still there too. What should they do now?

"Let's go back to our room," Kaely said to her. "I want to talk about this guy. See if we can add anything else to the profile."

"I'll talk to Terry and join you all later," Logan said.

"Just come to our room when you're done," Alex said. "And could you ask Terry if there's someplace else we can work? Our rooms are too small. We need a dry-erase board. And a large corkboard."

"This place is crazy with them," Logan said. "I'm sure that won't be a problem."

"Just tell Terry we want to refine our profile. See if we can give them any more information that will help find the UNSUB," Monty said.

"All right." Logan got up and went to the front of the room to talk to Terry. As Alex and Kaely stood to leave, Donald Reinhardt turned around and looked their way. His expression changed when he saw Kaely. His mouth thinned, and his eyes narrowed. The hostility in his face was chilling.

As she left with Monty and Kaely, Alex couldn't help but wonder about Reinhardt. Kaely thought he couldn't be their UNSUB, but at that moment, Alex wasn't so sure.

Satisfied, he reviewed the events of the previous night as he ate a breakfast picked up from a diner a few blocks away.

He'd watched Jefferson Cole's demise from a dock farther down the river's edge until his body was taken away. Everyone—from the passersby who'd dived into the frigid water to the EMTs—had failed to save the man. Then after he'd tossed the daughter's cell phone into the river, he'd pulled his jacket closed against the cold wind before driving away. He'd also slipped the envelope into a mailbox with a late pick up to ensure its arrival this morning.

Number four was finished. The police and the FBI's so-called behavioral analysts were no match for him, and it was time for his next work of genius. His magnum opus. He smiled. Two more, and then he'd leave the country. He had a place ready where no one knew him. Where he could start over. He would have a new life. And no one would ever come looking for him. He'd make sure of that.

Once the analysts were gone, Terry led Logan, Gorman, and Reinhardt into a small conference room. Cooper and Palmer had left as well, as had the police officer from George-town after speaking to Gorman for a few minutes. Once the four men were seated, Terry asked Logan if he already knew Donald Reinhardt.

"I'm not sure we ever spoke, sir," Logan said to the man. "But you taught interrogation techniques when I was a new recruit. Good to see you again."

Reinhardt raised one eyebrow and wrinkled his nose as if he were sniffing rancid food. "I don't remember you. I'm sorry."

"That's okay. You taught a lot of us."

Reinhardt nodded, then turned his attention back to Terry. "Look, I appreciate your concern for me, but I'm not convinced I need to stay here. I no longer work for the FBI. I'm retired. Those in charge made sure of that. I don't feel the need to follow your instructions."

"We're worried about you," Terry said. Logan could see signs of the tension Terry was trying to suppress. "Every book page left behind after a death has given us a clue to the next killing. You're not mentioned by name, but you are referred to on the page we found with Monty Wong's grandmother. You may be in grave danger."

"*May* be?" Reinhardt repeated. "I have a life, and I know how to take care of myself. I don't need a babysitter."

"Look, no one's saying that. We . . . we could use your

expertise with this. You have a lot of experience that could prove invaluable to us."

Terry was obviously trying to appeal to Reinhardt's ego since nothing else seemed to be working.

"So you kick me to the curb, but when you need me, you think you can pull me back?" Reinhardt said. "I don't think so."

"You know that's not true," Terry said. "We all have to retire at fifty-seven. You weren't singled out. And you were a great teacher here at the academy. You shared your wisdom with many trainees. You left with our appreciation and esteem. Not many people have the kind of career you've had with the FBI."

"I don't want to talk about that," Reinhardt said. His words were sharp and quick, like bullets ripping through a target. "I'll stay for a while, but if I decide to leave, I'm not asking anyone's permission."

"That's up to you." Terry turned to Logan. "I want you, Alex, Kaely, and Monty to keep working the profile. See if you can narrow it down any more. We need all the help we can get."

The door to the room opened, and an agent with a box in his hands stepped inside. "Oh, good," Terry said. "Craig, you're confident these will work?"

The agent nodded. "As sure as we can be. We're certain everyone will be protected."

Terry looked at Logan. "Since you and the other agents in your unit can't use your own cell phones, CIRG is giving us these phones for you to use. They have no video or photo apps and no voice mail. No one can call you or text you unless they have one of these phones. You can call out just like a regular phone, but don't call or text anyone outside of the people who've also been issued one of these phones unless it's an emergency. If you get a call and the name of the caller on the screen isn't the name of an approved caller, don't answer it. I really don't believe that will ever happen. CIRG is confident these phones are secure. No matter how good the UNSUB is at hacking, he can't get to these."

If the FBI's Critical Incident Response Group said these phones were safe, Logan was certain they were. CIRG was the best in the country at what they did.

"Remember, landline phones are also available on the first floor," Terry went on. "But I doubt you'll need them. Please distribute a phone to all seven agents in your unit and explain what I've just told you. They're labeled. Every phone has the names of the people who can be called listed under Contacts. And tell your team they still need to be on their guard. I don't want them taking any chances."

Craig held out the box to Logan, who took out the correct eight phones, including the one for him.

Terry took three more phones from Craig and handed them to Chief Gorman. "Advise your team they need to use these when they're here, not their regular phones. The same goes for you, Chief. I know it seems like our analysts are the UNSUB's target, but we shouldn't take chances. If he knows you're working with us, you and your detectives are at risk."

"I understand," Gorman said.

Craig held out two additional phones. Terry put one in his pocket, but when he offered one to Reinhardt, the man huffed, "You're not taking my cell phone. That's ridiculous."

Terry's face flushed, but he controlled his temper. "I'm not taking your phone. I would advise you not to use it, though.

If you don't listen to me, you may be putting yourself or a family member in danger."

He held the phone out to Reinhardt, who hesitated before finally taking it.

"We'll talk more about this later. Just please turn off your phone for now until we have a better plan. We're trying to save your life."

"I'm starting to realize how addicted we are to our phones," Chief Gorman said. "Not sure that's a good thing."

"Well, it certainly isn't right now," Terry said with a sigh. He turned to Reinhardt. "I've asked Craig to show you to your room. You'll have one to yourself. No one else is in Jefferson except the agents in BAU 4. If you need anything to make yourself more comfortable, please let us know."

"I know what the rooms are like in Jefferson," Reinhardt said. "Not much chance of being comfortable."

Logan was getting tired of his attitude. "You do realize all this is being done to protect you, right? I'm not sure you understand how much danger you might be in."

Reinhardt glared at Logan. "I was catching dangerous criminals and tracking down terrorists when you were still in high school. I am more than able to take care of myself. I don't need this place, and I don't need you. I'll do as Terry asks—for now. But if at any point I should decide to leave, I will *not* argue with anyone about it. And if I want to use my own phone, I will."

His eyes flashed with anger. "On your best day, you haven't done the things I have. I was in my twenties when I worked with John Davis and Evan Bayne. I helped to develop the BAU. You have a job because of me. I will not be talked down to or treated with anything but respect. I hope I've made myself clear."

He gestured at Craig. "You may show me to my room now." Without another word, he stomped out, the unfortunate Craig hurrying after him.

When the door closed behind them, Terry grunted. "I'm about this close to telling him to go it on his own."

"I feel a little sorry for him," Logan said.

"You're a better man than me," Terry mumbled.

"And me," Gorman added.

"I hope your people respond to these phones better than Reinhardt did," Terry said to Logan. "I know this is difficult, but we're trying to do everything we can to protect you."

"I know that. And they do too. Anything else?"

"Yes, there is," Terry said. "Now that Reinhardt's gone, I need to talk to you about something. It won't take long, but it's important."

Alex felt like she was trapped in one of the nightmares that had chased her for so long. How could Jeff be dead? Questions assailed her mind like frightened birds trying to find a place to land. Nothing seemed to make sense anymore.

Monty followed Alex and Kaely back to their room. "These rooms are really small," he said. "I like Logan, but that could change by the time this is over."

"They're going to be even tighter for the four of us to work in," Alex said. "I hope Logan finds us another place soon." Alex took a seat on her bed while Kaely and Monty sat down at the table.

"I . . . I can't believe Jeff's dead," Monty said. "Two people I care about gone in just a matter of days. It's . . . it's hard to take in." He looked away from them.

"I know," Alex said. "I'm so sorry, Monty. We're going to catch this creep. He's not perfect. He's made mistakes.

We just need to figure out what they are." She paused for a moment and then said, "Monty, are you sure you want to work this case?" She knew the answer even before he said anything. He felt the same way she would if the situation were reversed.

"I have to be involved," he said simply. "I just have to. It . . . it helps to keep my mind off my grandmother. Really."

When someone knocked on the door, Alex called, "Come in."

The door swung open. Bethany, Todd, Robin, and Nathan all stood there. They looked as shocked as Alex felt.

"We'd like to help," Todd said, his voice unsteady. "We know too many people working a profile can cause chaos, but it doesn't make any sense for us to just sit around and do nothing."

"Thanks," Monty said. "I agree. Since he's acting chief now, why don't you talk to Logan? I'm certain we could use your help."

"We'll bring it up and see what he says," Bethany said. She looked down for a moment. When she raised her head, she had tears in her eyes. "This guy has to be brought to justice. He killed Jeff."

"We understand completely," Alex said. "Let us know after you talk to Logan. We'd be grateful to have you on board."

"Okay," Todd said. "See you all later."

After Nathan pulled the door shut, Monty said, "I totally get it. I'd feel the same way if I was in their shoes."

"Let's get our notes together," Kaely said, "so we're ready to work when Logan gets back." She took a deep breath before saying, "Look, I just came on, so I didn't know Jeff well, but I know you two are really hurting. I just want you to know

I'm committed to doing everything possible to help find this UNSUB."

Alex could see Kaely had also been moved by Jeff's death. "Thanks. We appreciate that," she said. "I haven't been at the BAU for long either, but Jeff had become important to me. Logan and Monty worked with him for several years." She got up and grabbed her notebook while Kaely found the file they'd been working with.

"This is personal," Monty said. "I want this guy."

"I do too," Alex said. "For Jeff. And for your grandmother."

"And for John Davis and Evan Bayne," Kaely added. She frowned. "We could use more information from Australia. Hope that's coming soon."

"I'm sure the authorities will work with us," Alex said. "There's no reason for them to hold back. They have some great behavioral analysts there too. They can even bring them in to help."

They talked about the case until they heard a knock. Alex again called out, "Come in," and Logan opened the door.

"We've been assigned a classroom," he said.

"We're ready," Alex said. "Lead on."

Alex looked at the sky as they walked down the glass-covered hallway. The dark clouds overhead looked like snow.

"This is it," Logan said, opening a door. He led them into a room with a large table and eight chairs. Both a dry-erase board and a corkboard sat on portable easels for easy positioning. There was even a copier.

"This will work great," Alex said.

"The rest of our unit stopped by Alex and Kaely's room," Monty said. "They want to help."

"You're the analysts assigned to this case," Logan said, "but

I'll brief them later today. They can work on questionnaires for the police, review the victimology for common elements, and help the police develop investigative strategies."

"Are you still going to work with us?" Monty asked. "I mean, now that you're so important?"

His attempt to provide some humor actually helped a bit. Alex felt the tight muscles in her neck loosen.

"Yes, I'll be working with you," Logan said. "Things won't really change. I guess someone has to act as unit chief, but trust me, the title is in name only. I'm not Jeff, and I could never replace him."

The silence that followed his words was a testament to the truth of his statement. No one could ever take Jeff's place.

"So Chief Gorman will brief us about Jeff's . . ." Alex couldn't finish. Jeff was dead, but no one wanted to say it out loud.

"Right. He'll be here shortly to give us what he has. He's not in charge of this latest . . . incident. The Georgetown police are. But they're working with Gorman and feel it would be smoother for us to deal with him directly. I don't think Terry wants to have anyone else coming here anyway. It all worked out okay."

Logan leaned over and picked up the briefcase he'd carried into the room with him. He opened it and took out some files, which he then placed on the table. "Before we get started, I need to give you your new phones." He took out a box and handed each person a phone, then explained the new procedures.

"So we're to use them only to call each other?" Monty asked.

"Right. I know it's difficult trying to handle funeral arrangements on a landline downstairs, but we need you to stay safe. You can call the funeral home if you have to, but they can't call you back on this phone." He frowned. "Do you have a date for the funeral yet?"

"Not yet. My grandmother will be cremated, and the funeral home will keep her remains for a while. I'm hoping my parents will change their minds and decide to attend. Then we'll have a service." He looked around at everyone. "I hope you'll all come."

"It would be an honor," Logan said.

"We'll all be there," Alex added, trying to rein in her emotions.

After a few seconds of silence, Logan cleared his throat. Then bringing everyone back to the matter at hand, he said, "Just remember these phones are the safest way for us to be in touch. Check the contacts list. Everyone on this system is there, including our whole unit, Terry, and Gorman and his detectives. Even Reinhardt since he's here. And don't give your number to anyone else. I mean that, okay? Even if no one else can call your number directly, we don't want to give our UNSUB a chance to make it look like one of us is calling you."

Everyone let him know they understood, so he moved on. "Let's start by going over our previous profile and asking ourselves if we need to change it."

"Logan," Kaely said, "I have to address the elephant in the room. We've discussed Reinhardt as a possible suspect, and now he's here. Near us. I don't think this is a good idea. I've said I don't believe he's a viable suspect because of his almost obsessive adherence to following the rules. I find it hard to believe he would break that strong personality trait to kill his coworkers. But he's still a suspect."

Logan nodded. "I agree. We're keeping an eye on him. He's alone in a room at the end of the hall."

"He gets his own room?" Monty said.

"Hey, you had your chance," Logan said with a smile. "Are you already tired of me?"

"Well, you do snore."

"You should probably consider yourself lucky. I could put you in with Reinhardt."

"No, thanks," Monty said. "You're fine."

Logan laughed. Then he looked around at everyone. "Okay, let's get to work."

A knock on the door interrupted them. "It's open," Logan said.

Chief Gorman walked into the room with Cooper and Palmer. He had files and papers in his hands. "We have a more thorough report from Australia," he said. "Terry asked me to bring it to you. We don't have Agent Cole's autopsy report yet, but I'm sure you realize the cause of death was drowning."

He put the files on the table. "An envelope was delivered to the Georgetown police station today. This was inside." He handed each one of them a copy of a page from a book.

"From *Dark Minds*?" Alex asked.

"Yes."

The three police officers sat down, and Gorman read the highlighted sentences. "'Bayne and I worked together on the Austin City Strangler case. We profiled the killer as someone who wore a uniform. Someone the victims trusted. Just like the so-called Raggedy Man in Des Moines. After the killer was captured, we found that he'd worn a police officer's uniform when he stalked his prey.'" Gorman added, "A number four was written on the back of the page."

Alex turned the words over in her mind before saying, "He can't be referring to Bayne. He's already dead. This has to be pointing to Kaely."

"With the Raggedy Man mention? Seems like it to me," Monty said.

"How does he intend to get to her here?" Logan asked, irritation evident in his tone.

"He might not have known she'd be here when he mailed this," Gorman said. "My guess is he's found out by now, though. You need to be especially careful."

"If this guy can get to Kaely, he's inside somewhere," Logan replied. "And unless it *is* Reinhardt, that's impossible."

"I don't know," Kaely said, speaking for the first time since they'd read the letter. "We've wondered how the UNSUB knows so much about us."

"Well, he doesn't know everything," Gorman said. "My guess is that the UNSUB believed Davis was armed, that he had his gun with him. That means he's not infallible."

"But how did he know Jeff was on his way to see his daughter last night?" Alex asked. "I find that concerning."

"The UNSUB must have followed him," Monty said.

"Maybe," Alex said slowly. "But I agree with Kaely. He knows more than he should."

"Are you saying you think the UNSUB is someone we know? Someone in the Bureau?" Monty asked, a look of surprise on his face.

"Not necessarily one of us," Kaely said. "But someone close to us. Someone who knows where we're going to be. Or maybe someone inside this case is giving him information."

After using her technique earlier, Kaely said she thought the UNSUB could be at the academy. But Logan had been reluctant to believe anyone in law enforcement could be the killer or even help the man when Alex told him what Kaely said. She was reluctant to believe it too.

"Chief Gorman," Logan said, "please don't be offended by this question, but can't these files be accessed by quite a few people in your department?"

"Yes, of course. But they can only read about the case. There's nothing in there to indicate where you are. I've kept that private, per the request I received from Agent Cole. The only people who know besides me are Detectives Cooper and Palmer." He nodded toward the two. "I trust them implicitly."

"Are you certain no one could figure it out?" Monty asked.

Gorman hesitated long enough to make it clear he couldn't give Monty the assurance he was looking for.

"If you're not sure, that means everyone in your station is suspect," Monty said.

Alex frowned. "Someone has to be working with our UNSUB. Someone who's privy to information that should be private. It's the only thing that makes sense." She shook her head. "I just don't think he's the only one behind this.

"You mean maybe his helper could be the one who went to Texas to film Davis's wife?" Kaely asked.

Alex nodded. "Exactly."

There was a long silence before Logan spoke. "Chief, I need you to quietly investigate your officers and staff. Check their phone calls. Emails. Find out if any one of them could possibly be working with our UNSUB. If you need help, bring in people you trust. But whatever you do, don't tell anyone else what you're doing."

Gorman's face turned red, and he started to speak, but Logan held up his hand. "I'm absolutely not accusing your people. Believe me. We just need to be sure. I'm going to be checking out our agents and staff as well. If we have someone working against us, we need to find them immediately. We need to know if we have a traitor in our midst."

The chief swallowed hard, but his color returned to normal. "All right. I can understand why you're concerned, but I know my officers. I guarantee you we're clean." He stood. "I'll give you some time to review your profile. I'll use Cooper and Palmer here to help me quietly investigate, but this could take some time."

Gorman left the room. Cooper followed him, but Julie Palmer held back.

"Look, I agree with the chief," she said to Logan. "Our people are clean. But I understand why you have to look at everyone. I'm sorry he got so upset." She shrugged. "If the people in your unit were accused of helping this awful man, you would probably react the same way."

"You're right," Logan said. "I'm sorry the chief was offended, but we have a dangerous, clever killer who isn't finished. I want him stopped. I can't be worried about anyone's feelings. I hope you understand that."

"Of course I do. And the chief will come to that conclusion too, as soon as he calms down. He's very protective of us. I think you're doing an incredible job. I hate what's happening, but I love watching you work." She paused a moment before adding, "If anyone at the station is involved in this, we'll find them."

She was headed toward the door when Logan called out, "Thank you, Detective Palmer."

When the door closed behind her, Logan sighed and said, "If any of you see anyone acting suspiciously, or even if someone makes you feel uncomfortable, come to me. If we do have a mole who's helping the UNSUB, we've got to find them. If we don't, the police might not be able to stop this guy. He'll continue to be one step ahead of us, and more people could die."

The four of them worked for a couple of hours, trying to think of anyone who could be accessing information about the case, but they made no progress. Logan hated bringing up Jeff's daughter, but that idea was shot down quickly. One of Jeff's hard-and-fast rules was to never share information about a case with anyone outside of work. Especially family.

"It's just not possible," Logan said. "I know it's not always easy to raise a headstrong daughter, but Jeff loved Stephanie. I saw them together a few times, and she loved him too. That was clear."

"She'll have to live with refusing to leave town when he asked her to," Monty said. "She may blame herself for what happened."

"If the UNSUB hadn't used her, he would have used someone else to manipulate Jeff," Kaely said. "I think he picks his target and then gets to them any way he can. He seems to be pretty dedicated to achieving his goals."

"I agree," Alex said. "We need to get back to our profile. We're getting distracted. Can we look at the information from Australia? I'm really curious about it. It's the only killing that happened out of our guy's comfort zone. Bayne is the odd man out."

"Sure," Logan said, "but how about some lunch first? It's almost two o'clock. I'm starving."

Alex was surprised to hear the time. She hadn't thought about food. For some strange reason, she kept feeling that she'd missed something, but she couldn't figure out what it was. It felt as if it was right in front of her, but she just couldn't see it.

Everyone agreed to break for lunch. As they walked toward the door, Alex said, "Are you sure those files will be safe?"

"I have a feeling the police officer guarding our door will be sufficient," Monty said.

Alex smiled. "I think you're right. Feels strange to have so much security. I mean, we're profilers, not field agents."

"You're right," Monty said. "But we still deal with unstable, violent criminals. We can always be a target for them, I guess."

As they left the room, Logan locked the door behind them and spoke to the officer sitting in the hallway. Then he caught up with the others as they made their way down the gerbil tunnels. "He'll be there for another two hours before the new officer checks in," Logan told them.

"I don't want to take too long," Alex said. "We need to work."

"We also need to eat and relax a little. I'm not at my best when I'm too uptight."

"Okay, I get it," Alex said. She smiled. "Look at you. Unit chief for such a short time, but you're doing a great job."

"Maybe. I think I like being an analyst better. Being in charge is . . . tough."

As they headed for the food court, Alex realized Kaely had been surprisingly quiet. "Everything okay?" she asked.

Kaely nodded. "Just thinking." But by the look on her face, Alex could tell something was bothering her. Alex ran everything that had been said through her mind, but nothing stuck out. Everyone was trying to narrow down the possible leak. Had Kaely seen something the rest of them missed?

They reached the food court, and Kaely went for Chinese. Alex ordered tacos, and the men asked for pizza.

On Alex's way toward a table, Logan came up beside her. "I'm surprised you didn't get Chinese food too."

"I'm *not* idolizing Kaely," she shot back.

She walked faster, getting ahead of him. She noticed the other half of their unit sitting around a table. She hurried over to them.

"Hey," Robin said with a smile. "It's weird we're in the same building but rarely see you."

"I agree," Alex said. "Maybe we could meet here for supper tonight?"

"That would be great," Todd said.

"You guys doing okay?"

"We're working hard to come up with the investigative strategies Logan asked for," Bethany said. "We're also using ViCAP to look for possible suspects. Nothing so far."

"We've been checking for possible connections to our victims as well," Nathan said. "So far we haven't found any names linked to all of them."

Alex sighed. "Our profile is being fine-tuned. This guy is something different. I've never seen anyone like him before."

"Neither have we," Nathan said. He smiled. "We'll keep at it, though. We'll get him."

"I hope you're right. Look, I'll talk to Logan about dinner. He'll get back with you so we can set a time, okay?"

"Sure," Todd said. "We'll see you tonight."

As she walked away, she was grateful none of them seemed upset about not being one of the agents working the profile. Jeff was the one who'd decided having too many people would add confusion. In her heart, she knew he'd been right, but it still felt awkward.

Alex had just sat down at the table across from Kaely when a tall man with dark wavy hair walked into the food court. Kaely saw him and smiled. He came over, leaned down, and kissed her on the cheek.

"This is Noah Hunter," she said, addressing the rest of them. "My fiancé."

As Kaely introduced each person at the table, Alex noticed she was beaming. Who knew she could beam? And her previous reticence had disappeared. Alex couldn't help but feel a little jealous. She'd never been in love. Never known anyone who had made her feel that way. Before she realized it, her gaze swung to Logan. She silently chastised herself. She had no romantic feelings for Logan, nor did he have them for her. For all she knew, he was dating someone and just hadn't mentioned it.

"Excuse me, please," Kaely said. She got up and walked with Noah to a table away from everyone. When she sat down with him, he took her hand in his. She seemed so happy.

Alex looked away. Maybe that would happen for her someday, but for now, she just wanted to focus on her job. Staying single-minded was vital to her.

Everyone finished lunch and then headed back to the classroom. The clouds Alex had noticed earlier had delivered on their promise. Snow was falling pretty heavily. She loved snow. Although it sounded odd, she'd always felt safer when there was snow. Especially when she was a child. School would shut down, and the strange people her aunt associated with stayed away. It was as if snow stopped everyone in their tracks. Even people with evil intentions. She wondered if their UNSUB would have to change his plans if they got a heavy snow.

She sighed to herself. Probably not. So far he'd stayed ahead of them, pulling off his deeds perfectly—except for killing Monty. But he'd hurt him. If that was his real goal, he'd succeeded. Four deaths. How many more before they caught him? She looked at Kaely, who was a few steps in front of her. Was the UNSUB really going after her next? How could that be? People who didn't belong had no way to get near them. And she still found it hard to believe anyone in the FBI or on Gorman's team would help this madman anyway.

She noticed Logan hand a cup of coffee to the officer outside their room. Thoughtful. Alex nodded at their guard, and he smiled in return.

Once inside, everyone gathered around the table while Logan stayed on his feet. "We have a profile based on our first impressions of the UNSUB," he said. "But I think you'll agree that he keeps acting outside the parameters we set for him. That doesn't mean we're wrong, but we need to narrow down our depiction of him. See if we can make it easier to catch this guy."

"Don't you think we should first find out if someone's working with him—and who?" Monty said. "I know it's difficult to believe he's getting help from within the Bureau or the police, but if someone is giving him information, until we root them out, we're vulnerable."

"I understand what you're saying," Alex said, "but if we get the profile right, that may lead us to whoever is helping him."

A knock sounded on the door, and the same officer opened it. "Your detectives are here," he said.

Ben Cooper and Julie Palmer came in. Julie smiled, but as usual, Cooper looked as if he wanted to be somewhere else. What was his deal? He was starting to get on Alex's nerves.

"Welcome," Logan said. "We were just talking about our profile. We want to see if we can refine it to help you find the UNSUB."

"Did you discover anything at the station?" Alex asked. "Anyone who might be working with our UNSUB?"

"No," Ben said sharply. "No one there would be involved with someone like this."

"He means we're still looking," Julie said. "So far we haven't turned up anything, but we intend to keep at it."

Julie slipped into a chair next to Monty, but Ben grabbed one at the end of the table as if he wanted to distance himself from the group.

"Why don't you sit closer to us, Ben?" Logan said. "It's easier to share the information in these files that way."

"Sure," he said as he got up and sat next to Monty. Then he gave them all a quick, forced smile, but the tension rolled off him like waves of stench. What was wrong with him?

"Ben, we're trying to stop a murderer," Alex said. "He's killed four people. Two of them were close to our team. I'm sorry, but I get the feeling you don't want to be here. We need you fully invested in this case. Is there something we need to talk about?"

"Alex," Logan said, "you're not in charge of this group. Step back, please."

She looked at Logan with surprise. He'd never spoken to her that way. Before she had a chance to get offended, though, she realized he was right. She'd overstepped her boundaries. Logan wasn't her colleague now. He was her acting unit chief.

"I'm sorry," she said. "I was out of line."

"But she has a point," Kaely said slowly. "None of us want to challenge your authority, Logan. But you know as well as I do that we need to work as a team here." She looked at Cooper. "Someone with a bad attitude can be distracting."

"That's enough," Logan said. He turned toward Cooper. "Step out into the hall with me for a moment."

At first, Alex didn't think Cooper was going to go with Logan, but he finally followed him into the hall. Logan pulled the door closed behind them.

"I'm sorry about him," Julie said. "He's just having a tough time." She shook her head. "I can't tell you about it because it's personal, but he has nothing against any of you."

Alex didn't say anything, but she was worried about Cooper. Lives were on the line. If he couldn't get past his personal problems, he needed to be removed.

She rubbed the back of her neck. The muscles were hard and tight, and she could feel the beginnings of a tension headache. She had a terrible feeling the UNSUB was going to strike again. And soon.

He was almost ready for his next target, and this plan was more creative than anything he'd done so far. He laughed to himself. He'd prove he was truly in charge.

He hadn't decided how far he would go, though. When he would feel satisfied. He had two targets in mind. Would he bring down both of them? Or was the next one enough? He wasn't sure. He was waiting to hear from his eyes and ears on the inside. He didn't plan to leave anyone behind who might turn on him. No loose ends. Truth was he really didn't like traitors. He would make sure justice was delivered. Judgment was right around the corner, and it would be dispensed soon.

———

Alex, Kaely, and Monty started going through the files again, but Alex had looked over everything so many times that the information was burned into her brain.

"We decided he's male," she said, "maybe in his late fifties or early sixties, but he could be older. Have you noticed that we haven't seen him do anything that required physical strength?" She looked at Monty. "Your grandmother was elderly. Wasn't able to fight back."

"Is he killing this way because he has physical limitations?" Kaely asked. "He's smart, but maybe we've been looking at this the wrong way."

Alex thought about her comment. "You could be right. I was thinking he was trying to be clever, but maybe his MO is born out of necessity. He had to come up with a way to pull off his murder spree without being confronted by the person he wants to kill." She thought for a moment before saying, "We decided his motivation for killing is his passion to prove he's smarter than we are. Does everyone still feel this way?"

"I'm sure that's part of it," Kaely said. "But it might not be the only thing that's driving him. It would help us to know what triggered him. If he is older, I have to wonder just how recently his plan was hatched."

"We thought he might be someone who'd been turned away from the BAU," Monty said. "But if we're right about his age, that would have been years ago."

"And if he knew Davis and Bayne, even longer," Alex said.

"So why wait all this time to take revenge?" Kaely said. "That still doesn't make sense. I don't think our idea about him being rejected from the FBI—or at least the BAU—is viable."

"Right. Why wait until you're past retirement age to strike back?" Monty said.

"If you don't mind a comment from someone without your training . . ." Julie said.

Alex smiled at her. "Of course. You're a part of this team."

"Wouldn't this guy, the one you call your UNSUB, need time to put this together? If he operates out of this area, didn't he have to wait until John Davis was here? The Murder Will Out convention is held only once a year."

"That's a great point," Alex said. "This thing could have taken up to a year to plan. And most people don't know anything about drones, so he would have had to train himself for that."

"We're checking drone sales in the area, by the way," Julie said. "So far, nothing. We haven't found anyone who seems suspicious or can't account for their whereabouts when Davis died."

"He may have bought the drone somewhere else," Kaely said. "If I were him, I would buy it used from someone selling it on Craigslist or through newspaper or online ads. It would be almost impossible to track him then."

"We won't give up," Julie said. "But I tend to think it's a wild-goose chase at this point."

"Let's talk about Bayne," Monty said. "I know we brought this up earlier, but it really bothers me. I doubt his death was easy to plan. How could our guy know Bayne would jump off the cliff? Seems rather sloppy."

"Doesn't that confirm Davis's death was the most important to him?" Alex said. "That's why he's using pages from Davis's books. And you're right, Monty. He took more of a chance with Bayne."

"How can you say he took a chance?" Julie asked. "Most people who jump off cliffs die when they hit the bottom."

"But how did he know where Bayne was?" Alex said. "I mean, he obviously knew he was in Australia. It wouldn't be that hard to find that out. But how did he know he was near a cliff? What if Bayne had fallen on something below the cliff edge and hadn't ended up at the bottom? How could the UNSUB know? He would have hung up right after seeing Bayne jump, right?"

"But we know that didn't happen because people saw his body wash out to sea," Monty said.

"Look," Kaely said, "I don't believe the UNSUB knows everything you're giving him credit for. He didn't tell Bayne to jump. He just told him to put the phone where he could watch him die. And when you give people thirty seconds to kill themselves, they'll find a way. Step in front of a bus. Take a knife from the kitchen and stab themselves. Or jump off a cliff."

"Maybe . . ." Alex said.

"Let's go back to the idea of an associate for a moment," Kaely said. "Could this person have traveled to Australia so he could make sure Bayne died?"

Alex turned that over in her mind. "It's possible, but I can't quite believe that. That could make Bayne the most important target. I just don't think he was. It feels like he was significant only because of his relationship with Davis."

Alex was about to say something else when Logan and Cooper returned. Logan sat down, but Cooper didn't.

"I owe you all an apology," he said, his voice shaking. "My wife has a gambling problem. I didn't know anything about it until recently. She would go to Baltimore with her friends for what she called a girls' weekend. I had no idea she was really going to the casino. She . . . came to me a few weeks ago and told me she'd cleaned out our savings account." He shook his head. "She lost over two hundred thousand dollars. That was college money for our two girls. My father left us the money in his will for that purpose. With my salary alone, we'll never be able to cover the cost."

He blinked back tears. "I realize this is personal. I wouldn't have told you except I need to explain my behavior. That's why I've been so upset. It's not you." He looked at Logan. "I've been angry, but I had no right to take it out on you." He managed a small smile. "I'm sorry. I hope you'll all forgive me."

"I'm sorry for your troubles, Ben," Kaely said.

His smile widened. "Thank you. And no more attitude. Whatever I can do to help . . ."

"Sit down, and let's get to work," Logan said.

When Ben slipped into his chair, Monty patted him on the back.

"What have you come up with so far?" Ben asked Alex.

Alex quickly brought both him and Logan up to speed.

Logan didn't say anything right away. Finally he said, "That makes perfect sense. But we still don't have anything the police can really use. We suspect the UNSUB is older and that Davis was his primary target. But why not stop after Davis? Seems to me that he made his point, so why keep killing? Wouldn't it be harder on him to carry out this plan? Don't get me wrong, I know a lot of older men are strong and capable of anything, but I think we have to ask ourselves that question."

"I really am starting to believe someone on the inside is feeding him information," Monty said. "They have to be."

Kaely looked at Logan. "You've been keeping the other agents in this unit informed as to what's going on, right?" He nodded. "Maybe that needs to stop," Kaely said. "We need to be incredibly careful."

Logan's eyes narrowed. "You're new to us, Kaely, but I'd

put my life in the hands of any of our people. I understand
your concern, but please be careful about casting aspersions
on anyone in this unit."

Kaely's cheeks flushed pink. "I'm sorry. I wasn't trying to—"

Logan held up his hand. "Stop. I guess Ben isn't the only
one who's under pressure. You're right to try to figure out any
way information could be getting out. I'm sorry. Even though
I trust them, I'll be careful. I was going to bring them in at
some point so they could know what we've come up with,
but I won't do that." He shook his head. "I still can't believe
any of them would betray us, though."

"I understand," Kaely said. "Of course, if the UNSUB *is*
in league with someone else, it would be unusual. Usually
serial killers like to work alone."

Alex nodded. "If he does have a minion, I certainly
wouldn't give a nickel for that person's life."

"What do you mean?" Julie asked.

"He's planned this meticulously, and his world revolves
around himself. He won't leave any open doors. He'll kill his
crony to ensure his own safety," Alex explained.

"Where's Reinhardt?" Kaely asked. "I haven't seen him
since this morning."

"He's still here," Logan said. "And before you ask, we don't
think he's our UNSUB. Nothing points to it. He has alibis
for every killing."

"I'm sure he liked having to defend himself," Kaely said.
"His ego is enormous."

Logan smiled. "I'll agree with that."

"He couldn't be working with the UNSUB," Alex said,
"because he hasn't been privy to anything about us. At least
not until he arrived here."

"Right." Logan sighed. "So we're still looking for someone connected to Davis."

"I think so," Alex said. She tapped her fingers on the table as she turned over everything they knew so far in her mind. "Could these other killings simply be attempts to hide his main target—Davis?"

"But why send us pages from *Dark Minds*?" Monty said. "He's not diverting attention away from Davis. He's drawing us to him."

Alex leaned back in her chair. "You're right. Why doesn't this guy fit any profile we can come up with? His first target is John Davis. So we focus on people who might have a grudge against Davis. But the UNSUB continues to kill. Bayne is next, so we decide he's angry with the BAU. Because he killed Davis and Bayne, we decide he's older. But who waits so long to get back at people? And then he murders Monty's grandmother."

She looked at Monty. "What was your grandmother's first name? Calling her 'Monty's grandmother' most of the time feels a little disrespectful, and Mrs. Wong seems rather formal."

"Her name was Chunhua. It means 'spring flower.' As she got older, she used to tell me she was simply losing petals."

Alex cleared her throat, trying to choke back the emotion that suddenly overcame her. She'd never known her grandmother, but she'd wondered what it would be like to have someone like Chunhua in her life.

"Then he kills . . . Chunhua." She tried to pronounce it the way Monty had but failed rather badly. Monty didn't seem to notice. "Anyway, that's a variation. One that shouldn't be there." She groaned. "It's like we're trying to put together a puzzle, but someone has mixed the pieces with another puzzle's, and we can't put together the finished picture."

"Did the person who killed my grandmother move like an older man?" Monty spoke slowly as if still forming his thought.

Alex turned to look at him. "Do you mind if we look at the video to see?" she said. "You can leave the room."

Monty looked grim. "Go ahead, but you're right. I can't watch that again."

"That reminds me," Logan said. "I've got video from Georgetown. The police there sent it to Chief Gorman, and when he told me about it, I knew we needed to see it."

He removed his laptop from his briefcase and put it on the table. "Let's look at that first, and then we'll go over the video from Monty's . . . from Chunhua's house."

Logan connected his laptop to the video system in the classroom. Alex steeled herself. Would Jeff's death be caught on this video? The last thing she wanted was to watch Jefferson Cole die, but if they hoped to help find his killer, she had no choice.

T he first thing we're looking for is the theft of Stephanie Cole's phone," Logan told the assembled group as they all turned to face a large television screen on one wall.

He thought he saw Alex relax a little, but generally an atmosphere of gloom permeated the room. He didn't know how to dispel it. Jeff was able to stir up his people, inspire them, provoke their determination. But Logan was just as confused as everyone else in the group. Profiles weren't easy to create, yet they usually followed a formula. Some criminals thought they were unique. Unable to be categorized. But that wasn't true. Years of studying dangerous offenders had unlocked truths about them that led to their captures. That's what profiling was.

For instance, some serial killers included a sexual component when they killed. Those who didn't but showed anger toward female victims often had issues with some woman or women in their past. That wasn't true every time, but it was valid enough of the time to make it easier to profile them. And handing a profile to the police that was so on target that it led to the capture of a killer was an incredibly satisfying experience. It's why FBI agents became behavioral analysts.

But there was nothing sexual about this case. The UN-SUB's reason for killing, his motive, was something else. They knew he wanted to show them how superior he was to them. But there had to be more. What was his trigger? They had to refine their profile, but would it be before someone else died? Would it be Logan's fault because he wasn't Jeff? Wasn't as skilled as Jeff?

Logan hit a key, and the video popped up. "This is from yesterday afternoon. Stephanie is certain she still had her phone earlier that morning. We know she took a phone call around nine, so that confirms it. Here we can see her and the shop's owner, Roger Burredge, serving customers later that morning. Gorman said Burredge has seen this. He also said business is slow since it's winter. Some people still take out their boats or arrange for cleaning or repairs, but the shop isn't as busy as it is in summer. The chief said to watch carefully at around ten thirty. Burredge goes into the storeroom, and Stephanie is in the restroom."

He paused the video, stood, and pointed at the screen. "Burredge confirmed every customer on this recording but this one." Logan waited for the time in the video Gorman had mentioned. They watched as a man walked around the counter and seemed to be looking at something on the wall behind it. Then he turned around. For just a moment, his hand was behind the counter, out of sight. Then he walked away. By the way the light changed in the room, it was clear that the entrance door was opened and shut.

"Looks like this is the guy who stole Stephanie's phone. But he's wearing a stocking cap and keeps his head down the entire time," Logan said. "We can't see his face. He's wearing gloves and a thick winter jacket. Black jeans. Because of the heavy coat he's wearing, it's hard to tell his build. His height is hard to determine too because of the camera's angle, although we can tell he's not real tall when measured against the counter's height." Logan paused the video again. "Neither Burredge nor Stephanie saw him before or after this was recorded."

"Do they usually leave the front unattended like this?" Kaely asked.

"Burredge said that especially in winter, they know almost everyone who comes into the store. Besides, not too many people would rob a boat shop anyway. Their equipment is specialized. Also, the front counter was unattended for only a few minutes."

"So how did our guy know Burredge and Stephanie were going to be away from the counter long enough for him to steal her phone?" Alex asked. "That doesn't make sense."

Logan frowned at her as he considered her comment. "No, it doesn't, does it? If he'd waited inside the shop for them to both step out, they would have noticed him. And they wouldn't have left the room at the same time."

"Maybe our UNSUB planted a device in the store so he could watch them," Ben said.

"And sat outside for days, hoping Stephanie would leave her phone unattended?" Julie said. "I don't see it."

"Actually, he probably knew it wouldn't take long for that to happen," Monty said. "I worked in a small shop when I was a teenager. It was just the owner and me. Lots of times we both stepped away for a minute or two. Our guy was taking a chance, but he knew there would be an opportunity. And sure enough . . ."

"Ben, will you call your chief?" Logan said. "Ask him to contact the Georgetown police to send some officers over there and look for a recording device."

"You won't find it," Alex said.

"Why?" Logan asked.

"The guy took too long to reach the door. He probably grabbed his camera on the way out."

"I think Alex is right," Kaely said. "He's so organized he would have taken any camera he planted. It makes sense."

Logan turned to Ben again. "Okay, tell the chief the camera is probably gone. But even though the chances are slim, I'd like to think he left something behind that will help us find him."

"I keep wondering about his next move," Alex said.

Logan nodded. "I do too. He has an endgame, but what is it?"

"I don't think Jeff was his final target," Alex said. "But after targeting Monty, he had to assume we'd be put under protective custody."

"Why couldn't Agent Cole have been his last?" Ben asked. "Maybe the UNSUB considers his death his crowning achievement."

"But again, we have to look at his unstable MO. First he goes after the founders of the BAU, then he targets Monty and kills an elderly woman. After that he goes after Jeff, the agent in charge of our unit. So now what?"

"The last message he left pointed to Donald Reinhardt," Julie said. "I have to wonder if he's the next victim."

"I hope he stays here where he can be protected," Monty said.

"I don't know," Alex said, her face tight. "This UNSUB seems to always know what's going to happen next. Maybe he thinks Reinhardt will bail."

Logan cleared his throat. "The security camera in the boat shop's parking lot didn't show the thief leaving. He must have stayed close to the building, under the camera's view. Again, I think he knew exactly what he was doing. Probably parked down the street where there weren't any security cameras from other businesses."

He paused. "It will be difficult to watch the next video. I wasn't sure if we should even do it, but maybe we all need to see it. It's from a security camera by the pier."

"Have you seen it yet?" Alex asked, her voice tight.

Logan shook his head. "I haven't had time." He took a deep breath and brought up the video. Although it was dark, streetlights made it possible for them to see the road near the pier. Suddenly, a dark-colored car zoomed into the camera's range and hit one side of the pier, shooting straight into the water. Little by little, the car slipped under the black water.

It was over in less than a minute.

When Logan turned off the video, there was silence in the room. Then Monty excused himself, and they watched the video with his grandmother and the UNSUB. Unfortunately, they couldn't gather much additional information about him.

The team spent the next few hours trying to rework the profile. Alex had a hard time concentrating after watching Jeff speed toward his death and Chunhua pleading with Monty not to kill himself. She was frustrated. It felt as if they were simply repeating themselves. She ran everything they'd already surmised over in her mind. The UNSUB was obviously an organized psychopath who felt the need to prove he was smarter than anyone in the BAU. He was so passionate about pulling off his carefully constructed plan that he was willing to kill Chunhua himself. This meant he was totally committed to his agenda, and that made him especially dangerous.

They also believed he was an older man of medium height

and overweight, although it was possible he was trying to appear heavier than he really was. He may have known John Davis. He definitely held anger toward Davis and probably Bayne as well, but they had no idea why. They all agreed he was likely single and unemployed because he had a lot of time to engineer his plan and pull it off. He could be retired with some kind of pension, and he definitely had money, at least for this. Drones weren't cheap. He had the ability to travel, although his comfort zone seemed to be near Bethesda. That didn't mean he lived in the area, just that this was where his targets were, other than Bayne.

The FBI had gone through flight manifests with the airlines, trying to find someone suspicious who traveled from Bethesda to Houston, where Susan Davis lived. But the video of her sent to Davis was taken months before he used it to force Davis's suicide, and the UNSUB could have traveled there by car so he couldn't be tracked through the airlines.

If only Davis had looked closer, he might have realized the video wasn't live. Instead, he spent the last thirty seconds of his life searching for a way to die—and finding one.

The team had recommended that the authorities hunt for someone who had a beef with the BAU or with Davis or Bayne—maybe both. They suggested that he may have worked in the technology field. He knew how to hack the phones, and he was able to handle a drone. They recommended looking for someone who was wrongly convicted based on a profile given to police by the BAU. It might not have been for the UNSUB but for a friend or family member of his. Although that was a solid deduction, it didn't feel right to Alex. Not that kind of revenge. But that wasn't surprising. Nothing felt right about this entire case.

The team had thrown out the idea that the UNSUB was angry about not being accepted into the BAU because of his age. But even that didn't narrow down the possibilities. Who was this guy? Why couldn't they get a handle on him?

"If only we knew the trigger," Kaely said with a frustrated sigh. "It has to be recent. I know it took time to implement this plan since he waited for the Murder Will Out convention, but the trigger had to have happened in the last year or two. I know why we're saying he worked in the technology field, but what if his accomplice is the one with that kind of knowledge?"

"Still not convinced he has an accomplice," Monty said. "It would detour from the norm."

"We've established that already," Kaely said sharply. She shook her head. "I'm sorry. This is getting to me. We're just going in circles."

"I feel the same way," Alex said. "I just don't think we're giving the police anything they can really work with."

"Well, maybe we have," Logan said. "We believe John Davis is the most important victim. He's center to everything. That may be enough to find the guy." He frowned at Ben. "Has the chief asked Susan Davis if she suspects anyone?"

Ben nodded. "She gave him some names, and we're following up. But the FBI in Houston have taken over that part of the investigation. I think they can do a better job than we can." He sighed. "The person she said he had the biggest conflict with was Evan Bayne. He'd be the perfect suspect, but he's conveniently dead."

Alex couldn't help but laugh. "I'm sorry," she said to Ben, "but we're all punch-drunk and worried. You only said what we're all thinking."

"I still question Davis being the focal point of the UNSUB's killing spree," Logan said. "If that is true, why not stop after his death? Or at least after Bayne's? What's he trying to prove by going after other analysts? He outsmarted the men who started the BAU—who invented behavioral analysis."

"I don't know!" Alex said, revealing how she really felt—exasperated. "I've looked at these files until my eyes feel permanently crossed. I think we're missing something. You know, like when you're trying to remember the name of a song or the title of a movie, and it's just out of your reach?"

Monty laughed. "You say stuff like that a lot."

Alex couldn't help grinning back at him. "But I've been right every time, haven't I?"

The smile slipped from Monty's face. "Now that you mention it, yeah. Hey, please figure it out, okay? My brain is starting to hurt."

Logan pointed at him. "Well, keep that brain working. You're on this team for a reason. We need everything you've got on this one."

"I don't know how you guys do this," Julie said. "I'm used to being out in the field. This would drive me crazy."

"It's not exciting," Alex said, acknowledging the point. "Working a profile is boring, detailed work. Very repetitive. Certainly not everyone's cup of tea. But when you realize how much it can help the authorities track down suspects, it's more fulfilling than you might think."

"I guess," Julie said with a smile. "I've never been more thankful for my job, though."

Alex laughed. "I understand."

"That passage from *Dark Minds* says a couple of other agents helped Davis and Bayne in the beginning," Monty said. "We've assumed Reinhardt was one of them, but do we know who else it could be referring to?"

"Probably Bridget O'Fallon," Kaely said. "She was a psychologist and instrumental in developing the Enders Psychopathy Checklist in the seventies. Of course, over the years it's been changed by experience and a better understanding of the psychopathic personality, but her wisdom helped kick off the process we still use today. She was killed in a car accident around ten years ago."

"Anything between her and Davis?" Julie asked.

"I don't know, but I heard she and Evan Bayne were close . . . for a while. Then he got married, so that was the end of that. Bridget lost control of her car on an icy highway. It was ruled an accidental death. No one to blame. That road leads to a dead end, I'm afraid."

Logan sighed. "Reinhardt's out as our UNSUB. Terry says he has an alibi for every death."

"But Bayne was killed from far away," Kaely said. "And the killer used a drone to watch Davis die. We didn't see anyone suspicious hanging around when Jeff drove his car into the river. We may want to keep that in mind. The UNSUB could be orchestrating most of these killings from another location. So even though Reinhardt seems to have alibis, I don't think we should take him off our list yet."

"Good point," Logan said.

"What about D. J. Harper?" Alex asked him.

"Again, alibis for every death. Besides, Davis was his friend. He was really hurt by his death."

"What about Davis's funeral?" Kaely asked. "Many times the killer shows up for funerals. It's kind of like firebugs showing up at the scene of fires they set."

"Private family service," Logan said. "I thought of that too, but only immediate family members were there. No one noticed anyone hanging around outside the church or following the family."

The group looked at each other, but Alex couldn't come up with anything else. They just didn't have enough to go on. "Did anything come out of questionnaires and investigative strategies the other members of our unit have been working on?" Alex asked.

"I haven't been briefed yet," Logan said. He looked at Julie and Ben. "Can you tell us anything else?"

Julie shook her head. "People who attended the convention have been questioned. Hotel workers too. We're also looking at other guests at the hotel around the time Mr. Davis was . . ." She sighed. "We really can't say he was murdered, can we? I mean, he killed himself."

"Yes, that's true," Logan said. "But the UNSUB caused his death, and he'll be held responsible when he's found."

Julie nodded. "We showed everyone the sketch drawn from D. J. Harper's memory of the rather strange man he met at the convention, but no one else remembers him."

"That seems odd," Alex said. "And nothing from the security cameras?"

"No," Ben said. "No one like that showed up anywhere. Not outside the building or inside."

"I don't get it," Monty said. "Is this guy a ghost?"

"No," Alex said. "But maybe he wore a disguise. Maybe more than one." She looked at Logan. "It's possible the sketch we have is our UNSUB. All he had to do was make sure Harper saw him in his disguise, to throw us off. Then he shed it before packing up everything and leaving when everyone else did. He didn't stand out. He fit right in. Maybe we need to look for someone who'd never attended the convention before. Someone who stayed to themselves."

She leaned back in her chair and crossed her arms. "He's smart, but we're smarter. We have to find him—and his accomplice. I'm afraid we're running out of time."

27

I t was late, they'd missed the chance to have dinner with the rest of their unit, and the cafeteria workers were preparing to close. The hot foods were gone, but sandwiches and chips were still available. The four of them grabbed what they could and ordered a drink. They were each given a paper cup, and the beverage machine doled out ice and whatever drink they wanted.

Alex chose root beer since it didn't have caffeine. Kaely's restlessness the night before had kept her up, but she had no plans to say anything. She didn't want to make her uncomfortable. It was obvious the case was on her mind 24/7. She was even working on it in her sleep. Even though Alex wasn't getting much rest either, the idea of being alone right now didn't appeal to her.

It might seem like overkill to have FBI police officers scattered all around the building and outside, watching out for the members of their unit, but Alex felt more secure with them there. Of course, everyone in their unit was armed as well, so if someone was inside the building working for the UNSUB, it would be hard for that person to hurt them. But Alex found herself looking around anyway, wondering if the people around her were who they seemed to be.

Kaely sat down at a different table, and minutes later, Noah came in and joined her.

As Logan and Monty ate with Alex, neither mentioned the case. She was pretty sure it was because they were as tired of thinking about it as she was. Were they finally close enough to really help the agents and detectives who were looking for the UNSUB? Or was their profile falling as short as she feared?

When they were finished, everyone, including Kaely, headed to the elevator. They passed one of the police officers and said good night. When they got off the elevator on their floor, Alex was surprised to see another officer. They said good night to him as well, then entered their rooms.

"Why the extra security out there?" Alex asked when she closed their door. "Is it because of what happened to Jeff? Or a new threat?"

Kaely shrugged. "If there was a new threat, Terry or Logan would tell us. They're not trying to keep anything from us."

"I guess you're right. This case is making me squirrely."

"Me too." Kaely frowned. "I'm usually pretty accurate when it comes to writing profiles, but this time . . ."

"I know. Do you get the feeling we're missing something?"

Kaely laughed. "I always feel that way until the UNSUB is apprehended."

Alex grinned at her. "Good point."

Kaely was quiet for a moment. "Look, that dream you had last night? About the woman in the maze?"

Alex nodded. "Yeah. Do you understand it?"

Kaely looked away from her. "Are you sure you want to hear this?"

"I . . . I think so."

"From what you've told me, you grew up without a role model."

"That's true." Alex's body tensed remembering what Logan told her. Surely Kaely hadn't come to the same conclusion. Did she think she was the ghostly figure in Alex's dream? "Before you say anything else," Alex said, unable to keep a note of bitterness out of her voice, "I'm not obsessed with you. I admire you, but I don't want to *be* you."

Kaely's eyes widened. "I wasn't going to say that. Why would you come to that conclusion?"

Feeling embarrassed and wishing she'd never told Kaely about her dream, Alex said, "Logan accused me of trying to emulate you. He thinks I'm trying to be you."

To Alex's surprise, Kaely laughed softly. "Oh, Alex. Heavens no. I'm so imperfect. I'm growing, but I still have a long way to go. My childhood was so traumatic, and I've been trusting God for healing ever since I met Him. No one should want to be like me."

"But you seem so . . . self-confident. And you're the most talented analyst I've ever heard of."

Kaely removed the band holding her curly auburn hair in a messy bun. Then she ran her hand through her hair in an attempt to tame it. Alex could tell she was stalling, trying to think of what to say. Finally, Kaely looked at her. "Sometimes what seems like self-confidence is just plain stubbornness. You see, I just won't give up. Ever. But I've been lost and confused. After my father was apprehended and we learned who he really was, my mother became emotionally distant."

"But . . . you needed her then. You were just a child."

"Yeah, that's true. But she wasn't there for me or my brother. I left home as soon as I could."

"So did I."

Kaely nodded. "Because you thought it would give you another chance at life."

"Exactly. I knew what I wanted to do and who I wanted to be. I put everything I had into getting to Quantico."

"I did the same thing," Kaely said, her expression serious. "But then it was taken away from me. I lost everything I cared about. I . . . I've never admitted this to anyone before, but I considered suicide. I really didn't know who I was, or even why I was alive."

"But now you're back in the BAU, so you've found yourself again."

Kaely shook her head. "No, Alex. I did find myself, but it was before I got here. It was even before I ended up in St. Louis. I reached out to the only Person who could show me who I was truly meant to be. I found God. Without Him, I have no idea where I'd be right now. You see, positions, success, praise from people—none of that lasts. If you judge yourself by human standards, you'll fail. The only way to truly know yourself is to know the One who created you. Without Him, we'll never find our way. No matter what happens, nothing will ever rob me of my identity again. And even though now I can actually give myself to another human being, which was impossible for a long time, I will never see myself just through Noah's eyes. I've learned to see myself through God's eyes. Do you understand?"

"I think so. . . . But the dream?"

"You're not chasing me, Alex. You're chasing yourself. You're not sure who you are. You're afraid of things because you're trying to retain control of your life. The fear of germs, keeping your distance from people, these are the tools you use to protect your heart."

"But when I cried out to God . . ."

Kaely smiled. "The light came. Inside, you know all this. You're just afraid to embrace it. To put everything you are into God's hands. To trust Him completely with your life."

Alex had clenched her hands into fists before she even realized it. "No one has ever proved trustworthy. My parents. My so-called friends. No one."

"Have you ever had a close friend try to kill you?"

"Uh, yeah."

Kaely's eyebrows shot up, and for some reason, it made Alex laugh.

Kaely broke out in laughter too. "I didn't expect that response. Boy, we certainly have a lot in common—and very interesting lives."

"I guess that would be a fair assumption. Wow." Alex wiped her eyes. "I'm sorry. You were making a point?"

"My point is this," Kaely said. "You're stuck at a place called There."

"There?"

"Yeah, there. You see, I could have camped out at the discovery of who my father really was. And how my mother acted. Or even at the friend who betrayed me. I could have stayed There at that point in my life. But I don't want to live tied to events from my past. I want to live here. I want to keep following God, becoming the person He created me to be. But I can't do that if I stay There."

Tears filled Alex's eyes. "But what if you don't know how to get here? What if you're really stuck at There?"

Kaely came over to where Alex sat on the edge of her bed. She joined her and reached for her hand. "Alex, you are so special. You're strong. Strong enough to make it through circumstances that would have stopped most people cold. You're talented, and you're compassionate. Many people who closely guard their hearts don't have any way to offer love to others. I saw how you reacted to Chunhua's death. You've managed to hold on to your compassion. But unless you find a way to move on, you'll never be able to give yourself to another person. Get married. Have children. Enjoy the life God gave you."

"I don't want marriage and children."

Kaely shrugged. "Hey, not judging. If you don't feel called to be a wife or mother, that's between you and God. But if you're ruling it out because you're afraid . . ."

"Then I'm camped out at There, and I can't go forward."

Kaely nodded. "The hardest part of leaving There? Forgiving. You have to forgive your father for taking off. Forgive your mother for taking her life and leaving you behind. And forgive your aunt for not being who you needed her to be."

Kaely took a deep breath. "The toughest person I had to forgive? Me. I made so many mistakes because of the past. Because I let it shape me. But the longer I've known God, the freer I've become. I don't want to live There anymore. I have too much to look forward to. Jeremiah 29:11 says, "'I know the plans I have for you,' declares the Lord, 'plans to prosper you and not to harm you, plans to give you hope and a future.'"

Alex wiped tears from her cheeks. "Logan told me about that Scripture, but I hadn't really applied it to me."

"Maybe it's time."

"Maybe it is." Alex gave Kaely a hug. "Thank you. I guess I need to stop chasing myself and stand still and let God lead me." She sighed. "I'm afraid trusting Him might not be easy for me."

"The funny thing is you'll find it's easier than you expected. He has a way of healing us on the inside. I've always said that one of the ways the world should be able to see that Christianity is real is to watch the way it changes people. We can't change ourselves. False religions or self-help gurus can't change hearts. Only Jesus Christ can create a brand-new human being."

"Thanks," Alex said. "Really. I won't forget what you said."

Kaely went to her own bed. "Actually, you probably will. It's a process. I fell down so many times on my way to learning this lesson. I can't say I'm perfect at it, but at least I'm headed in the right direction. And I'm more at peace. I know I'm not alone." She laughed lightly. "I'm so stubborn. No matter how many times I've blown it, I just don't give up. I never will."

"I'm glad you have Noah."

Kaely smiled broadly. "I am too. And I'm grateful I was finally able to open my heart to another person. But I want to be strong on my own. So confident in the Lord that if tomorrow Noah said he didn't want anything more to do with me, I'd be okay. I don't need him to keep me grounded. I have God."

Alex thought about what she'd said. She didn't have a fiancé, so she couldn't really relate to that, but she knew it was hard to lose someone you loved. She thought about Monty.

He'd lost his grandmother, but he had to go on. She'd lost her parents. Now she needed to rely on God to heal her heart and the empty places inside.

"First shower?" Kaely asked, pulling Alex out of her musings.

Alex shook her head. "Go ahead. I'll probably take mine in the morning."

After Kaely stepped into the bathroom, Alex changed into her sweats and T-shirt. Then she turned down the lights and got into bed. She turned toward the window and watched the snow falling while she thought about everything Kaely said. Finally, she closed her eyes and silently asked God to help her leave her past behind and find the life He had for her.

Within minutes, she was drifting off to sleep.

When Alex woke up, she realized she'd slept straight through the night. She turned over to look at the clock on the nightstand. It was after eight. She rarely slept this late. Even though this was only a twin bed, it was pretty comfortable. She suddenly had the strangest feeling, though—as if someone were trying to tell her something. She flipped over on her back and tried to still her mind. What was it? She couldn't shake the impression that something was wrong.

Logan had told them to take the morning off while he met with Gorman about the profile. After lunch, Gorman would let them all know what his team was doing and what kind of progress they were making. That wasn't the usual procedure. In most cases, once the profile was delivered, the analysts moved on to the next case. She wondered if they would be called in on something else while they were here. It was certainly possible. The plan was to keep them here until the

UNSUB was captured, but how long would that take? They couldn't stay here forever.

She turned back over and looked out the window. It was still snowing. Beautiful. She tried to enjoy it, but once again, that odd feeling came. She couldn't ignore it. She turned over again and sat up. Kaely wasn't in her bed. She must have already gone down for breakfast. Alex looked around. She would have felt better if Kaely had at least left a note to tell her where she was.

Alex got out of bed and took a shower. Then she dressed in jeans and a light-blue shirt, which she tucked in. Yesterday she'd dressed more formally, but when she saw almost everyone else was wearing casual clothes, she'd decided to join them today. She reached into a pocket of her bag and pulled out a pair of earrings she loved to wear. Jordan Stewart, Shirley's eight-year-old son, had given the silver pistols to her at Christmas. He'd purchased them with his own money saved from his allowance. Shirley told her she certainly didn't have to wear them if they were in bad taste, but Jordan thought they were "cool," and Alex did too. She wore them whenever she could.

Monty and Logan had teased her about them more than once, but she didn't care. She treasured them because Jordan had given them with love. She quickly put them on, then pulled on her boots and brushed her hair. She started to put it into a ponytail, but at the last minute she changed her mind and left it down. She wasn't working this morning, so why not? She hurried out of her room. Maybe she could catch Kaely before she finished breakfast.

She closed the door behind her and was on her way to the elevator when she noticed the door to one of the unused rooms was open. She started to close it, but then she noticed a man lying on the floor inside. She ran over and recognized him. It was one of the FBI police officers. What was his name? Dennis. Dennis something. She couldn't remember. He was on his side with his eyes closed. She felt for a pulse, but she knew he was dead as soon as she touched him. He was cold.

A quick look around didn't turn up any signs of violence. He was just . . . dead. What in the world had happened? She reached for her phone and called Logan. When he answered, she told him what she'd found. He sounded as stunned as she felt. She tried to keep her attitude professional, but this man had died while trying to protect her and the other BAU agents.

She went back out into the hallway and waited. A minute or two later, the elevator began its ascent to their floor. When the doors opened, Logan and an officer stepped out.

"Show me," Logan said.

Alex led them to the room. "The door was partially open. That's the only reason I looked inside."

"Dennis?" the officer said.

"I'm sorry," she said to him. "He's dead." The officer, whose badge read *Shawn Driscoll*, started to approach, but then he stopped. Even though the death looked like natural causes, at this point they couldn't assume anything. They had to keep the area as clean as possible for the crime-scene investigators.

"Do you have any idea what happened?" Logan asked her.

"No. I checked to see if he was alive, but I quickly realized he was gone. No visible signs of trauma. It looks like he simply died."

"When did Dennis come on?" Logan asked the obviously distraught officer standing next to him.

"Two a.m.," Driscoll said, his voice breaking.

"Why would he enter this room?" Alex asked. "It's being updated. No one was staying here."

"Maybe he heard something and was checking it out."

"Or he was just curious," Logan said.

"The way he's positioned, he could have simply fallen against the door after suffering a heart attack," Alex said. "Maybe it was slightly ajar."

Driscoll was fighting to maintain his composure, and Alex felt bad for him.

"Let's call the ME," Logan said. "Until he gets here, we need to leave Dennis where he is." He looked at Alex. "Was he lying on his side when you found him?"

"Yes. I just checked for a pulse and then called you."

"Okay, let's go downstairs. Will you stay here with him?" he asked Driscoll.

The officer nodded.

Logan turned to look at Alex. "Where's Kaely?"

"She's not here. She left before I got up."

"Okay." He addressed the officer again. "Shawn, no one is allowed on this floor without my permission. And no one leaves. I believe all my people are already downstairs, so none of them should be up here. It looks like Dennis's death was natural, but I want to make certain. Do you understand?"

He nodded. "Yes, sir."

Logan started to take his secure phone out of his pocket. "I want my own phone back," he grumbled. "I had numbers stored on mine. I need the number for the ME's office."

"I can give it to you," Shawn said. He looked at his phone, and in a few seconds, he read the number to Logan.

Logan had just finished talking to the ME when the elevator doors opened, and several FBI police officers stepped out.

"We heard something happened to Dennis," one of the men said.

"I'm sorry," Logan said. "Yes."

"Do you know how he died?"

"No, it might have been a heart attack, but we'll have to wait for the ME's report to be certain. I'm sorry for your loss."

"I don't understand," one of the officers said. "Dennis was in great shape. Took care of himself, you know?"

"Sometimes a death doesn't make sense," Alex said. "I'm so sorry."

The officer who'd spoken just nodded his head. He was blinking back tears. Dennis was more than a colleague to these officers. He was family.

"I'd like you to check all the other rooms on this floor," Logan said. "Just to be sure no one is up here who shouldn't be. I honestly don't see anything that makes me think this was foul play, but don't touch anything just in case."

"Yes, sir. We know how it works," another officer said.

"I know you do. When you're done, please come downstairs and report to me. I only want Shawn with Dennis for now. We need to do our best to keep the scene clean."

"Yes, sir, we understand," the same officer said.

Alex got on the elevator with Logan. As they began their descent to the first floor, she said, "We need to make sure the ME gets us a tox screen ASAP."

"Why?" Logan asked. "Do you suspect something?"

"I don't know. His young age. His physical condition. Just a precaution."

Logan nodded. "I'll ask, but you know how long those tests take."

"Yeah, I know."

Something suddenly occurred to Alex. It almost took her breath away.

"Are you okay?" Logan asked.

"He was cold."

"Dennis?"

"Yes. He was *cold*. If Kaely had gone down for breakfast, she would have seen him. I noticed the open door. And if I did, she would have. He couldn't have died after she came through here. He would have still been warm." She swallowed hard. "Have you seen Kaely this morning?"

"No."

"Did you have breakfast?"

He nodded. "Sure, in the food court . . ." He looked into Alex's eyes. "Don't jump to conclusions. One thing doesn't necessarily have to do with the other. Maybe she went the other way down the hall. She could have been meeting another one of our group for breakfast, and I just didn't see her."

"Yeah, maybe." Logan could be right, but she still felt apprehensive.

When the elevator doors opened, Donald Reinhardt stood there. He glared at Logan as they stepped out.

"I'm sorry," Logan said. "But you can't go up to your room."

"Fine. But I'm done," Reinhardt said. "This whole thing is outrageous. I know how to keep myself safer than you do, it seems."

"Are you talking about the officer who died?" Logan asked. "It looks like natural causes."

"Sure it is. Kind of a big coincidence, though, isn't it? I've gone along with this long enough. You have no right to keep me here." He took the FBI-issued phone out of his pocket and handed it to Logan. "I'm getting out of here before I die of so-called natural causes."

"Look, it's not safe—"

"I've given the FBI everything," Reinhardt said, his voice getting louder. "They threw me aside like yesterday's newspaper. You can't tell me what to do anymore."

"We've been over this, Don."

Reinhardt stuck his finger in Logan's face. "You don't get to call me *Don*. I'm Supervisory Special Agent Reinhardt."

Logan, who'd obviously had enough, said, "Actually, you're not. You're *Mr.* Reinhardt. You need to stay here. You have to be interviewed."

"Either have me arrested or stay out of my way." He stood toe-to-toe with Logan, and they stared at each other for several seconds. "I thought not," Reinhardt said. "You have no way to keep me here against my will. I'm leaving." He turned on his heel and stormed away.

"Should we try to make him stay?" Alex asked. "Isn't he still a suspect?"

"I'll call Chief Gorman and ask him to assign an officer to watch him," Logan said. "But he's right. We have no authority to keep him here. The police don't have any evidence to arrest him, and he doesn't work for us anymore. Besides, I have more important things to think about. I need to call Washington and let them know what's happened."

The Washington field office had jurisdiction over Quantico. But since the death appeared to be natural, calling them was just a formality.

Logan walked over to talk to the officer standing near the elevators, and Alex hurried to the food court. It was pretty empty. Just their unit and a few officers.

"Where is everyone?" she asked as she approached the table where Monty sat.

"The rest of the trainees are checking out," he said. "Most of them left last night. Other than that, nothing's going on down here."

"Have you guys seen Kaely?" she asked.

"No," Robin said, "but we just got here." She looked at Todd. "You came down early. Have you seen her?"

"No," he said. "Sorry."

"You all took the elevator near your rooms to come downstairs, right?"

"Sure," Robin said. "Why?"

"What about you, Monty?"

"Todd and I planned to go down to breakfast together. I met him outside his room." Monty frowned at her. "Why are you asking these questions?"

As Logan joined them, Alex quickly told them about Dennis.

"Seriously?" Monty said. "Maybe if I'd used the other elevator I could have found him soon enough to save him."

"No, he'd been dead for a while," Alex said. "It must have happened sometime early this morning. Are you sure you haven't seen Kaely anywhere? Did anyone make breakfast plans with her? Could she have used the elevator on your end?"

"Not as far as we know," Robin said. "What's going on, Alex?"

"We don't know where she is." Alex took the phone from her pocket, found Kaely's name in her contacts list, and called her. The phone rang and rang, but no one answered. These phones didn't have voice mail, so there was no way to leave a message.

"I wouldn't jump to conclusions," Bethany said. "Kaely knows how to take care of herself. She could be anywhere. Maybe she went over to the training field."

"No one's supposed to leave the building without permission," Logan said. "And why wouldn't she answer her phone?"

"Maybe it's not working," Todd said. "I've had some trouble with mine."

"Yeah, maybe," Alex said.

They had no proof anything was wrong, but the odd uneasiness Alex felt when she'd opened her eyes this morning was turning into cold, paralyzing dread. Somehow she knew Kaely was in trouble.

"Maybe she left," Nathan said. "I realize no unauthorized person is allowed on campus, but I doubt the guards would question someone going out. We're under protection, but we're not prisoners."

"She wouldn't do that," Logan said. "She knows better. And even if for some odd reason she wanted to leave the grounds, she would have told me."

He tried to call her on his phone, but after a minute, he put the phone back in his pocket. Alex could tell he was worried too.

"Before we call in the cavalry," Monty said, "let's see if we can find her."

"Okay," Logan said. "But first let me find out who left early this morning. Stay here."

As Logan walked away, Alex prayed they would find Kaely quickly, yet her gut told her it wouldn't be that easy. Even though she knew there'd be no answer, she called Kaely again. Every ring made it clear to her that Kaely was in real danger, and they had no idea how to help her.

Did anyone come through here last night? After two a.m.?" Logan asked the officer standing guard near the food court entrance.

"No one came past me except Agent Wong," he said. "He came downstairs for some hot chocolate. Went right back up. That was it."

Logan took a deep breath, trying to settle himself. "Did anyone check out of this building last night?"

"Sure. Some of the folks in training this week. Staff. Agents through with their shifts. They don't live here, you know. They're allowed to go home."

"Look, Agent Quinn is missing, and she didn't just grow wings and fly out the window. Plus, we have a dead police officer upstairs," Logan said. "I'm sorry if I'm taking my frustration out on you, but right now all I care about is finding out why the officer died and getting my agent back. I might be overreacting, but she's not the kind of person to go off without

telling someone where she'd be. Will you check the gates
to see who left either late last night or early this morning?"

The officer's expression softened. "Okay. I understand. I'll
call the gates and check the tapes from the security cameras.
I'll also check with the staff and other officers. Can you de-
scribe her? I think I know which agent she is, but . . ."

Logan gave him a thorough description, which the officer
wrote down.

"Thanks," Logan said as soon as he was finished. "As fast as
you can, okay? If we don't find her quickly, I'll have to bring
in someone from the Washington field office."

"Sure. I get it."

The officer hurried away.

Logan headed back to the food court. "They're calling the
gate at the Marine base as well as the officers at the west gate,"
he told his team. "I want to wait here until I hear from them."

"I feel so stupid," Alex said. "How could I not know she
was missing?" She sighed. "The last time I saw her was right
before she went into the bathroom to take a shower. I fell
asleep." She shook her head. "I don't remember hearing her
come out. I slept really well last night. Never heard her leave
the room."

Logan noticed Ben standing close enough to hear everything they were saying. "What are you doing here?" he asked.

"You finished your profile, right? Chief Gorman sent Julie
and me over to see if you had anything else for him. And to
find out if you need anything more from us before we check
out of our motel."

"I'm glad he did. Do you mind helping us look for Kaely?"

"Of course not. When did you notice she was missing?"

Logan quickly brought Ben up to speed.

"So she could have been gone all night?" Ben asked.

"It's possible," Alex said. "Her bed wasn't made when I got up, but you can't tell much from that. I don't make my bed every morning." She frowned. "I think she would've left me a note to let me know if she left early for some reason. She wouldn't want me to worry." She shrugged. "At this point, I have no idea where she might be."

"Break up into teams and look for her," Logan said. "I'll stay on this floor in case someone down here saw her. I also want to find out if the security cameras caught her. Monty, you're in charge of the search teams. This will have to be quick. If we don't find her within the next hour, I'm calling the WFO for help."

As he walked away from his team, he prayed that time wasn't running out for Kaely Quinn.

Monty pointed at Todd. "You and Robin check the first floor, then head over to the library. Maybe she went there. Bethany, you check out the second floor. Alex just told us all the rooms are being checked by police officers, but I'd like one of us to look around too. Kaely could be somewhere they might miss. Just don't touch anything. Tell Officer Driscoll I sent you. If you have a problem, call me. I'll come up there."

"Let me do that," Alex said. "I want to check our room to see if there's anything there that might tell me where Kaely could be."

"Okay, but then come back down as soon as you can. I really don't think Kaely would leave the building, but I guess it's not impossible. So I want you to drive through the grounds. Check for any signs that she might be somewhere on the property. Bethany, why don't you go with her?"

"Could I go?" Ben asked. "The rest of you trained here. I've never seen Hogan's Alley. I know this isn't the best time to ask . . ."

Alex couldn't blame him. As a simulated town constructed to teach investigative techniques, firearms skills, and defensive tactics, Hogan's Alley was an interesting area. Scenarios involved investigations of terrorist activities, planning and making arrests, processing evidence at crime scenes, conducting interviews and searches, using ballistic shields as protection, and clearing areas and buildings so they're safe to enter. Agent trainees weren't allowed to carry live weapons. Instead, they were issued guns with no firing pin. Their actual handguns were secured in the academy's gun vault and used only for firearms training.

The town consisted of a bank, post office, drugstore, laundromat, hardware store, barber shop, pool hall, and even a theater. The Biograph was modeled after the theater in Chicago where the FBI took down John Dillinger in 1934. Of course, it wasn't a real theater. It actually housed an FBI office.

"No, that's fine," Monty said. "You two drive around the campus. If you see anything that concerns you, don't get out of the car. Lock the doors and call me. I'll order an SUV for you."

"Okay," Alex said. "I'll get my coat while I'm up there."

"Are you sure you don't want me to go upstairs with you?" Ben asked.

Alex shook her head. "At least one officer is posted there. I'll be safe. But thanks."

"Bethany, you come with Nathan and me," Monty said. "We'll check out the Washington and Madison dorms. The training class was housed in Washington, so someone could still be there. Robin, Todd, check the gym, the pool, and the weight room. I need everyone back here within forty-five minutes." His gaze scanned the team. "Call me if you find anything or have any questions."

Monty looked around. "Where's Julie?"

"She was here a little while ago," Ben said. "She doesn't know what's going on."

"Okay. We'll find her as we're looking for Kaely and bring her up to speed." Monty frowned at the group. "Any questions?"

No one said anything. Monty hesitated for a moment, then said, "Okay, everyone. Let's get going."

Alex started to leave but then stopped. "Could you get the car, Ben? You could be warming it up instead of waiting around down here. I'll catch up to you."

"I'll get one of the officers to meet you in the parking lot," Monty told Ben. "He'll get you an SUV."

Ben nodded. "Okay." He turned and headed out.

Alex hurried to the elevator. She really did intend to quickly check out all the second-floor rooms again, but she also had something else in mind. She needed a few minutes to herself, without anyone else around. When she got out of the elevator, she told Driscoll she had permission to go to her room.

"Have all the rooms been gone through yet?" she asked him.

"We've searched every single one," Shawn said. "They're good."

"Okay. Thanks. I need my coat, and I want to take a look

around our room one more time to make sure we didn't miss anything. You've probably heard Agent Quinn is missing."

Driscoll frowned. "Okay, but make it quick. There really shouldn't be anyone up here until the floor is officially cleared."

"I understand. I won't be long." She felt a little guilty deciding not to look through the other rooms for Kaely after all, but she was confident the officers had done a good job. Besides, something told her Kaely wasn't in the building.

She'd just finished talking to Driscoll when the elevator doors opened and a man with a medical bag stepped off. He was with two other people wearing jackets that identified them as being from the medical examiner's office.

"Sorry we took so long," the man with the bag said. "The snow slowed us down." He was clearly in charge and obviously the ME. "Where's our victim?" he asked.

Driscoll turned his attention to him while Alex rushed to her room. This was taking too long.

After she pulled the door shut, she did a quick search of the room. Nothing told her where Kaely was. Then she grabbed the files on the table, the ones Kaely had been going through. She took a deep breath and sat down. "God, I need You to show me the truth," she prayed out loud. "Please help me find Kaely. And please, Lord, keep her safe." What was that Scripture she'd heard in church? "Your Word says You give Your angels charge over us to keep us in all our ways, so I'm believing that Your angels are with her. Watching over her. And over me right now." She had to believe that God would protect her, and that she wouldn't see the dark image that had appeared the last time she'd tried this.

She calmed herself and stared at the chair on the other

side of the table. She knew how little time she had. Could she do this? And could she do it in time?

"Okay, we know you're angry. Most of what you've done so far was directed at John Davis. But you're continuing to kill. And you're taking chances. Why? If you really cared only about Davis . . ." She paused as something popped into her mind. "Maybe you really don't care about these other killings. They're just . . . incidental. You *are* just using them to direct our attention away from the first killing." Although she'd suggested this before, no one had really explored the possibility. As Alex tried to see the case in a new way, something Sherlock Holmes said drifted into her thoughts. *"When you have eliminated the impossible, whatever remains, however improbable, must be the truth."*

Alex didn't see anyone in the chair across from her. Maybe her imagination wasn't as vivid as Kaely's. But she suddenly knew what had been bothering her about this case. She took another minute to consider the possibility. Could it be? Why hadn't she seen this before?

She took her phone out of her pocket and called Logan. He didn't answer, so she sent him a text, asking him to meet her in the food court. Then she grabbed her coat and started to leave the room. But at the last second, she turned back and removed her vest from her go bag. After slipping it on and adjusting her holster, she left the room, took the elevator to the first floor, and jogged to the food court to wait for Logan.

30

lex stood alone at the entrance of the food court. No Logan. She tried calling him again, but he still didn't answer. His phone just rang. She texted him once again, this time telling him more, but then she began to worry that his phone might not be working. Todd had said he'd been having problems with his. They were pretty new. She thought about calling someone else, but her theory could be completely wrong. She wasn't confident enough to tell anyone except Logan, and besides, she wasn't certain who she could trust.

Should she try to find him? But Kaely could be running out of time. She had to leave. She ran over to one of the staff working at the bakery, sure he couldn't possibly be involved with Kaely's disappearance. The guy had to be barely out of his teens. She asked him for something she could use to write a note, and he gave her a paper menu and a pen. She quickly scribbled a message, folded the menu, wrote Logan's full name on it, and then handed it back to him. His name tag read *Kirk*.

"Please, you've got to give this to an FBI agent named Logan Hart. It's very important. You can't give it to anyone else, okay?"

"Okay, I guess. I mean, I just serve food. I'm not an FBI agent or anything."

Oh, crud. "I realize that, Kirk. I just need you to get this to him. Please. He has dark blond hair, blue eyes, and he's fairly tall." She reached into her jeans pocket, then peeled off several bills and handed them to him. "I wrote his name on the note. Okay?"

"'Kay. Thanks for the tip."

Alex took another quick look around. Still no Logan. But between the last text and this note, she'd done all she could. Throwing up a quick prayer, she hurried out the front entrance and found Ben waiting in the SUV. She opened the passenger side and stuck her head inside.

"Let me drive, Ben. You don't know where things are here, and I do. It will be faster."

Although he didn't look happy about it, Ben got out and slid into the passenger side while Alex got behind the wheel.

He disconnected his phone. To think he'd almost called off the last part of his plan. But now things were back on track. No matter what, everything would work out just fine. They were just pressed for time.

He smiled at the small redheaded woman in the chair. "Just a little longer, my dear. Then I'll be finished. I'm almost sorry I won't be watching you die firsthand, but I'm sure you can understand I have no choice. I have to make my getaway."

"You won't get away with this," Kaely said.

He laughed. "Oh yes, I will. I'm sure if you think about it, you'll see how easy it will be for me. I've planned every detail, even arranged for unexpected surprises. You can see that, can't you?"

Kaely was silent as she stared at him. Finally, she said, "You've underestimated the agents in the BAU. They're much smarter than you are, and certainly more honorable."

He advanced on her and slapped her with enough force it left a red mark on her cheek. She barely moved and never lost eye contact with him.

He laughed in her face. "That's supposed to intimidate me, isn't it? Good try, but it doesn't."

"That's because you're a psychopath," she said.

Rage nearly made him strike her again, but he wanted her fully aware. "You don't call me that, you understand?"

"Why? Because it hits too close to home?"

He took several deep breaths, trying to calm himself. "No, my dear. Because it isn't true. You're just trying to get me to make a mistake."

Kaely didn't respond.

He laughed again. "Nothing you say or do will make any difference. This is your last day on earth, Kaely Quinn. No one is coming to save you. I've beat you once and for all."

Alex drove slowly down Hoover Road, then turned onto Investigation Parkway. Nothing looked out of place at the laboratory or the DEA Justice Training Center. She rolled down the window and shone her flashlight over the area. It was snowing so hard it was difficult to see, but she didn't notice any lights or tire tracks at either facility. Any tracks left by the training camp had already been covered under a layer of white.

As she pulled onto Forensic Way, Ben said, "We need to move faster. Remember, we don't have much time before Logan calls Washington."

She smiled at him. "Don't worry. We're almost to Hogan's Alley. I just want to be certain she's not here." She cocked her head to the right.

"I seriously doubt Kaely would have an interest in the Tactical Emergency Vehicle Operations Center garage," Ben said, his voice tight as he read the sign on the building out loud.

"I can't see her coming out here by herself anyway," Alex said. "But if Washington takes over the search, we'll lose control, and Kaely's career could be over."

"Do you really believe she just took off on her own?" Ben asked.

Alex sighed. "No. That doesn't sound like her. I think someone took her."

She entered Hogan's Alley, then slowed the car to a stop and looked at Ben, her foot on the brake. "So where is she, Ben?"

His eyes widened. Then he pulled up his jacket and removed a gun he'd tucked into the waist of his slacks. "How did you know?" he asked, his voice quavering.

"It had to be either you or Julie. I couldn't believe anyone on our team would leak information to our UNSUB." As she said the words, she realized she hadn't been completely sure.

If she had, she would have been more specific in the note and text to Logan. She'd known she was taking a chance by going with Ben alone, but she honestly couldn't think of any other way to locate Kaely. Of course, she could have asked an officer to come along, but that would have made Ben suspicious.

And if she'd been completely sure about him, she also would have pulled out her gun first. Not doing so had been a mistake. She wasn't a field agent, but she should have known better.

"Does anyone else know?" Ben asked.

"They may be suspicious, but they're not certain."

Alex could see the gun shaking in his hand.

"How could you?" she asked. "How could you betray your brothers and sisters in law enforcement? Is he paying you?"

"Shut up."

Alex was surprised by the expression on his face. He looked tortured.

"Give me your gun," he said. "Now."

Alex reached for her holster and slowly removed her gun. She thought about shooting him right then, but she couldn't take the risk. She still had no idea where Kaely was.

"Did he threaten you? Who does he have? Your wife? Your kids? Ben, it's not too late. One call, and your family will have protection. You don't have to do this."

"I told you to shut up," he said, his voice breaking. He took the gun from her hand and stuck it in his waistband.

"Has it occurred to you that he's bluffing? If he's here — and you're here — I'm betting no one's anywhere near your family."

"I said shut up!" he yelled. "Just be glad you and Monty

made it easy for me to get you out here. I didn't want to . . ."
She could see his twisted expression in the light coming from
the interior car lights, but then his face tightened with resolve.
"Drive to the pool hall. Now!"

Alex headed to the pretend pool hall. She pulled up in
front of it and stopped.

"Park behind the building, then turn off the engine and
the lights."

After she followed his instructions, he held out the hand
without the gun. "Give me the keys."

Seeing an opportunity, and realizing that Kaely was probably nearby, she leaned closer as she held out the keys. Then
she knocked the gun out of his hand and tried to grab it. She
didn't want to hurt him, but she had to get control of the
situation. He was obviously uncomfortable with what he was
doing. Maybe they could get help to Kaely without tipping
off the man who was holding her.

She wrapped her fingers around the barrel, but Ben
grabbed the grip, and they struggled. Alex almost had it when
the gun went off. She felt something hit her with force. It
took several seconds to realize she'd been shot.

Ben opened the passenger-side door and was coming around the car. Alex couldn't catch her breath, but she managed to do something she hoped would help her team find her.

Ben yanked her door open and pulled her out. Then he stuck the gun in her side with one hand and put his other arm around her to support her.

"Wait," she said. "I . . . I can't breathe." The snow made her feet slip, and Ben's grip tightened.

"You're going to be all right," he said. "The bullet hit your vest."

"I think I broke a rib."

"I'm sorry. I really am. But I can't help you. I just can't."

He dragged her to the pool hall's side door and knocked on it three times. The door swung open.

"We don't have much time," Julie said. "They'll come looking for them both soon."

"I know that." Ben pulled Alex along as the pain in her chest increased. She fought to stay conscious.

"Put her over here," Julie said. "It took you long enough."

Ben helped Alex into a chair. "I got here as soon as I could."

"Now get the van. We have to leave soon."

"Okay. But we need to be careful. She says the others might be suspicious of us."

As Alex fought against the fog that threatened to overtake her, she tried again. "Look, if he's threatening you or your families, we can help you. Please listen to me." She searched Ben's face, trying to find a sign that she was getting through to him. But all she could see was fear.

When he walked away, Alex took in her surroundings. The fake town had been used just yesterday, but now it was deserted. Obviously Ben and Julie had been waiting for this.

She blinked several times, trying to clear her vision. She realized someone was in a chair a few yards away. Thank God. It was Kaely.

"Are you okay?" Alex asked her.

"Yes, I'm fine. So far. Tell me you brought backup."

"No. Sorry. I'm sure Logan thinks I'm safe since I was accompanied by a trusted detective. Too bad he's crooked." Alex glared at Julie. "They'll find us, you know." The last thing she wanted Julie and Ben to know was that she'd left a note for Logan. She hoped he was on his way. She tried to take a breath, but the pain was too intense.

"I don't think so," Julie said. "We'll be gone before they search here."

But most of my team heard Ben say he wanted to see Hogan's Alley.

"Where's your phone?"

"I don't have it. I left it in my room. I was in such a hurry—"

"Liar." Julie held a gun on her while she patted Alex down. If she wasn't in so much pain, she could probably take her. But it was all she could do to try to stay conscious and wait for Logan. It was possible the bullet had cracked more than one rib.

Julie straightened up. "I guess you're telling the truth." She walked over to a nearby bag and took out a pair of handcuffs. While she wasn't looking, Alex quickly left the same bread crumb she had in the car. It was a long shot, but she had to do something.

Julie walked over and pulled both her arms behind the chair. A sharp stab of pain caused Alex to cry out.

"Be quiet," Julie said. She bent down and opened Alex's jacket. "Guess the FBI's bulletproof vests aren't everything they're cracked up to be," she said. She removed the vest and tossed it on the floor next to them. The inside was red with blood. Alex looked down and saw blood on her shirt too. The bullet had actually pierced the vest. She couldn't tell how bad her injury was. Julie put the cuffs around Alex's wrists, then came around in front of her.

"You're helping him," Alex said. Her voice was weak. "Why, Julie? We checked out everyone who worked with John Davis, but we never thought we needed to run background on you." She struggled to take another breath. "Why?" she asked again.

"For money. Isn't it always for money? I make a little over forty thousand a year. I have two kids. My ex-husband isn't paying child support because he's a bum. My kids deserve a chance. To be something better than me."

"I'm sorry you think so little of being a part of law enforcement. You help people. Protect their lives."

"Save it. I made a decision. My son's running with the wrong crowd, and my daughter's on drugs. This is my chance to take them somewhere else. Start over."

Alex could hear the anger in her voice. Julie hesitated for a moment, just long enough for Alex to see the pain in her face. She was struggling. Just like Ben, who probably had worse problems than losing his daughters' college money. Leave it to a grand manipulator to find someone's weakest spot and exploit it.

"Julie, he's not going to give you anything," Kaely said. "He'll kill you once he's done with you. Can't you see that? He can't afford any loose ends. Which is exactly what you are."

"You're wrong. He cares about me. He . . . he says I'm the daughter he never had."

"Oh, come on," Alex choked out. "You can't be that naïve."

Julie walked up to her. "If you don't shut your mouth, I'll put you in even more pain. Do you understand me?"

Julie was past reasoning. Alex prayed that Kirk had given the note to Logan. Where was he?

Logan waited in the food court for everyone to return. None of the guards had seen Kaely leave. The only people who'd checked out of the academy were supposed to, and none of the FBI cars were missing.

Todd and Robin came back first. He looked at them questioningly.

"Sorry. Couldn't find her," Robin said. "We thought she might be in the library, but she wasn't. It was actually closed until a little while ago. We waited for the librarian, but she hadn't seen her."

"Has anyone heard from Alex?" he asked Todd, who shook his head.

"Ben asked to go with her to drive around the grounds," Robin said. "He wanted to see Hogan's Alley."

"Alex isn't a tour guide," Logan said, frowning.

"She knows that," Todd said. "It will probably take them a while to check out all the buildings. Ben will help her get it done faster."

"They should only be looking for signs of life," Logan said. "All the new recruits have cleared out by now." He wanted to chew Monty out for not sending more people to look through the grounds, but it wasn't his fault. Monty was doing the best he could with the number of people he had.

Monty, Nathan, and Bethany walked into the food court. "We couldn't find her," Nathan said. "Madison was locked up tight. The only people in Washington are the staff cleaning the rooms and gathering dirty laundry."

"Where's Alex?" Monty asked.

"Not back yet."

"She checked out their room one more time before she left with Ben," Monty said. "She wanted to make sure she hadn't missed something. Maybe a note from Kaely or anything that could help us find her."

"Has anyone seen Julie?" Bethany asked.

"I got a text from Ben," Monty said. "All it said was that Julie is with them. Didn't he text you?"

Logan shook his head. He took the phone out of his pocket and tried to check his texts. Nothing. "I think this thing is dead."

"Did you charge it?" Bethany asked.

"Of course." He sighed. "Great. If Kaely tried to call me . . ."

"If she couldn't get you, she would have called one of us," Monty said. He handed Logan his phone. "Take this. At least you can contact Alex if you need to."

"Thank you." Before his phone quit working, he'd tried to call Kaely several times, but the phone just rang and rang. "Anyone else try to call Kaely?"

"We all did," Bethany said. "No answer."

He didn't like being out of touch with his team. He tried to call Alex with Monty's phone. No answer. Maybe her phone was down too. At least she had police detectives with her. She should be safe. He really didn't expect them to find anything. The idea that Kaely would find a way to leave the building without a car, and in the middle of a snowstorm, was ludicrous. But where was she?

"I checked with the guards," Logan said. "Kaely didn't leave the building through any of the gates. No cars missing. She's got to be here somewhere. We'll wait to hear from Alex, Ben, and Julie or for them to get back and let us know they found her."

"Can we eat while we wait?" Robin asked. "I'm starving. I haven't had breakfast."

"Sure. Go ahead."

Logan was hungry too, but he was wound too tight to eat. He checked his watch. If Alex couldn't find Kaely, he had no choice but to call Washington. A missing FBI agent was a big deal and never taken lightly. He was getting more and more concerned. It was hard to accept that Kaely had somehow gone off by herself, but since he didn't really know her, he just couldn't be certain.

He glanced at his watch again. Then he tapped his fingers on the table while he waited for everyone to get food or coffee. Monty walked up to the table and put a plate in front of Logan. "I know you love bagels and cream cheese. Eat. You need your strength." He smiled. "That guy who usually works the bakery is on break." His gaze swung back to the breakfast bar. "His replacement is pretty cute."

Logan followed Monty's gaze. A petite blonde was working behind the counter. She smiled at him when she saw him looking her way.

"Too young," Logan said.

Monty glared at him. "Hey, man. Don't burst my bubble."

Logan laughed even though he wasn't in the mood. He picked up the bagel, gave thanks, and took a bite. Fifteen more minutes and that was it. Whether he'd heard from Alex or not.

Julie lifted another bag from the floor, then put it on the pool table, unzipped it, and removed a plastic case. She opened it and took out a vial and syringe.

"No," Kaely said. "If you give us too much—"

"Then you'll join our friend Dennis," Julie said. For just a moment, Alex saw a look cross her face that revealed she was actually bothered by his death. Was it possible to reason with her after all?

"Listen, Julie, it's not too late. We can still turn this around."

"No, it is too late. We've already committed murder. I can't go back."

"If you get caught or killed," Kaely said, "what will your kids think? Is this the way you want them to remember you? Don't you realize that you're betraying your code? Throwing away your honor?"

"I just can't take it anymore," Julie said. Tears filled her eyes. "My kids don't respect me. I work constantly, and I'm exhausted. And for what? It's not worth it. I want out."

Julie plunged the syringe into the vial. Then she walked over to Kaely, who squirmed in her chair, trying to get away from her. "I realize this is your second dose," Julie said, "but you'll be all right. I'm only giving you enough to knock you out for a while. He wants you alive—for now." She plunged the needle into Kaely's neck. Then she moved to Alex. "Sorry to use the same needle on both of you, but she's not sick. You'll be fine."

"Is this what you used to kill Dennis?"

Julie nodded. "Propofol. We had no choice. He saw us."

"How did you take Kaely?" Alex asked. "I would have heard you if you'd come into the room."

"Simple. I sent her a text and told her I needed to see her downstairs. Even though we were supposed to be at the motel, she didn't suspect me. She was quiet so she wouldn't disturb you. We grabbed her and gave her a shot. Thankfully, we still had enough after we took care of Dennis. No cameras anywhere in the dorms, and we took Kaely out through the stairs. Had a vehicle waiting. It was easy. Ben must have failed to close the door to that room all the way, or you wouldn't have found Dennis so fast."

Alex glanced at Kaely. She was out. As Julie advanced toward her, Alex yelled, hoping someone might hear her, but Julie didn't hesitate. As the drug flowed through her veins, Alex prayed.

***

Logan was torn. He was ready to request help from Washington, but he had to call Terry Burnett first. He was the one who would actually make the call. But now Logan was worried about Alex. He'd texted her several times. Then he tried Ben and Julie. No response.

He gave up and called Terry. "Are you missing one person or four?" he asked after Logan explained what was going on. His tone was sharp.

"I don't know. One for sure. Maybe four. We've been calling and texting them, but no answer. It seems we're having some problems with the phones, though." The way the unit chief spoke to him made Logan feel incompetent. How could this have happened?

"I'll contact Washington, but I'm not sure when they can get there. We've got blizzard conditions coming in. They're grounding flights."

"They don't have that far to drive," Logan said.

"I realize that, but it could still take them a while if this thing hits really hard." Terry paused for a moment. "Can you safely search the grounds? Look for your missing agents and officers?"

"Yes. I think so. I'll take some agents with me. We'll see if we can find them. Then I'll report back to you."

"As soon as possible, please. If Gorman's officers are missing, I need to let him know." Terry swore loudly. "For crying out loud, Logan, this is Quantico. The FBI Academy. How could anyone get inside, let alone capture our agents? It's just not possible."

"Well, if we can't find my agents and the two police detectives, I guess it *is* possible."

Terry didn't respond to that. "Get back with me. Let me know what you find."

Logan ended the call and hurried back to the food court.

"Monty, Bethany, Todd, come with me," he said loudly. "Robin, Nathan, stay here in case someone comes back. I'll call you if I decide I need you, but in this weather, I think it's best we have only one vehicle out. Don't leave the area, understand? I don't want to have to look for anyone else. We're headed to Hogan's Alley since Ben said he wanted to see it. They might be there by now."

"Yes, boss," Robin said. "We won't move. If they show up, we'll text you."

"No, call or text Monty's number. I'm using his phone."

Logan and his three agents went up to the second floor. Dennis's body had been removed, but Shawn Driscoll was still on guard. Logan told him what they were doing before they entered their rooms to get boots, hats, and coats. Logan told his people to also put on their bulletproof vests. He didn't need to tell them to take their guns.

He'd been waiting for the call telling him everything was under control. When his phone rang, he picked it up with a smile. Confirmation.

"When you arrive, let me know. I'll open the garage door. Drive the vehicle inside. They'll be looking for it soon, but they won't think to look here. By the time it's discovered, we'll all be gone."

When he finished speaking, he turned off his phone and put it in his pocket. He was still wearing a disguise— uncomfortable but necessary. When his acquisitions arrived, he'd remove this look and don a new one. He'd been seen like this too many times. Someone might remember him and give a description that could cause him trouble.

He laughed. One step ahead. Always. His performance had been legendary. But this was his pièce de résistance. No one would ever top this. Profilers would talk about him forever. Someone who broke all their assumptions. Beat them at their own game.

He walked to the area he'd staged for Kaely Quinn and Alex Donovan. His last two performers. His finale. Then he'd be gone, living in Switzerland. No one would ever find him.

Another laugh reverberated throughout the empty space—as if his joy echoed throughout all creation.

Alex fought against the drug that was supposed to put her to sleep. Ben came back and put tape over her mouth, and then he placed something over her head. It was scratchy, and she couldn't see. Alex tried to scream, praying someone could hear her even with the tape on her mouth. But the more she yelled, the thicker the shadows grew, until she finally had to give in to the darkness.

Logan drove slowly through the academy grounds, in part because of the snow but mostly because he didn't want to miss anything. But so far, none of them had spotted the SUV Alex and Ben took. At least the guards hadn't seen them leave the grounds. Other than the final new recruits, some instructors, staff, and a few FBI police officers, only a laundry van and mail truck had left the campus this morning. Everything aboveboard.

He finally turned toward Hogan's Alley. It almost looked cozy cushioned in snow. Monty and Todd were shining flashlights from the car's windows, looking for something, anything that seemed out of place or unusual. The snow wasn't helping. The dark clouds overhead made it appear like nighttime.

They had just passed the Biograph and turned the corner when Todd yelled out, "I think I see the SUV."

Logan forgot about the snow for a moment and slammed on the brakes. His own SUV slid, and he fought for control.

"Four-wheel drive, huh?" Monty said under his breath.

"Sorry," Logan said. "Driver error."

He backed up until he spotted the vehicle. It was parked at the Facilities Maintenance Center with other vehicles used by the maintenance crew. He started to back up farther when Bethany called out.

"The door to the pool hall is open. That's not right."

"Let's check the car first, then we'll look at that." Logan carefully drove up to the ramp that led to where the SUV was parked, then stopped and turned off the engine. "Monty, check this out with me. Todd, Bethany, wait in the car."

The two men got out and carefully climbed the concrete ramp until they were next to the SUV. It was unlocked and empty. No one was inside.

Monty shone the flashlight in the front seat and then the backseat. "I don't see anything," he said.

Logan was disappointed but also relieved. He was afraid they might find bodies. "So Alex isn't here. Neither is Ben or Julie. And we're still missing Kaely. This is ridiculous. I don't get it."

They were shutting the doors when Monty said, "Wait a minute." He bent down and picked up something from the floor. When Monty showed it to Logan, he didn't know whether to laugh or cry.

It was one of Alex's pistol earrings. "Why is this here?" he asked, more to himself than anyone else.

"I think Alex is telling us she's alive. Take it as a good sign."

"Maybe it fell off during a struggle," Logan said. "You don't know."

"Yeah, I do. Look closer."

Monty carefully dropped it into Logan's outstretched hand. "This is a pierced earring. The back is on it. If it had fallen off in a struggle, the back wouldn't be attached. Alex did this on purpose."

Logan blew out the breath he'd been holding. "You're right," he said. "At least when she left this car, she was alive. But what about Ben and Julie?"

Monty hesitated a moment before saying, "I think it's time we realize that one or both of them had something to do with this."

"I can't believe that."

"Well, how else did this happen? Because of increased security, we know no one suspicious came onto the property, and we know they were with Alex. She's gone. I think we have to assume they're involved."

Logan sighed. "Maybe you're right. Let's check out the pool hall, and then I'll contact Chief Gorman. He needs to look into Ben and Julie. Especially at their finances. I don't think either one of them is our UNSUB, but they could be working with him."

Logan fought back anger that felt as if it would overtake him. He had to keep his head straight. Play this by the book.

Alex and Kaely needed him at his best.

33

Alex was safe at home, and Krypto was beside her. He slept next to her every night, sometimes giving her less space on the bed than he had. But she loved reaching out for him. Feeling his warm body near her. She felt safe. Protected and loved.

She tried to touch him, but for some reason she couldn't move her arm. "Krypto, move over," she said. Her mouth felt like it was full of cotton. What was going on? She forced her eyes open, but everything was blurry. She blinked several times until her vision cleared. Confused, she looked around her. She was in a large building. Like a warehouse. She suddenly remembered what had happened at the academy. The shot Julie had given her. She had to blink back tears. Thinking of Krypto made her wonder if she'd ever see him again.

She realized someone was sitting in a chair a few feet away from her. Kaely. Her head was dropped onto her chest. She was still out.

Alex tried to take several deep breaths so she could clear the fog in her head, but as soon as she made an attempt, the pain in her chest made her eyes fill with more tears. She looked around but couldn't see anyone else in the building. Were they alone? Had they been dropped off and left here? Frankly, she was surprised they were still alive. Why hadn't Julie or Ben just killed them? Then she remembered Julie said someone wanted them alive. For now.

"Kaely," she called out. "Kaely, wake up."

No response. Alex's heart dropped. Was she dead? Julie had given her two doses of propofol. It was a dangerous drug. Michael Jackson had died when his doctor gave him too much. It was supposed to be used only as an anesthetic in operating rooms.

Alex strained against whatever they'd bound her with. Once again pain shot through her and she yelled out. She looked down at her shirt. The bleeding had stopped. She didn't think the wound was very deep, but the impact had been awful. She'd end up with a pretty bad bruise before long. She couldn't tell how many ribs were broken. Her only chance was to ignore the pain and do whatever it took to get her and Kaely out of there. Although her hands were behind her back, she could tell this time they'd used zip ties to bind her wrists together. Her feet were bound the same way. If she could use the right amount of force, she might be able to break them.

Alex tried to stand but realized the ties around her wrists were woven through the spindles on the back of the chair. She sighed and began to scoot it closer and closer to Kaely, until she was finally next to her.

"Kaely?" she said. "Wake up."

This time Kaely's eyes fluttered open. "Where . . . where are we?"

"We're in a large empty warehouse or something," Alex said. "We're tied up. We have to get free. Now."

Kaely nodded. It was obvious she was still fighting the effects of the drug. Thankfully, the tape had been removed from their mouths. Probably so they could breathe better.

"What do we do?" Kaely asked.

"I don't know. I don't see anyone. We could make some noise and hope someone hears it, but if we do that and the wrong person is here, things could get worse."

"They'll show up sooner or later anyway. I say we give it a try."

"Okay. One . . . two . . . three . . ."

Alex yelled as loudly as she could. Kaely tried to help, but she was still weak and could barely make a sound. Alex prayed someone would hear them and call the police. She also decided to use some of that vacation she'd earned after this case. She had lots of time off coming to her. She and Krypto deserved a chance to do something fun. Maybe they'd go to the mountains in Colorado. Krypto loved snow. He found such joy bouncing around in it.

Odd the thoughts that drifted through her mind as she and Kaely continued to call for help. She'd just tried to take another deep breath for the next round when a deep voice behind her said, "Shut up, ladies. Or I'll put a slug in your backs."

Hands grabbed Alex's chair and pushed it back where it was originally.

"You stay where you are if you want to live," he said.

The man walked around in front of them. He wore glasses

and was overweight, balding, and had a large nose. The man in the sketch.

"You won't get away with this," Kaely said. "People are looking for us."

"I'm afraid they won't find you." A smile cracked his face. He swung his hand around like a circus entertainer showing off the acts in his tent. "This will be the last place you ever see."

"Where are we?" Alex asked.

"This warehouse was left empty when the company moved out of town. It was easy to break into. It's the perfect place for me to make my exit."

"You've been wearing a disguise," Alex said. She could see where the makeup on his face had caked.

"Yes, so no one would know who I really was. And it's worked beautifully. Even you, supposedly the world's greatest profilers, have no idea." He walked up next to Kaely, his face only inches from her face. "The great Kaely Quinn. The daughter of a serial killer who's brought down so many criminals that no one can count them all. I followed your escapades in the papers. There was the Elephant Killer. Oh, and the Copycat Killer. What silly names."

"We didn't name them. The media did," Kaely said. Alex could tell she was trying to gather her strength, but her voice was still weak.

"Yes, I know that. You could never cheapen what you do by creating goofy nicknames for violent serial killers." He sighed. "There's no one you can't find, is there?"

"I don't find them. I only—"

"Please. Don't insult my intelligence. Without you, dangerous killers would still be walking the streets."

"Whatever you say."

He approached Alex. "And now we move on to Alex Donovan, who saved the world from a deadly plague. And what was the name of your little friend? Oh yes. The Train Man. Very dramatic."

"I absolutely didn't save the world."

"You're right," he said. "You *absolutely* didn't. Supervisory Special Agent Alex Donovan. Brave, true, and loyal." He put one hand over his heart. "I, Alexandra Donovan, do solemnly swear that I will support and defend the Constitution of the United States against all enemies, foreign and domestic; that I will bear true faith and allegiance to the same; that I take this obligation freely, without any mental reservation or purpose of evasion; and that I will well and faithfully discharge the duties of the office of which I am about to enter. So help me God." He moved closer to her. "And you believe that, don't you, Alexandra?"

"Don't call me that."

He straightened up, a look of feigned surprise on his face. "I seem to have touched a sore spot, haven't I?" He laughed again. "And here you are paired with Kaely Quinn, the legend. I'll bet she intimidates you, doesn't she? Are you insecure? Afraid you won't measure up?" He stared at her. "I can smell the fear in you. The insecurity. You'll never be as good as she is, and you know it."

Alex's heart thudded in her chest, and she couldn't breathe. "Shut up," she choked out.

"That's not true," Kaely said, disgust dripping from her words. "He's just trying to weaken you, Alex."

With effort, Alex dismissed the fear that had tried to overcome her reason. And her training. Kaely's assessment was right. They both needed to be at their best. She knew they'd defeat him. No doubt in her mind. But when? How long would it take for Logan to find them? What did this man have planned for them?

"You were never really one of us," Alex said. "You spit on that pledge without hesitation. You've killed all these people. You're a disgrace."

He glared at her. "You have no idea what you're talking about. 'I will bear true faith and allegiance to the same.' But the FBI has no true faith or allegiance to their agents, do they? Don't you two realize they don't care about you? That they will turn on you in the end?" He cursed loudly and backed up a few feet. "Neither one of you really understands who they are. You're ignorant."

"What are you talking about?" Kaely asked. "You make no sense."

Kaely was egging him on, trying to get him to talk. They needed time. Time to figure a way out of this on their own — or to give their rescuers a chance to find them.

He shook his head and turned away for a moment. "I know what you're trying to do," he said when he faced them again. "You're stalling for time." He looked at them with a quizzical expression. It was impossible to see most of his face. The putty from his nose extended to his cheeks. And his jaw had been enlarged as well. His ears were covered, and Alex was pretty sure he was wearing fake eyebrows. She knew who he was, but she wouldn't let him know that. Not yet. She was afraid he'd grow angry. Feel that she had bested him.

If that happened, she and Kaely would probably die.

Logan took Monty, Bethany, and Todd with him into the pool hall. They held their guns in front of them since they had no idea what they would find.

The lights in the building were off. Monty was behind Logan, ready with his flashlight to help them find their way.

When they reached the door, Logan turned to look at his team. He nodded, silently letting them know he was ready to move in. Logan pushed the door open and stepped inside. He felt for the light switch next to the door and flipped it up. The lights came on, and they found themselves alone with just a pool table and some chairs. Two of them were out of place, but other than that, everything looked normal.

Logan pointed at Monty and made a gesture telling Bethany and Todd to stay where they were. There was a back room that held equipment. He and Monty walked quietly to that door, then Logan opened it slowly. He felt for another light switch, but there wasn't one.

He held his hand out for the flashlight. "Cover me," he told Monty.

With Monty behind him, he swung the flashlight around the room. At first he found only chairs and pool equipment. But when he moved the light to his left, he found something else.

A body.

"Who is it?" Monty asked.

"I don't know. I've never seen him before." He moved closer to the man. He felt for a pulse, but it was too late. He was gone. Shot. He had on an undershirt but no outer shirt. Logan patted him down, looking for some kind of identification, but he couldn't locate any.

Logan backed out of the room. He told Bethany and Todd what they'd found, then took Monty's phone out of his pocket and dialed Terry's phone number. When Terry answered, he brought him up-to-date. Told him they hadn't found Alex and Kaely, nor Ben and Julie.

"I think Gorman's detectives may be involved," he told Terry.

"What do you mean you *think* they're involved?"

"I'm about as sure as I can be, but I can't prove it."

"Until you can, I'm not accusing Chief Gorman's people. Washington is on the way. They'll get to the bottom of things."

Logan acknowledged Terry's words, but he wasn't so sure Washington would get there in time. Maybe he wasn't supposed to be looking for Alex and Kaely, but he was going to do it anyway. He couldn't just stand by and let them die.

He ended the call but kept the phone in his hand.

"Follow me," he said to Monty. "I want to look at something."

As he started toward the pool hall's entrance, Bethany stopped him. "You need to see this," she said.

"What is it?"

"We're certain Alex and Kaely were here," Todd said.

Logan frowned at him. "How can you be sure?"

"Kaely's phone is on the pool table, and I found this on the floor." Todd opened his gloved hand.

Logan looked. "Alex's other earring."

"There's something else," Todd said.

"I hope it's a note telling us where she is."

"No. I wish it was."

He pointed at a spot near the chair. It was blood. Logan's heart sank.

"And that's not all." Todd pulled something from beneath the pool table—a bloody vest with a hole in it.

"It's Alex's," Logan said.

"Or Kaely's," Bethany added.

No one said a word as realization set in. One of their agents had been shot. Might be dead.

"Whoever it was, she was protected by the vest," Todd said. "That means they're probably alive."

"Right," Logan replied. He couldn't show his team how frightened he was. He pulled up all the courage and faith he had inside. He would find his agents, and they would be alive. Period. He couldn't accept any other outcome.

"The guy in the back was shot," Logan said, "but there's hardly any blood. I think he was killed somewhere else and then moved here." He pointed toward the front door. "Follow me, but stay behind me."

Logan stepped outside and looked around. When he was certain it was safe, he motioned for Monty to join him. Once he did, Logan pointed the flashlight onto the street.

"What are you looking for?" Monty asked.

"The snow has covered most of what looks like a large vehicle's tracks, but some are still here." He stared at them for a moment before saying, "I think I know how they got them out of here."

"How?"

"The guards at the gate here and at the Marine base told me everyone who left after Kaely and Alex disappeared. One was a laundry van driver who entered the academy grounds to pick up dirty laundry. I think he's the dead man. That's why his shirt is gone. It probably had the insignia of the company on it. He was killed, and someone took his place. Also stole his ID, not only in case a guard asked for it but also to throw us off when we found his body. A mail truck left here too, but it's smaller, and the same mail carrier comes every day. The guards know him. But the laundry van driver? If he—probably Ben—looked okay and had identification, the guards would let him through."

He sighed. "The UNSUB had to know we'd figure that out. By now they've either dumped the van or hidden it. We need help, Monty. We've got to find Alex and Kaely and bring them home."

"We will," Monty said. "They're smart. If Alex found a way to tell us she was here, she's got something else up her sleeve."

"I hope so."

"You taught me that when things look their worst, we have to put the situation in God's hands. And we need to have faith. Didn't He say if we call on Him, He'll answer us? That He will deliver us? Then we need to pray and believe that God's the One who's a step ahead. We need to take Him at His word that He'll deliver Alex and Kaely."

Logan wanted to ask Monty how he could believe that after losing his grandmother the way he did, but he couldn't.

"Look, Logan, I don't understand why my grandmother died," Monty said as if reading Logan's mind, "but I do know she was a believer, and she was excited about seeing heaven. She wanted to go. And she wanted to protect me. I have a peace about that. It's what's getting me through this."

"I didn't know your grandmother was a Christian. I assumed she was Buddhist . . . or something."

"No. That's why I finally gave in. With both of you talking about God, I never stood a chance." Monty smiled.

"Well, I'm glad. And you're right about putting Alex and Kaely in God's hands. We need His direction. Even though I think I know how our UNSUB got them out of here, I don't have a clue how to find them now." He paused for a moment before saying, "Let's go. The rest of us need to do what we do best. See if we can help the agents from the WFO find Alex and Kaely."

He went back inside and told Bethany and Todd they were all going to wait in the SUV until agents arrived to secure the scene. Once they were in the car, Logan called Terry again and told him about the vest, the earrings, and his suspicions about the laundry van. "I don't think they'll find the van," he said. "It's probably hidden somewhere. But I think the UNSUB—or one of his accomplices—killed the driver. Alex and Kaely were probably carried out of here in laundry bags. Even if a guard at the gate had checked the back of the van, he would only have seen those bags."

He took a deep breath, not really wanting to say the words that came next. "Our agents wouldn't have stayed still and silent if the van was searched. The UNSUB couldn't take a

chance that they would call out for help, so I think he probably drugged them. My guess is he used the same stuff on
the guard in the Jefferson dorm."

The women could have been silenced another way, but
he couldn't say it out loud. Two things gave him hope that
they were alive. One was that this UNSUB liked putting on
a show. He'd want to kill them in some kind of dramatic
way. The other was that if they were dead, why take a chance
smuggling their bodies off the property? He would have just
left them behind.

"That's good investigative work," Terry said.

"Spent a lot of time in the field before joining the BAU. I
guess it never goes away."

"Well, I think you're being humble. It's good information.
I'll find out who our dead guy is and put out a BOLO for the
van. I know what you said, but we have to try. In this weather,
maybe they haven't gotten too far."

"Any idea when Washington will be here?"

"As soon as they can. Their vehicles can handle the snow,
but they have to take it slow and steady. It's getting worse out
there." Terry's deep sigh showed his frustration. "You all get
together and see if you can send me an updated profile that
could help us. It sounds as if you're finally getting a handle
on him."

"Maybe, but if we'd had something better, sooner, maybe
Alex and Kaely would still be here."

"You've done the best job you could with what you've had.
You know better than to internalize this."

Logan appreciated Terry's encouragement, especially after
their previous conversation, but he couldn't shake the feeling that they'd all missed something important. Something

that would have kept Alex and Kaely safe. "Terry, I think you might want to locate Donald Reinhardt. He fits the profile we have so far, and he walked out of here this morning when we found the dead guard. I shouldn't have let him leave, but I had no legal way of holding him."

"Done. Look, I know we believe the UNSUB is focused on Alex and Kaely, but you need to be extra careful. Don't take any unnecessary chances, okay?"

"Okay. That reminds me. We're having some problems with the phones. I'm using Monty's now."

"I noticed you've been showing up as Monty's number." He paused for a moment. "Look, just keep using this phone. I'll contact CIRG and see if they have any way to fix the problem. You call the Evidence Response Team."

"Okay. Thanks. I'll keep in touch."

After making the call, Logan put Monty's phone back in his pocket. He still wanted his regular phone, but Terry was right. They all needed to be even more careful now. The wrong move could put Alex and Kaely in further danger.

As the four of them waited in the warm SUV for ERT, Logan prayed silently for his two missing agents. *God, You promised to deliver us when we called out to You. I'm calling out. Please protect Alex and Kaely. Keep them safe.*

Monty was right. He had to put them in God's hands and trust Him. With no way to figure out where they were, there was nothing they could do anyway. God was their only hope.

L ogan and the rest of his unit gathered around a table in the food court. The Evidence Response Team was processing the crime scene at the pool hall, and the dead man was quickly identified as the driver of the laundry van. He was checked in by one guard but let out by another, who didn't ask for his ID because his vehicle was leaving the property. Service vehicles weren't normally checked when exiting.

"Where's the file Kaely had?" Logan asked.

"It's probably in her room," Bethany said.

"Go get it, will you?" Logan said. "If anyone gives you a hard time, come back and tell me. I'll talk to them."

Bethany returned with the file a few minutes later. Logan pored through it. "Nothing new here. Just copies of what we already know. We found Kaely's phone in the pool hall, but we didn't see Alex's. I imagine whoever took them was smart enough to take her phone, but I'll call CIRG and ask them to triangulate it just in case. I realize it's a long shot, but we have to try." Logan looked at Bethany. "Did you see Alex's phone in her room?"

She shook her head. "I looked around just in case, but I didn't see a phone. I'm sure it wasn't there."

Logan couldn't help but feel a spark of hope. Alex was smart. Maybe she hid it where the UNSUB couldn't find it. He was about to call Terry to tell him they needed to triangulate his agent's phone when the kid who worked at the breakfast bar counter came up to them. "Is one of you Agent Logan Hart?"

"I am."

"I was asked to give this to you a while ago. I hope it wasn't too important."

Logan took the paper the kid held out. "Thanks," he said. When he opened it, he could hardly believe what he read. He stood. "We need to triangulate Alex's phone now. There's no time to waste." He handed the paper to Monty. "Alex has a hunch who our UNSUB is, and she may have given us a way to find her and Kaely."

"Where are Ben and Julie?" Alex asked. "We know they helped you."

He grabbed a folded metal chair leaning against the back wall, then brought it over and sat down in front of them.

"Julie was a fan. She followed me for years. Wrote to me. I cultivated her. Made her think she was special. I waited until she trusted me, and then when I gave her a chance to make a lot of money, she took it. She needs it for her children, you see. And to be honest, she's greedy. And Ben? He's been a reluctant helper. Julie brought him on. It wasn't hard." He clicked his tongue several times. "She found out our Ben was a very bad boy. He took some money from a drug bust. Needed to cover his wife's gambling debts. We threatened to tell the chief about his indiscretion. I also offered him a great deal of money. If it makes any difference, he felt bad about you ladies."

"Who took Stephanie Cole's phone?" Alex asked.

"Oh, that was Ben. I couldn't take the risk myself. Since everyone got rid of the phones I'd hacked, including Cole, I needed another plan. It worked out well, didn't it? He read the text I sent him because it actually came from his daughter's phone. I'm nothing if not adaptable."

"Did you let Ben and Julie go?"

His eyes widened. "Heavens no." He leaned closer, as if studying them. "You're smarter than that."

"You couldn't take a chance that they'd turn on you," Kaely said. "Julie might have kept quiet for a while, but she could hold what you've done over your head. She would probably ask for more money later. And Ben was liable to have an attack of conscience. He's the one who would crack first."

He grinned widely, cracking more of the pancake makeup on his face. "Ding, ding, ding! Very good. Exactly right."

"So you killed them," Alex said. It wasn't a question. It was a statement of fact. Alex knew the answer, but she needed to hear him say it.

"Yes, dear. I had no choice, did I?" He cocked his head toward the room he'd just come out of. "Their bodies are waiting in that office. Julie traveled here with you. She was in a laundry bag too. Of course, she had to put you to sleep because we couldn't take a chance you'd make noise or try to work your way out of the bag and jump out. Then when she and Ben got here, I thanked them for their help before I shot them."

"How could you do all this?" Kaely said. "You were respected. Even if you disliked me, almost everyone else thought you were one of the people responsible for creating the BAU."

This time he looked truly surprised. "Just who do you think I am?"

"Only one man fits the profile and has a grudge against the BAU. You refused to stay at the Jefferson because you had things to do. You were there long enough to communicate with your two helpers, though. It all fits."

"So say my name. And don't worry that the knowledge will put you in danger. You're going to die anyway. Go for it."

"You're Donald Reinhardt," Kaely said. She didn't sound confident. Although everything fit, Alex could hear the uncertainty in her voice.

The man swung his gaze to Alex. "Do you agree with her?"

Alex slowly shook her head.

"Really?" Again the man looked surprised. "I want to hear your thoughts."

"It has to be him, Alex," Kaely said. "Doesn't it?" She turned her gaze back to him. "Wait a minute. You're not tall enough . . . ."

Alex could tell Kaely was still coming out from under the effects of the drug.

"You're the man who wanted to prove he's smarter than Davis—and all analysts," Alex said. "The man who killed several people simply to divert attention from himself. But what nailed it for me was a line from a Sherlock Holmes novel, *The Sign of the Four*: 'When you have eliminated the impossible, whatever remains, however improbable, must be the truth.' I realized you could be only one person."

She looked over at Kaely. "Reinhardt fit so much of what we knew, but I decided you were right. He would never break the oath he took when he joined the FBI. Reinhardt might be unfair and egotistical, but a serial killer?"

"I never actually accused him . . . before now."

"I know. But why is that? Wasn't it because you had doubts?"

"Yes, I did. I still couldn't accept it was him. I've been thinking about it ever since Ben and Julie took me, though, and—"

"Excuse me. I hate to interrupt you, but I can't sit here all day and listen to you two prattle on and on about who was right and who was wrong." He glared at Kaely. "Too bad you missed it this time, my dear. You could have been rescued." He turned his attention back to Alex. "My goodness, I think you really do know who I am. I'm impressed. Too bad you won't have time to tell anyone."

"How do you know I didn't?" Alex said.

He sighed loudly. "Because if you had, you wouldn't be here now, would you? Again, don't insult my intelligence."

Kaely gasped and looked at Alex. "I should have caught it. We were so busy looking in another direction, I missed it. I'm sorry, Alex."

"It's not your fault. He knew how to play us. We forgot to ask the questions that should have been asked." She looked back at him. "Once I realized who the perfect suspect was—regardless of the circumstances—there was only one possibility. Improbable, maybe, but true nonetheless."

The man removed his glasses. "May I introduce myself, ladies?"

"It's not necessary," Alex said as he pulled the putty off his face, then dropped it onto the floor before stripping off his fake, bushy eyebrows and the head covering that made him appear bald.

"Say my name. I just want to hear you say it."

"You're Evan Bayne."

Logan sat down with his unit after getting off the phone with Washington. He was keeping them all apprised of the situation.

"When will they be here?" Robin asked.

"There's a pileup on the highway coming out of Washington. Both lanes are shut down, and they don't know how long they'll be stuck there. They'd send out a helicopter, but the winds have picked up. It's too dangerous."

Logan ran his hand through his hair. "The Hostage Rescue Team is being alerted, but they need a location. They also need local police to help us find our agents. Until the weather clears, they can't use a helicopter either, so they'll deploy their emergency vehicles, including their Humvees. As you know, HRT is trained to operate in this kind of weather. They'll get through the snow, but they're slow. We need that triangulation. Not only for Alex's phone, but also for Cooper's. Julie's too. I don't know if she's part of this or if she's a victim, but we need to look for her phone as well."

Logan quickly called Chief Gorman. He asked for Cooper's and Julie's normal phone numbers. After the chief gave them to him, he asked why he needed them. At this point, Logan wasn't certain who he could trust. He wasn't ready to tell the chief he thought his two detectives were working for the man they'd been looking for. Or that he wasn't certain they were still alive. He told the chief he would talk to him about it later. Then he called CIRG and gave them the additional phone numbers.

"Can we use our other phones now?" Monty asked.

"Not yet," Logan said. "They're probably okay, but until we have our agents back, we can't take any chances. I'm not losing anyone else."

As Logan waited to hear from CIRG, every minute seemed like an hour. He prayed that God would lead them to Alex and Kaely. And that they would be alive.

"It will be okay," Monty said. "God will protect them."

Logan was surprised that Monty had talked about God in front of the rest of the team. Expressions of faith in the workplace, especially for those in the federal government, were discouraged. An agent could even receive a reprimand.

"Amen," Robin said.

The other agents nodded their approval.

"Well, I guess we're all in agreement," Logan said with a smile. "We'll get them back alive."

"Ben put a thought into my head that wouldn't go away," Alex said to Kaely. "I didn't realize that was what was bothering me all this time until I sat in our room and used your method. That's when it came to me—that and the quote from Holmes."

"And what was that thought?" Bayne asked. "I'd really like to hear it."

"Ben said you'd be the perfect suspect if you weren't dead."

"We just accepted that you'd died," Kaely told him.

"As you were supposed to. You see, if I'd been the only one who died, you would have figured out my suicide was fake. That's why I had to add it into the mix. Get your attention on Davis as the first and most important victim and the rest as an attack against profilers." He chuckled. "Sorry. Behavioral analysts." He wagged his finger at them. "You realize no one wants to say that mouthful. That's why everyone calls you profilers."

Alex was trying to do anything she could to stall him. She had no idea what he was going to do next, but she was certain he wouldn't just shoot them. He wanted to end his spree with something memorable. "I became convinced when I considered that the only person who actually saw your body wash out to sea was your wife," she said. "That's when I realized that what we saw on the video could have been rigged."

Kaely stared at him for a moment before saying, "How did you do it? Although no one else reached the edge in time to see your body wash away, people did see you jump."

"A lot of crevices sit below that cliff edge. Early that morning, before anyone was around, we set up a cable and attached it firmly to a rock near the top. Then when I *fell*, I grabbed the cable to my right and easily swung over to one of the jutting rocks below. It wasn't that far, and I'd found a way to practice at home. Build up some calluses on my hands. Then

I jumped onto several other rocks that led me back to the top but far enough away that no one noticed when I climbed back up. When Gloria dropped down to her knees, she unhooked the cable and let it fall into the sea. Her performance kept all the attention away from me. We had a car waiting, and I just drove away. By the time anyone could reach her, the cable had washed away."

"Clever," Kaely said. "Very clever."

"Yes, it was," Bayne said. "We had to make it happen in real time to fool you. So there you go. As you said, everyone's attention was on the spot where my poor mangled body had been dragged out to sea, just waiting for the sharks to feast on my remains." He pulled up his shirtsleeve and flexed his muscle. "Good thing I'm in shape, or it never would have worked. Pretty good for a man of my age, don't you think?"

Alex wasn't impressed or surprised with his self-aggrandizing. "And Gloria? I guess she's the only person who knows what you did. Will you let her live?"

A man like Bayne would value his own life above everyone else. Even those he professed to love.

His eyes widened. "Of course. We planned this together. She's dedicated to my plan. Now, if that ever changes . . . Well, I'll deal with that possibility then."

Of course he would.

"But I still don't get it," Kaely said. "Again, you were respected by every behavioral analyst who came through the BAU. You and John Davis are the fathers of behavioral analysis. Why would you destroy your reputation? Your legacy?"

His face grew dark, and his expression twisted into one of rage. "John Davis believed he was the only one who was

instrumental in creating the BAU. He took credit for everything. I hated him."

As if she understood that they needed to keep him talk-
ing, Kaely said, "But you wrote all those books. I read them.
They were great. Your contribution in the early days of the
BAU is clear."

He glared at her. "My books? You and Julie were among
the few people who bought them, then. Everyone wanted *his*
books. Not mine. My books didn't sell close to the number
his did."

"You left the FBI before retirement age," Alex said. "If
you'd stayed, you would have sold a lot more."

Bayne strode to Alex's chair, a venomous hatred flashing in
his eyes. "I left because I couldn't take it anymore. Couldn't
abide another minute with Davis and his insufferable ego.
He ruined my career, destroyed my book sales. And then
his publisher sued me, saying I'd claimed one of his cases
as mine! But we worked that case together. Why was it so
important that he get top billing, especially when *I* am the
superior profiler and always have been? He said he tried to
talk his publisher out of taking me to court, but I didn't believe him. They all wanted their pound of flesh. We finally
settled out of court, but it left me nearly bankrupt."

"So you *were* after the insurance money," Kaely said. "It
was brought up as a possible motive, but I didn't take it seriously."

Bayne took a deep breath as if trying to regain control.
"I deserve that three million dollars. I need it. But I had to
be patient. Wait until it wouldn't matter if my jumping off
that cliff was considered suicide so the insurance company
would still pay."

His expression darkened again. "The chance to see Davis dead was the icing on the cake. And then the two of you getting accolades just like he did. . . . You and your arrogant colleagues all fit into my final plan perfectly. The more analysts your UNSUB killed, the less the focus would be on little ol' dead me."

Bayne sighed. "I thought Davis would have his gun with him, but he had a knife, and that was good enough. I just wish I could have seen him die in person. But I was busy in Australia, setting up my own death." He chuckled. "Then I used a fake passport to fly here without detection. Agents learn how to spot fake documents and IDs in the FBI, you know. That, of course, teaches us how to create them too."

"But you were the man in the sketch," Kaely said. "The man Harper talked to at the convention."

"That was Derrick Williams, a two-bit criminal who needed a break. I had him dress up in the same disguise I've been using to hide my identity so it would plant the seed that a crazy fan could have been involved in Davis's death." He shrugged. "I hoped it would send the police in the wrong direction. And since I'm not very knowledgeable about today's phones and . . . What are they called? Apps? Anyway, Williams was the master behind all that. He made certain all Davis could see on his phone was his wife. He also was careful not to leave any clues that might lead back to me. And he operated the drone so I could watch Davis kill himself. Julie oversaw everything else. Made sure it was handled correctly. She did a wonderful job, didn't she?"

"Is Williams still alive?" Kaely asked.

"Ah no. Unfortunately, Mr. Williams died of an overdose after helping us." He shook his head. "So sad."

"Who killed Monty's grandmother?" Alex asked.

"I did that. I told Cooper to do it—even if Monty killed himself first—but he refused, and I had to change my plan. You see, I'd initially promised him he wouldn't have to take a life." He shrugged. "It was too late in the game to get rid of him, and the window of opportunity was closing. I wore the fake stomach but decided not to use the makeup and wig. Another red herring, you see." He sighed. "I'm still upset about losing my favorite leather jacket. But oh well. Easy come, easy go."

Bayne gave them a wide smile. "As much as I've enjoyed this interesting exchange, the weather is worsening, and I have to get going. I'm not really worried. Even if I have to hole up in the area for a while, my new disguise will protect me. No one will be looking for me anyway. You'll both be dead, so you won't be able to tell anyone who I really am. Hopefully, by the time they find you, I'll be long gone."

He made a sweeping gesture with his hand as if he were bowing. "I have to leave you for a moment, but I'll be right back. Don't go anywhere." He laughed as he walked toward the other side of the large warehouse and opened the door to a room that looked like a small office.

"Kaely, listen," Alex whispered. "I left a note for Logan telling him I suspected Bayne. I should have told him I was concerned about Ben and Julie too, but I wasn't as certain about them. I waited for Logan as long as I could, but I finally had to take off so I had to leave it with someone else. I'd stalled so long I was afraid Ben would get suspicious. I thought I could find you, neutralize Ben if I had to, and then call for help." As she explained her actions to Kaely, she couldn't help but wonder if she'd made a fatal mistake. One that would lead to both their deaths.

"Who could you trust with that note?" Kaely asked.

"I gave it to someone who couldn't possibly be involved." But now she was second-guessing herself. She'd thought the bakery guy was probably a safe option, but was trusting him one of the dumbest things she'd ever done? Or had he followed through? Knowing she needed to show Kaely some confidence, she smiled.

"And there's something else." She looked around carefully, not only to make sure no one could overhear her but also for any kind of listening device. But Bayne was overconfident. In her opinion, he couldn't hear them. He considered them too stupid to ruin his great strategy.

She lowered her voice even more. "I told Logan I put my phone in my boot, just in case. Ben and Julie never looked there."

Kaely's eyes filled with tears. "If I could reach you, I'd kiss you."

"If they triangulate my phone, it will give them an area to search. Empty warehouses should be their first thought. They could also be looking for Ben's and Julie's phones." She paused a moment before saying, "It's not a slam dunk, Kaely. It's just a chance, but I think it's a good chance."

"I agree. Let's pray it's good enough to get us home alive."

Alex heard a door close. Bayne was coming back. Time was running out. If they weren't found soon, it could very well be too late.

37

Logan kept staring at the phone. What was taking so long? The seconds were ticking away. Bayne probably wouldn't keep Alex and Kaely alive for long. He had to leave the area before the weather made it impossible.

When the phone finally rang, he jumped. CIRG. He listened and took notes. When he ended the call he said, "We've got it."

"Please tell me she's close," Monty said.

"We don't know exactly where it is, of course, but her phone is somewhere in Woodbridge, just twenty-five miles from here in Prince William County. We can be pretty sure they won't be in a populated part of town. That would be too many people for Bayne. But several large warehouses are in one area, three of them owned by an industrial company that's left town. They're all empty. CIRG thinks our agents could be inside one of them. They contacted the Prince William County police chief, Chief Barfield, and his officers are going to check them out. They have the number for the HRT chief, and HRT will stay in touch with me."

"This has to be done so carefully," Nathan said. "If Bayne sees them or hears them, he'll kill our agents."

"We have to let the officers do their job," Bethany said. "If they're working with HRT, they'll know exactly what to do. We have to trust them."

"I know you're right," Logan said. "But I'm going to Woodbridge. We can get to them before HRT. It will take them some time to prepare. We have four-wheel drive, and it's only twenty-five miles."

Todd stared at him. "You do remember that Washington can't get here because the highway is blocked with multiple accidents, right? That means the roads are dangerous out there."

"Yes, and I realize the police may find them before we can. But I want to be there anyway. No matter what happens." He stood and looked around the table. "No one needs to come with me. This is my own decision."

"We know," Monty said.

Just then, Noah Hunter walked into the building. Logan had completely forgotten about him. His mind had been so focused on finding the women that he hadn't thought about Kaely's fiancé.

"I just heard," Noah said. "I want to help. I know what to do in a kidnapping." It was impossible not to see the fear on his face. "You need me."

Logan nodded. "All right." He looked at the agents sitting at the table. Without saying a word, they stood, one by one. "Are you sure?" he asked. Each one nodded. "The SUV holds

six people. It will be tight with seven, but it makes no sense
to take two vehicles in this weather."

"Good thing we all like each other," Monty said. "We'll
make it work."

Logan nodded. "Okay, let's go."

He ran toward the exit, six agents behind him. He was sure
time was running out. Alex and Kaely's lives depended on
what happened next.

Bayne returned from the office, carrying a large wooden
box and a small laptop. He placed the box a few yards in front
of Alex and Kaely and set the laptop on top of it. He fetched a
long pole with a hook on the end that had been lying on the
floor. Then he moved next to Alex and reached up to grab
something. She thought about trying to stand and knock him
over, but she was bound to the chair with very little chance
of success. Bayne was strong. Waiting for help was their best
bet, so she stayed still. Surely Logan would be here soon.

A rope fell from the ceiling. She looked up to see it had
been looped over a large metal pipe. As it swung in front of
her, she realized it had a noose tied to it. Bayne moved over
to Kaely and used the pole to pull down another rope.

Alex tried to control the terror that surged through her.
Was he going to hang them? But surely his intention for them
wasn't that mundane. That wasn't Bayne. He prided himself
on making his killings unique. What was he planning?

"You're probably wondering what I have designed for you."
He laughed. "Oh, it will be special, trust me." He looped the
nooses over both their necks. "It takes ten to twelve minutes
for a human being to die from hanging, but you'll have a

little longer." He walked a few feet away and pulled an old desk chair toward them. "You'll be able to stand on this for a while. It will take more time, but you will eventually die. You see, when one of you gets a respite from your *situation*, the other one will be slowly choking to death. You must pass the chair back and forth between you."

He patted the back of the chair. "Although this is well made and not prone to tipping over, if you should panic and exert enough pressure to the back of it, it could fall, and then you'll no longer be able to delay your demise." He looked at each of them again. "Do you understand?"

"You won't get away with this, Bayne," Alex said. But she couldn't stop her voice from shaking.

The look he gave her was one of amazement. As if the idea that he would fail were as real as unicorns. "I know you think you're smarter than me," he said. "But you're not. I created you. Don't you understand that?" His eyes were wide and mirrored the insanity that drove him. He was caught up in his own delusion and truly believed no one could stop him. People like Bayne could control their mental illness for years, but when they were finally triggered, like Bayne had been when Davis humiliated him publicly with the lawsuit, his psychopathic tendencies erupted into unreasonable hatred and a desire for revenge.

But he certainly wasn't hiding his insanity now. Not in front of agents he thought could do nothing to stop him.

Bayne got so close that Alex could smell his breath. He'd been drinking. She was surprised he'd risk being out of control, but then he had supreme confidence in himself. He believed he'd won. He'd defeated Davis and everyone else who was a threat to him.

"You exist because of me," he hissed. "Both of you." He moved to Kaely. "Without me you two would probably be working in some two-bit job that robs you of your soul. You should actually be thanking me."

He stepped back and smiled at them. Then he pointed at the laptop he'd set up. "This will record your deaths. I wish it could be live, but then your friends might be able to track the laptop or see something pointing to this location. So instead, I'll leave them a couple of presents. First, this wonderful recording. A souvenir to remember. A gift that will keep on giving, shown to law enforcement personnel down through the years. Profilers will talk about it. Have nightmares about it."

He grinned widely, his face a mask of madness. "The feed is being sent to another computer for safekeeping should anything happen to this laptop. Which leads me to my other surprise." He picked up a bag a few feet away. "When they do get here—too late—they'll also find this." He opened the bag and took out a box with wires.

His smile turned lopsided. Crazed.

"The last thing our friend Derrick did for me. So now we begin our last act. The deaths of Alex Donovan and Kaely Quinn."

The storm had definitely turned into a blizzard, and Logan was having trouble keeping the SUV on the road. The real problem was the blowing snow that made it hard to see. He kept his speed down and prayed all the drivers in front of him were using their lights. When he did come up on a vehicle's taillights, he slowed down to keep from hitting it.

"This is taking too long," Monty said.

"We can only do what we can do," Logan said. His phone buzzed, and he picked it up. He'd had no choice but to use his own phone now. He had to stay in contact with the local police in Woodbridge as well as HRT.

It was a text from Chief Barfield. He and his men were ready to check out the first building. HRT had reminded him to make sure they were quiet so they wouldn't alert the UNSUB of their presence. If Bayne knew the police were closing in, he might immediately kill Alex and Kaely. Logan texted back, asking Barfield to let him know what they found.

"Anything?" Bethany asked from the back.

"They're at the first building," Logan said. "Getting ready to check it now."

"What if the police find them?" Monty asked. "Wouldn't it be better to let them enter and try to secure Alex and Kaely? By the time HRT gets there . . ."

"HRT will make that decision," Noah said, irritation in his tone. "They know what they're doing."

"If Bayne follows his previous MO," Logan said, "he's going to do something dramatic. Something memorable. That takes time, and that works in our favor."

"How much longer?" Monty asked.

"Eight miles."

Everyone was silent as they waited to hear from the Prince William police. Logan prayed they'd follow HRT's instructions to the letter. That none of the officers would decide they knew more than trained hostage-rescue agents and blow the operation.

He took a deep breath and let it out slowly, trying to calm himself. He was letting his personal feelings interfere with his training. It had to stop. He looked in his rearview mirror and saw the tension in Noah's face. They both had to see Alex and Kaely as kidnap victims who needed to be rescued, not women they loved.

Logan was startled as he realized he'd just admitted to himself that he loved Alex Donovan. He'd certainly had feelings for her, but love? He felt anger rise in him. Had he put his team in danger because of his feelings for a woman who didn't return them? Who might never return them? Should they have stayed at the academy and allowed HRT and the police to do their jobs?

He glanced in the mirror again. If he hadn't jumped into the SUV and headed toward Alex in the middle of a snowstorm, Noah would have. And he couldn't have allowed Noah to go alone. Did love mean you completely lost your mind? That you'd shove your professionalism aside and put other people in danger? He shook the thoughts from his mind. He had to concentrate on the road ahead. He needed to keep everyone in this vehicle safe since it was his fault they were out here. Besides their physical safety, had he also put their careers on the line? What would the FBI think about his decision?

He couldn't turn back now. He prayed they'd find Alex and Kaely alive—and that his decision to take his team out in a blizzard would be seen as heroic, not completely irresponsible.

Bayne put the noose over Alex's head and tightened it. She felt sick to her stomach as his sour breath seeped into her pores.

"We'll beat you," she said quietly. "By the end of the day, you'll either be in custody or dead. If you survive this day and end up in prison, you'll only be there a short while. You remember that Virginia has the death penalty, right? Either way, you're going to be dead soon."

Bayne shrugged. "You can tell yourself anything you want, but the truth is I'll soon be living in Switzerland. Gloria will join me there as soon as she gets the insurance money. Who can blame a widow for taking a little trip? No one will be looking for us, because you're the only people who know who I am."

Alex wanted to tell him he was wrong. That by now, law enforcement knew exactly who he was and was probably tracking the location of Alex's phone. But that could anger him and cause him to kill them right away. For now, she needed him to think he was going to get away with his plan. She was so thankful she'd hidden her phone in her boot, ringer off. She knew someone had been trying to reach her because the phone had silently vibrated against her skin many times.

There were two places to hide something you didn't want found. A place where someone might not look—your shoes and your hair. But her hair was down, so that hadn't been an option. Although the small phone was uncomfortable, it was doing the job.

Bayne walked over and slipped the other noose over Kaely's head. "The famous Kaely Quinn. You've been a target more than once, haven't you? It took me to bring you down. I hope you realize this proves I'm the greatest profiler who ever lived."

Kaely grunted when he tightened the rope. He stood back and surveyed his work. "Perfect." He reached behind him and pulled out a gun. "Now I'm going to help you stand up on your chair." He peered at Kaely. "If you try anything, I'll shoot your friend. She's already experiencing quite a bit of pain. A bullet in her leg won't help her. Do you understand me?"

"Yes, I understand."

Alex exchanged a look with Kaely. Their only hope rested on a guy who served breakfast food in the food court. What had she done?

39

lex was struggling. Pain ripped through her body, and she could hardly breathe. Had a broken rib collapsed her lung?

Bayne lifted another bag from the floor, then put on a blond wig and glasses before pasting a beard onto his clean-shaven face. He looked so different from his first disguise. No one would guess who he was unless they knew him well and got a close look at him.

He walked over to Alex. "I believe you have a pierced lung, so this will be painful for you." He swung his gaze toward Kaely. "Alexandra won't need the desk chair to stand on for very long. Yes, my desired plan may delay your deaths for a while, but help still won't come in time."

He took a deep breath. "Well, I need to be on my way." He peered into Alex's eyes, then smiled. "This will be interesting.

Will you die to save your colleague's life?" Then he stared at Kaely. "Or will you sacrifice yourself to save hers?"

He laughed as if he found their situation highly amusing. Then he lifted his gun from the box next to the laptop and walked over to Kaely. "Stand up."

Kaely hesitated for a moment, and he slapped her with his free hand. "Stand up, or I'll shoot you in a spot that won't kill you, but you'll certainly suffer. You'll also lose all hope of survival. It's up to you."

Kaely slowly stood to her feet, her eyes locked on Alex's. Alex was certain they were both trying to figure a way out of this. She needed to break the zip ties around her wrists, but she couldn't do it while Bayne was still here.

"Now onto your chair," Bayne said, his nasally voice sharp and irritating.

"I can't," Kaely said. "Not unless you untie my feet."

He sighed dramatically. "I see the problem. Yes, I can do that." Then he glared at her. "I'm not stupid. I thought we'd already established that." He put his arms around her and lifted her up until she was standing on her chair. "Good. Now you." He turned to Alex.

Alex's brain clicked through every scenario she could think of to stop Bayne's plan. She decided she'd find a way to kick him with all her might when he tried to help her onto her chair. But for that to work, he'd have to fall hard enough to either knock him out for a while . . . or kill him. She couldn't help but wonder why Kaely hadn't tried it.

But when Bayne put his arms around her, the pain almost brought her to the point of unconsciousness. There was no way she could carry out her plan. By the time he stepped away from her, her entire body was racked with pain. She couldn't defend herself against him.

Bayne walked to a concrete support beam next to Kaely and began cranking a handle hooked up to the other end of the rope around her neck. Little by little, the rope tightened. Kaely looked over at her and smiled. Alex knew she wasn't going to give Bayne the satisfaction of seeing her fear. But as the rope continued to tighten, Kaely's smile slipped. He finally kicked her chair away. She was hanging in the air without any support under her. Her eyes were wide, but she didn't cry out. Bayne looked disappointed. Then he rolled over the solid-wood desk chair and put it under her. Her feet couldn't quite reach it, so he loosened the rope around her neck. When she was able to stand on the chair, she took a deep, raspy breath and coughed several times.

Bayne moved to Alex. "Your turn, my dear. I'm sure you'll react a little more than your friend did."

She didn't say anything as he went over to the support beam, where there was another hand crank. He began to turn the wheel. Alex tried to stand on her toes as she was raised higher and higher. When she was no longer in contact with her chair, the rope choked her. She tried desperately to get air, but she couldn't draw any in. If they weren't found within the next few minutes, she would die.

Bayne took the chair away from Kaely, then rolled it over to Alex. As soon as she stepped on it, she was able to suck in a little air. Not enough to sustain her, but at least it was something. She looked over at Kaely, who was trying to be brave but was slowly dying.

Bayne went over to the box that supported the laptop. He picked up a cap lying next to it and put it on. Then he reached over to a hook on the wall and grabbed a thick parka, which he slipped on. He went to the laptop, then turned it on and pointed it at them before clicking the keys several times. "We're recording," he said with a smile.

He was careful to stay away from the front of the laptop. He obviously didn't want to be seen. He had his new identity and was ready to leave.

"Good-bye, ladies. Sorry I can't stay. I have no idea how your FBI friends will find you, but they will eventually. Of course, Agent Donovan will be dead by then. It's highly unlikely they'll get here before you die too, Agent Quinn. But if they do discover you in time, their rescue attempt will be their final act of bravery."

He pointed to the only regular door in the building. The other doors were huge garage doors that opened electronically. They were heavy and would be almost impossible to get open manually. Alex's heart sank. Whoever found them would choose the regular door and be killed by the explosives Bayne had placed there. If by some miracle she and Kaely were still alive, the blast would kill them too.

"I need to get going," Bayne said. "Thank you for providing me with such wonderful entertainment. And of course, when I hear a huge explosion rocking this side of town, that will be the cherry on top of the delicious sundae I so carefully created." He paused for a moment and then smiled. "And by the way . . . I win. If one of you should survive the explosion, which I seriously doubt, be sure to tell your colleagues that I outsmarted all of them. This proves no one is or was as good as I am. Not even the great John Davis."

He took off his cap and tipped it to them. Then he walked to one of the large garage doors, picked up a remote, and opened it just enough to roll under it. Alex watched the door close behind him with a thump.

She and Kaely were alone.

———

Logan was struggling to keep his speed down. Other vehicles had slid off the road, and he couldn't risk being one of them. He'd given his phone to Monty, who'd texted their location to Chief Barfield. They couldn't do anything for him right now, but they had to keep going. At least no vehicles had been in front of them for a while.

His phone buzzed. "It's a text back from Chief Barfield," Monty said. "The first warehouse is clear. They're moving to the next one."

Logan nodded. The chief had sent him the addresses of all three possible warehouses. He'd written them down. He took the list out of his pocket and gave it to Monty.

"Mark that one off, okay? Where are they going next?"

"He didn't say, but my guess is they'll move to the building closest to the one they just left." He read off that address.

"Okay. Then we'll keep going to the last one. We're almost there."

Logan looked behind him. Although he couldn't see much through the snow, he didn't notice any headlights. Where was HRT? They should be right behind them. Why did it have to snow today? For crying out loud, it was March. Where was spring?

He slowed down so he wouldn't miss his turnoff. His GPS showed it was just ahead. He couldn't see a sign, but he trusted what he saw on the screen and turned. Sure enough, he was soon driving slowly through Woodbridge, and thankfully, the industrial area was on this side of town. With Monty directing him, it didn't take long to find the empty warehouses.

He pulled over, trying not to get too close to the final building. "How are we supposed to see anything in this storm?" he asked.

"Well, it's kind of a blessing, isn't it?" Monty asked. "Because he can't see us either."

Logan looked over at him. "You're right. Sorry. I'm just—" He started to say *frustrated*, but he decided to be honest. "Frightened."

"I am too," Noah said.

"We all are," Bethany said. "That doesn't mean we're not skilled agents. It just means we're also human. And that's okay."

Logan was moved by what she'd said, but he forced himself to concentrate on what they needed to do next. "I'm going to back up and park around the corner. That should keep the car hidden. Noah, why don't you and I scout things out? The rest of you just stay in the car. If we need you, I'll send Monty a text. If it says nine-one-one, it means I want you to join us. If I text the letter *H*, it means get out of here. Get backup. The police are on the row of buildings behind us."

"Leave without you?" Bethany said. "We can't do that."

"You can and you will. I'm in charge. You'll do what I tell you to do."

No one said anything. Logan knew their instinct was to come to his and Noah's aid if they needed help, but he didn't want them walking into a trap. He took his phone from Monty and quickly texted Chief Barfield to let him know they were here.

"You ready?" he asked Noah.

"Let's go. I want to get this guy. And I want him to pay."

Logan should have told him to check his attitude and concentrate on securing their agents, but he couldn't. He felt exactly the same way.

40

Alex could hear the wind blowing and see the driving snow through the high windows at the top of the concrete walls. She wondered how Bayne intended to get anywhere in this weather, but he hadn't looked concerned. So far he seemed to have prepared himself for every possibility.

Although the pain was excruciating, Alex pushed the chair back toward Kaely, who was just able to reach it with her feet and roll it over. As soon as she stood on it, the color in her face returned to normal.

"We need to just keep pushing it back and forth," she told Alex. "Someone will come in time if we're smart."

Alex looked away from her. She couldn't talk with the rope cutting off her windpipe. Tears ran down her face, and it made her mad. She didn't want to die afraid.

Kaely pushed the chair to Alex, who used her legs to pull it underneath her. It was difficult with them bound together. "Can you try to break your zip ties?" she asked Kaely, her voice raspy and barely above a whisper. "I can't lift my legs to get into position."

Kaely tried to hit the bone at the base of her spine with the ties, but it didn't work.

Alex pushed the chair back to her. When Kaely was standing again, she said, "When I lift my legs, the rope cuts off my air. I almost passed out. I just can't do it. I'm sorry." Her voice was barely above a whisper. She pushed the chair back to Alex.

At first she didn't think she could talk. "I . . . I can't get enough air with a collapsed lung. I don't have long. You have to keep the chair. At least one of us will be alive when they get here."

Kaely tried to shake her head. "No," she croaked. "No."

Alex took the deepest breath she could. Pain shot through her chest and down her arms. "Please," she choked out. She didn't care about the tears that coursed down her face now. "Please ask the Stewarts to keep Krypto. He loves them." She kicked the chair back to Kaely, and then she whispered a prayer, asking God to save Kaely. As soon as she said, "Amen," she began to lose consciousness.

Logan and Noah kept their backs against the side of the building, trying to stay out of sight of any cameras that might be mounted on it. Since they could hardly see through the blinding snow, they had no idea if they were being watched. If anyone could even see them. Logan pointed to the high windows above them, then gestured toward some trash dumpsters beneath one of the windows. Logan held up his hand, letting Noah know he wanted him to stay where he was. Noah nodded.

Logan pulled himself up onto the top of the dumpster. Thankfully, the lid was shut. He tried to shield his eyes from the blowing snow with one hand while he used his gloved hand to brush snow off the window. He looked through the small spot he'd cleared and was horrified by what he saw—Alex and Kaely hanging by ropes tied to pipes near the ceiling. Alex wasn't moving, and her eyes were closed. Kaely was standing on a chair, looking around. Logan tapped on the window, and Kaely looked up. He pointed down the alley where he'd seen a door when they pulled up to the building. Kaely looked horrified and shook her head. Thinking she was disoriented, he held up one finger, letting her know they were coming in. Again, she shook her head.

Logan jumped down and went back to where Noah waited. "They're in there, but they're hanging from the ceiling. Alex isn't moving, but Kaely saw me. Let's try to get that metal door down there open." He frowned. "Kaely shook her head when I pointed toward it, but she probably doesn't know what she's saying if she's been deprived of oxygen."

They fought the wind and pushed their way to the large metal door. Logan was about to pull the handle when Noah grabbed his arm.

"Don't," he said. "I think it's booby-trapped."

"Why?"

"I think that might be what Kaely was trying to tell you."

Logan tried to tamp down the emotions raging through him. Alex wasn't moving. He had to save her. But what if Noah was right?

"So what do we do?" he asked Noah.

"We go through one of those windows."

A long drop to what surely was a concrete floor could cause

them physical damage, but Logan didn't care. And he knew Noah didn't either.

"All right," Logan said. "Let's do this."

He found a concrete block lying a few feet away and grabbed it. Noah jumped back onto the dumpster and put his hands out. Logan handed him the block, then jumped up beside him.

Before breaking the window, he showed the block to Kaely. She nodded but appeared to be fighting to stay conscious.

Noah lifted the block and hit the window with it. It didn't break, but spider-webbed cracks filled the glass. Again he lifted it and hit the window with more force. This time the glass shattered. Both men began to pull out the broken shards. If they cut themselves when they crawled through the window, they wouldn't be much good to Alex or Kaely.

Once the window was as clean as they could get it, Logan put his head through the opening. It was at least a nine-foot jump onto the concrete floor.

"I see a wooden box," he told Noah. "I'll put it under the window so you can lower yourself onto it. Make that call to HRT. Now."

"All right."

"Wish they were here already," Logan grumbled. He looked at Alex. She was blue. He had to go. Now. He climbed through the window feet first, holding on to the window sill. Then he let his body slide down along the wall so his landing wouldn't be so far.

God, help me, he prayed.

Then he let go.

41

A lex was walking through a field of beautiful yellow flowers. She'd never seen flowers like this before. It was as if the sun itself shone through them. Love surrounded her like a hug. It felt so good. She'd never experienced a love this pure and strong.

She could see a city on the other side of the field. It glowed like jewels, and she could hear something coming from it that sounded like the praise and worship music she'd heard at church. But this was way beyond that. It was incredible and seemed to fill everything. Even the flowers she walked through.

Alex suddenly realized she didn't hurt. The pain from her chest was gone.

She wanted to keep walking, but something seemed to be holding her back. At first she resisted, but then she realized someone was walking next to her. A Man. She tried to turn her face to see Him, but she couldn't.

"You are loved, Alex," He said. "Someday you and I will

walk this field together, but you still have a journey to complete on earth. As I am with you here, I will be with you there."

Suddenly, Alex felt hands pulling her. She could hear someone talking. The pain returned in a wave, and she began to cry. She wanted to go back to that incredible field. She didn't want to hurt. Didn't want to be alone. Then the words she'd heard came back to her. *"As I am with you here, I will be with you there."* The loneliness she'd felt almost every day of her life slowly faded. She felt complete. Loved.

"Alex, Alex," someone was saying. She forced her eyes open and saw Logan looking at her. Where was she? At first she couldn't remember. Then it all came back.

She tried to speak, but nothing came out. She tried again. "I-I'm alive," she croaked.

"Yes, you are."

She realized Logan had tears on his cheeks. She reached her hand up and touched his face. Why was he crying?

"Ka . . . Ka . . ."

Logan put his fingers on her lips. "Stop trying to talk," he said. "You might hurt your throat even more. Kaely is fine. You saved her life."

She smiled. Thank God. She tried to sit up, and Logan helped her. She looked around the room. Kaely. They were both alive. Bayne had lost.

"It . . . was . . . Bayne," she whispered.

"We know. I got your note."

Fear suddenly filled her. "The door," she whispered. "The door . . . There's a bomb."

"We know that too. Can you get to your feet? I think you'll be more comfortable in a chair."

She nodded and tried to stand, but even that small movement caused pain. She cried out and touched her chest. "It hurts," she croaked.

"I know. I'm already aware of everything you're telling me, Alex. Please quit talking. Please."

As Logan helped her to her feet, the pain from her broken ribs ripped through her body. The room swirled around her, and she grabbed hold of him.

"Are you dizzy?" he asked.

She gave him a small nod, trying not to move her neck any more than she had to.

"Hold on to the sides of the chair," Logan said. "I need to help Noah."

"I'll sit next to her."

Alex looked up to see Kaely smiling. Her neck was bruised and red. Her eyes were red too. Alex realized that was from petechiae, small blood vessels that had ruptured from the pressure of the rope against her neck.

Alex began to cry again. She reached over and put her arms around Kaely. Kaely cried too as she encircled Alex with a hug.

"You saved me," Kaely said, her voice hoarse. "I tried to send the chair back to you, but you were already unconscious. Why would you do something like that?"

Alex thought the answer was obvious. She let go of Kaely and looked into her eyes. "Because I wanted you to live."

Tears dripped down Kaely's cheeks. "Alex Donovan, I pray I can be more like you someday."

Alex tried to process what she'd said as Kaely hugged her again. How could someone like Kaely want to be more like her?

"There's more," Kaely said. "We can't find another opener for the garage doors." She pointed toward the door where Noah and Logan were looking at the bomb Bayne left. "And remember the laptop Bayne was using to record our . . . deaths?"

"Yes."

"When Noah turned it off, the bomb began a countdown. If that thing goes off in here, it could be serious."

"This is a large building. If we move to the back—"

"Logan says the whole place could collapse. We'll have to go out the same way Noah and Logan got in—the window up there."

"Then why haven't you tried to climb—" Alex realized the answer. "You were waiting for me to wake up? You shouldn't have done that. At least you could have made it out."

"No man or woman left behind, my friend," Kaely said with a small smile.

Alex struggled to her feet. "Well, I'm conscious. Let's get the heck out of here."

"I agree." Kaely looked over at Noah and Logan. "How much time?"

Noah looked grim. "Ten minutes. We're not sure how to disarm it. I'm afraid if we try, it will blow."

"Then let's go," Alex said.

Noah shook his head. "We have to wait for the HRT. You're in no shape to climb up to that window, Alex. Neither are Kaely and—"

Logan's phone rang, and he picked it up. He gave directions to whoever called before hanging up. "They're here." He looked at the timer. "They'd better hurry."

For the first time, Alex noticed Logan's right ankle was

bound with a cloth, and he was using a board as a crutch. "What's wrong with Logan?" Alex asked Kaely, pointing.

"When he jumped from that window, he broke his ankle. We're a rather pathetic group."

"We need to get you closer to the window," Noah said. "Someone is going to rappel in here and take you both up. Logan, did you text Monty and the others?"

"Yeah, they should be out of the area by now. I told them they can't do anything to help us, that HRT should be here soon, and we don't know when this building will blow."

Alex looked at the bomb's counter. Six minutes. She wanted to ask if they could all get out in that amount of time, but she knew it wouldn't help the situation.

Noah was quiet as he led Alex to the wall with the windows. "They'll have to put their harness around your chest. It might hurt some."

Alex wanted to correct him. It would hurt a lot, but they couldn't do anything about that.

Suddenly, a man rappelled through the window and down the wall. Without saying a word, he attached a harness to Alex. Then he yelled, "Okay. Get her out."

The pain was so bad, Alex wanted to tell them to stop, but she bit her lip until she felt blood. When she reached the window, hands grabbed her and pulled her out. She fought the darkness that tried to overtake her, but finally, it won the battle.

42

ogan forced himself to ignore the severe pain that shot up his leg when he put weight on his right foot. No time to think about that now. Noah had found a stack of rags inside the office on the other side of the room, where he'd found Cooper's and Palmer's bodies. Then he'd smashed a wooden chair from the same room, removed two slats from the back, and fashioned a splint. Without Noah's help, his situation would be a lot worse.

As the Hostage Rescue Team member pulled Alex out, Logan was relieved to see her free but still worried about her condition. Broken ribs could cause other serious injuries. They could collapse a lung, cause damage to other organs, or in some cases puncture her aorta. He was angry to see her hurt so badly.

Bayne was gone, but he couldn't be far. Noah had given HRT a description they'd passed along to area law enforcement so they could send out a BOLO. Hopefully, someone would find him, though most of the attention was on the storm. Clearing the highway and rescuing people who had gone off the road would hamper the police from concentrating their efforts to find Bayne.

"Hurry," he said to Kaely. Another harness was lowered for her, and within a couple of minutes she was up and over.

"You're next," he said to Noah.

"Absolutely not. You're injured. You go first."

Logan looked over at the bomb. Ninety seconds. "We don't have time to argue." The harness dropped down. Without any warning, Logan hit Noah with a right hook, knocking him to the floor and disorienting him. Logan quickly put the harness around him and motioned for the agent above to pull him up.

"Get out of here," Logan told the HRT agent. "If this thing goes off while you're trying to pull me out, we're all dead. I'm going to try to disarm it."

"We've got someone here who—"

"No time!" he yelled.

The agent finally nodded. As Logan had, he realized there wasn't any choice.

Once Noah was clear, Logan hurriedly hobbled to the bomb. He wasn't sure he could disarm it—he certainly wasn't an expert—but he had a better shot at it than Noah. His time in Afghanistan had given him some knowledge of explosives.

The sticks of dynamite weren't the main concern. It was the block of Semtex attached to the dynamite. Semtex was usually mixed with explosive compounds that were powerful and unstable. It made the explosive material easier and safer to handle for the bomb maker. If mixed with pentaerythritol tetranitrate—PETN—the explosion it caused would not only bring down the warehouse but also some of the other buildings around it.

This was an extremely dangerous explosive.

Logan had a vague idea of how to disarm it, but bomb makers didn't always follow the rules. He assumed Bayne had paid someone to construct it, someone who obviously had connections to black-market suppliers with PETN. Logan stared at the wires going into the block of Semtex. Fifteen seconds. He'd heard the vehicles outside leave, so he knew Alex, Kaely, and Noah were clear. Noah had found a pair of wire cutters in the office, and they'd used them to cut the ties binding Kaely and Alex. Logan picked them up and studied the bomb.

Bayne had tried to outsmart them at every turn. A plain bomb wasn't his style. Wires connected the Semtex to the detonator and the timer. Usually the blue wire carried the power to the primer, so it was the wire to cut. That meant cutting the red wire would cause the bomb to explode. But Evan Bayne paid for this bomb. What were his instructions to the bomb maker? Was he determined to always have the last word?

Five seconds.

Logan took a deep breath and clasped the wire cutters around the red wire. He prayed and squeezed the handles.

When Alex opened her eyes, she realized she was inside a vehicle with agents from HRT sitting across from her.

"Glad you're awake," Kaely said from beside her.

"Me too." She looked around. "Where's Logan?" she whispered.

Kaely looked at Noah for an answer.

"There was a bomb," Noah said.

"I know that," Alex said crossly.

"Don't be angry," Kaely said. "Logan stayed behind to try

to disarm it." Her voice was so raspy Alex could barely understand her.

"Is . . . is he okay?"

Noah grinned. "Yeah. He stopped it with two seconds left. He took a big chance and cut the red wire."

Logan must have figured Bayne would use the wrong color wire so the bomb would go off even if someone knowledgeable tried to disarm the bomb. Genius.

"He's in the truck behind us," Noah said. "We're taking all three of you to the hospital. You both need to stop talking and rest your throats."

"I'm fine," Kaely croaked. She put her hand to her throat.

"See? Now quit arguing," Noah retorted. "You were hung from a rope. We need to make sure there isn't damage to your throat. A clean, comfortable bed, someone bringing you food, time to rest and catch up on your sleep. How can you even think of turning that down?"

Kaely sighed. "Sounds wonderful."

Alex had to admit it did sound good. "Bayne?" she asked.

Noah shook his head. "We have a BOLO out. Haven't heard anything yet. He can't get far, though. Especially since we have an updated description."

"He'll change again," Kaely said softly. "Especially when he finds out his bomb didn't go off."

Alex nodded in agreement.

"Let's not worry about it now," Noah said. "Let's just get to the hospital."

"I hear this storm's finally moving out," the agent driving the truck said. "But we could get more snow before we're all done. We've got ten inches on the ground. It's gonna be hard to keep the roads clear."

"Bayne can leave town before the next snow comes," Kaely whispered. "He said Switzerland."

"Well, that's new information," the agent sitting in the passenger seat said. "We need to watch the airports. Anyone heading out of the country. Especially with Switzerland as their end destination."

"I think he'll go somewhere else first," Noah said. "If he knows you're alive, he'll realize he made a mistake by telling you about Switzerland, and he'll have to change his plans. His wife has been detained in Australia and is being turned over to federal custody. I'm hoping we'll get some information out of her."

Alex suddenly remembered something. "Fake passport," she whispered. "He said he has a fake passport."

"Okay," Noah said. "Did you hear that?" he asked the agent in the front seat.

"Yeah, we'll pass it along," one of them replied.

"I don't suppose he told you the name he was using?" Noah asked.

Alex slowly shook her head. It hurt to move her neck. "I wonder if he'll go back to Australia to get his wife."

"I wouldn't bet on it," Kaely said, her voice barely audible.

"You think he'll leave her behind?" the driver asked.

She nodded. "Psychopath. He doesn't care." What little voice Kaely had was now gone.

"That's cold," the driver said. "So anyone who cares about him is just tossed aside when he's through with them?"

"That's right," Alex croaked. She looked out the window at the snowflakes drifting lazily around the car, then took a deep breath and whispered, "If you do a deal with the devil, you have to be prepared to pay the bill."

Alex's eyes fluttered open. A nurse stood next to her bed.

"Where am I?" she whispered.

"In recovery. You made it through the operation just fine."

The last two days slowly came back to her. She'd had to wait for surgery because the snowstorm had trapped the surgeon, who lived well beyond the outskirts of town. She was just grateful it was over. Even with medication, the pain had been excruciating, and it was hard to breathe.

Thankfully, another doctor treated her when she first checked in and determined her injuries weren't life-threatening. "You're lucky," he'd said. "Hanging can cause significant damage to your throat." He smiled. "Your friend Logan says getting you to stay quiet will be a challenge, but you have to if you want to get your voice back."

She'd started to respond to him, but instead, she just gave him a thumbs-up.

Then he'd laughed. "Good job. Keep it up."

He also confirmed that she had three broken ribs, and that one had punctured a lung. "When the surgeon gets here, she'll get you fixed up. Make it easier for you to breathe. We don't see any damage to your internal organs, but she'll check that out too. You'll need to rest for six weeks or so, but you'll be fine."

"We'll move you to a room when you're really awake," the nurse said. "The doctor will talk to you soon. In the meantime, we'll give you lots of nice drugs to keep the pain manageable." She pointed to the IV bag next to Alex's bed. "Morphine now, then we'll switch you to something else."

"Thank you." Alex didn't like pain medication. Anything that made her feel she'd lost some control bothered her. But this wasn't the time to take a stand. This was the time to shut up and let the doctors and nurses do their work. Right now all she wanted to do was sleep.

"I'll come back in a few minutes."

Alex thanked the kind nurse again. She reached down to touch her chest. It was wrapped tightly. She tried to take a deep breath. It was uncomfortable, but at least she could breathe easier than before.

She nodded off more than once. But she wanted the privacy of her own room, so she fought to keep her eyes open. Finally, the nurse and an orderly returned.

"Ready?" she asked.

Alex nodded.

The orderly wheeled her out of recovery and down a long hall, the nurse keeping pace. So did one of the agents who'd been with her since she arrived. When they reached her room, the agent stayed in the hall, and the orderly pushed the padded gurney inside, where he and the nurse helped her into bed.

"Take it slow and easy," the nurse said. "We don't want to put pressure on those ribs."

It took a while for Alex to finally get comfortable, but when she did, it felt heavenly.

The orderly pushed the gurney out of the room, and another nurse came in to take over. She covered Alex with a sheet and blanket, then hung her IV and attached another bag to the side of the bed.

"You're hooked up to a catheter. For now just enjoy knowing you don't have to get up." She frowned. "You haven't eaten in quite some time. I can give you something light, but nothing heavy yet."

"I'm not hungry," Alex whispered. "But maybe some water? To be perfectly honest, I just want to sleep."

The nurse stepped to the side table, then filled a glass with water from a pitcher. "Just a little at a time," she said when she brought it to Alex.

Alex took a few sips, then put the glass on her tray.

"I'll get you a specially warmed blanket. Then you can get some sleep. And if you wake up in pain, push this button." She pointed to a machine near the bed.

"Thank you."

Alex was already drifting off when the nurse covered her with the second blanket. At that moment, she thought it might be the best thing she'd ever felt.

Logan had finished his lunch and was watching the news when Noah walked into his hospital room.

"How are you doing today?" he asked.

"Well, let's see. They put screws in my ankle, put this stupid cast on my leg, and stuck my foot up in the air." Logan pointed at his leg, elevated on top of a foam pillow. "How do you think I'm doing? But at least the doctor said I can go home later today, and I've been able to switch to over-the-counter pain meds. I'll be fitted for a boot before I leave, and I have to use crutches for a while."

"Doesn't sound too bad."

"Hey, man, thanks for what you did for me at the warehouse. Your makeshift splint probably kept this from being a lot worse."

Noah smiled. "No problem. I'll break a chair for you anytime you want."

Logan laughed. "How's Kaely?"

"Good. She gets to go home later today as well. She and Alex both could have had serious neck injuries from what Bayne did to them. Especially in Alex's case. Kaely told me Alex had given up right before we broke into the warehouse. Pushed that chair over to her so one of them would hopefully survive. She could have easily died, Logan." He shook his head slowly. "She saved Kaely's life. She's quite an agent— and human being."

"Yes, she is. And so are you. I'm sure glad you didn't let me open that door. None of us would have made it."

"God was with us," Noah said. "That's all I can say."

"Boy, Bayne didn't miss a beat, did he? What a monster. He killed Cooper and Palmer as soon as they delivered Alex and Kaely to the warehouse. I mean, what they did was awful. Especially Palmer. But I almost feel sorry for them."

"Alex said something when we were on the way to the hospital, and it stuck with me," Noah said. "She said, 'If you do a deal with the devil, you have to be prepared to pay the bill.'"

Logan nodded. "I guess their bill came due."

"They still haven't found Bayne." Noah shook his head. "He may be long gone, I don't know, but I still have to wonder if the storm slowed him down. Maybe he's closer than we think. Of course, he's a planner, so I'm sure he had a contingency plan in place. Terry says his wife claims she doesn't know where he is, and maybe she doesn't."

Noah sat down in the chair near Logan's bed. "How long will you have agents outside your rooms?"

Logan shrugged. "I don't know. I guess they just want to err on the side of caution." He frowned. "They didn't find any pages from Davis's book at the warehouse. I guess Alex and Kaely were his last victims, so he didn't need one."

"You don't look convinced."

"He's a psychopath. He loves attention. For him to just slink away . . ." He looked out the window. It had snowed twice more since the storm, but only lightly. Still, it was a mess out there.

"So you think running away is—"

"A rather anticlimactic ending? Yeah."

"Don't forget the bomb. He thought there would be a major explosion, and we'd all die. That's pretty dramatic."

"Yeah, that's true," Logan said slowly. "Still, he likes to take credit for things. Maybe we're not hearing from him because he failed." Logan grunted. "I'm sure he doesn't like to lose." He paused for a moment. "Hey, can you find me a wheelchair? I want to see Alex."

"She just got out of surgery. I expect she's resting."

"I know. I just want to talk to her a minute. If she's asleep,

I won't bother her. I haven't spoken to her since yesterday, and our conversation was limited since she could barely talk. I want to know what she thinks about Bayne's next move. Maybe we can help the police narrow down their search if we can figure out where he's headed."

"Shouldn't you wait a bit, man? I mean, seriously. Let her have some time to recover."

Logan knew what Noah said made sense, but he couldn't shake the feeling he needed to see Alex. "I won't stay long."

Noah sighed. "You BAU people really don't take any time off, do you?"

Logan smiled. "It takes over your life. We analyze everything. It's a sickness, I guess."

Noah's expression tightened. "Yeah, I believe that. Kaely's thinking about Bayne too." He stood. "Stay there while I look for a wheelchair."

Logan laughed. "Like I'm going anywhere."

Noah had just walked out of the room when Monty came in. "So how long are you going to milk this?" he asked, grinning.

"Hey, I'm already tired of it." He was glad to see Monty, who gave him a quick hug.

"Glad you're alive, brother. I can't stand to lose anyone else I care about."

"Thanks, but I'm still mad at you for not getting out of there when I sent you that text."

"Couldn't leave you, man. No one in the car wanted to go."

"If that bomb had gone off . . ."

"Then we'd all be singing hallelujah," Monty said with a grin.

"I guess that's true."

Noah came back into the room with the wheelchair.

"I'm going to talk to Alex if she's awake," Logan said. "I'm concerned about Bayne. He failed to pull off his pièce de résistance, so now what?"

Monty was silent for a moment. "Yeah, that bothers me too, but if he has any sense, he won't be hanging around."

"With more than ten inches of snow, travel's been really affected. What if he's nearby? I'm not convinced he's gone."

"Terry just told me Bayne cashed out his dwindling bank accounts before coming here from Australia, leaving his wife just enough to get by until the life insurance came through. After he paid the settlement from Davis's lawsuit, he was pretty much wiped out, but he probably has enough to keep him going for a while."

Noah spoke up. "He despised Davis for years. Was jealous of his success. Then when Bayne was hit with the lawsuit, it triggered his hatred. His instability. He started putting his plan into place, although the authorities in Australia now think his wife might not have known about all the killings he planned, let alone the methods he employed. They don't believe she's as twisted as he is. She just wanted the insurance money. Anyway, he targeted other profilers in an attempt to make it look like Davis was killed because of his profession, not because of who he was. Kaely and Alex caught his attention because they made it into the media. He was jealous of what he considered their undeserved celebrity."

"So," Logan said, "Bayne hated Davis because of his success. That hatred simmered for years. Then when Davis took away his financial stability, his psychopathic personality burst forth. He couldn't hide it anymore. He figured out a way to take revenge and to make himself rich. And no one would suspect him because he was dead."

Noah frowned. "Now that he's failed, what do you think he will do?"

Logan hesitated a moment before saying, "I don't know. If he's smart, he's somewhere safe. Someplace he'll never be found." But even as the words left his mouth, something inside told him this wasn't over yet.

44

Alex was sitting near a beautiful lake, with Krypto next to her. She put her arm around him, and he laid his head on her shoulder. She kissed the gentle dog's face and then went back to watching the water. She felt so relaxed. She hadn't felt this good for a long time.

A voice began calling her name. It was so faint she could barely hear it. She didn't want to leave this place. The voice wanted something, but she had no more to give. Why couldn't whoever it was just leave her alone? She wanted to stay by the peaceful lake with Krypto.

When the voice called a little louder, Krypto turned around to look, his large head still on her shoulder as he gazed at something behind them.

"No, Krypto," she said gently. "I want to stay here with you. Please. If we ignore them, maybe they'll go away."

Someone reached for her hand, and she started to pull it away. "Alex?" This time the voice was closer. Next to her. Krypto began to wag his tail. This was someone he liked.

"Alex?"

She recognized that voice. Logan. She glanced once more at the lake before forcing her eyes open partway. She found herself peering into Logan's face and smiled.

"I thought that was you," she said. Her eyes flew open all the way when pain shot through her chest. She looked at the meds machine beside her bed. It wasn't just her chest that hurt. Her throat felt like she was still hanging from that terrible rope. Everything was sore. It felt as if her entire body was on fire.

Her surgeon came in. "You're awake?" she said. "I figured you'd be sleeping for a while longer."

"I'll sleep more soon," Alex whispered. She'd wait to push the button. She had to know if she'd be okay, and the meds would just make her drift away again.

The doctor looked at Logan, who sat in a wheelchair. Noah and Monty were here too. "Are these men family?" she asked.

Before any of them had a chance to answer, Alex said, "Yes, they're my brothers."

The doctor looked them over, her eyes lingering on Monty a moment longer. Finally, she smiled. "All right." She turned back to Alex. "No internal damage. I repaired your lung and placed a metal plate on your ribs to make sure they'll heal correctly. This will also protect your organs. You were lucky. It could have been much worse. You'll be here a few days until we're sure you can take care of yourself, and then we'll send you home. Recovery will take around six weeks. That means very limited activity. You'll need help, but I'm sure your *brothers* will pitch in." She raised her eyebrows and looked at them. "Right?"

Alex had to fight not to laugh. They all nodded solemnly.

"All right, Miss Donovan, if you have any questions, your hospital doctor will have your chart and my notes. He'll be able to help you."

"Thank you."

After she left the room, Logan said, "Do you feel okay to talk? I have concerns about Bayne."

She smiled at him and reached for the button. When she pushed it, the result was almost immediate. The morphine began to put out the flames.

"I'm sorry," she whispered. "I have to go back to the lake. Krypto's waiting for me."

Logan smiled at her. "Okay. You go on. I'll talk to you later. It will keep."

"Okay. I love you, Logan."

As she walked back toward the lake, she suddenly felt her legs give out. The clear sky filled with dark clouds, and a heavy wind surrounded her. It pulled her away from Krypto as she fought to breathe. Krypto ran over and started to bark. Something was wrong. Horribly wrong.

She tried to call for Logan, but her voice wouldn't work. Her whole body felt paralyzed. As she kept attempting to call for help, she found herself in the lake. Krypto stood on the shore, barking wildly. She tried to stay afloat, but she couldn't. As she slipped under the water, she took a deep breath. She knew unless someone pulled her out quickly, she would slip away forever.

"I don't know what I was thinking," Logan said as Noah pushed him back to his room with Monty alongside. "She's had major trauma. She needs to rest."

"I did mention that fact," Noah said.

"Did you hear what she said?"

"Yes."

"That was the heavy drugs, right?"

"I don't think they make you say things you don't mean, Logan."

"But . . . she's never given any indication . . ."

Noah laughed. "Boy, I could tell you stories about what I went through with Kaely. Look, I'm sure she means it somewhere inside, but I doubt she's ready to face her feelings for you in the light of day. Not yet anyway. Do you have feelings for her?"

Logan swallowed hard. "Yes. Yes, I do."

"Then just give her time. Don't push it. Let what's between you grow until she's ready—and undrugged. Okay?"

Logan wanted to think more about what Alex said, but something else was competing for time in his mind. "I just can't stop thinking about Bayne. It's really bothering me."

"Turn that off for a while too," Monty said. "You need to rest and get stronger."

"Not so easy. I find myself analyzing people in the grocery store. Even in church."

Noah and Monty both laughed.

Logan wasn't looking forward to more time in bed. He was afraid Bayne would get away, and he wanted him caught. Too many people had died because of him, and Logan was angry because of what he'd done, especially to Alex and Kaely. With the police and the FBI both looking for him, why hadn't they found him yet? Logan couldn't shake the feeling that Bayne wouldn't allow his total defeat at the warehouse to be his curtain call. Psychopaths were too egotistical for that.

"If they don't catch him, do you think we'll ever hear from him again?" Logan asked.

"I don't know," Monty said. "Sometimes people like Bayne fail. If they can't find a way to go out with a bang—sorry for the pun—they simply live with their failures." He frowned. "But if Bayne decides he can't do that, you're right. He may try to end things another way, be willing to take chances. He's used to careful planning, but if he's at the end of his rope—" He colored. "Sorry again. I'm not trying to be insensitive."

A sense of dread filled Logan. It was almost overpowering. He looked up at Noah. "Check on Kaely right now. Don't let anyone into her room, not even medical personnel."

"I don't understand," Noah said.

"I think Bayne's still here, and he has a grudge to settle. He wants to go out a winner. The one who had the final word after all." He motioned to Monty. "Get me back to Alex's room. Now!"

As Noah raced toward Kaely's room and Monty pushed Logan back to Alex's, Logan prayed he was wrong. But in his heart, he knew he wasn't.

───────────

As she sank deeper and deeper under the water, Alex looked down. It was dark below her. She hated the dark. She couldn't go there. She called out to God to save her.

Suddenly, a hand appeared. It reached toward her. She wanted to swim up to grab it, but her limbs wouldn't move.

"I can't reach you!" she called.

"Don't worry, child," a voice said. "No matter where you are, I am there with you."

The hand, which looked like it was made of light, reached down and picked her up, gently placing her beside the lake. Krypto was still there, and he licked her face. As she began to breathe better, the lake and Krypto slowly faded away.

45

When Monty and Logan got to Alex's room, she was obviously in distress. Monty ran out into the hall and called for help. Within seconds, two nurses sprinted into the room.

"Out," one of them ordered Logan. Monty pushed him into the hall, where they waited with the agent who'd been guarding Alex. The man was shaken when he heard their suspicions, but he left to find someone to shut down the hospital.

A few seconds later, a man in a doctor's coat came running down the hall and into Alex's room. Logan could only pray. He couldn't lose Alex. He really did love her. Maybe she'd never feel that way about him, but it didn't matter. She had to live.

Monty pulled his wheelchair near a row of chairs. He

pushed one next to the wheelchair, sat down, and grabbed Logan's hand. "Let's pray for her," he said.

Logan didn't care that other people were in the hallway. He just started praying, asking God to take care of Kaely and save Alex. He felt someone come up behind him and put a hand on his shoulder. He was grateful for anyone who would pray for this woman who had captured his heart. When he finished, he opened his eyes and wiped the tears off his face. He turned to talk to the person who'd prayed with them, but no one was there. In fact, a trash can sat behind him.

"Who was standing here with us?" he asked Monty.

Monty looked confused. "I don't know what you're talking about."

"Someone was standing behind me with a hand on my shoulder."

Monty shook his head slowly. "No one else was with us, Logan." He leaned over and looked around. "I can't believe I'm saying this, but maybe it was an angel or something."

A nurse came out of Alex's room and looked around until she saw them. "You're the brothers?" she asked.

Logan nodded. He felt a little guilty saying that, but the truth was they *were* family. The FBI bonded people in a way some blood relatives never experienced.

"Your sister had a reaction to something in her IV, but she's recovering. We're not sure what happened."

"I am," Logan said. "We're with the FBI, and this hospital is being shut down right now. We believe someone tried to kill Agent Donovan. He could still be here."

The doctor who'd rushed into Alex's room came out. "What's going on? You need to tone it down."

"Doctor," the nurse said, "this man says they're with the FBI, and their locking down the hospital."

The doctor, whose badge said his name was Wenden, looked back and forth between Logan and Monty. Then they all heard "This is a code silver. We are in complete lockdown. All security personnel to the exits and entrances."

"Who are we looking for?" Wenden asked.

Logan hesitated a moment. Who knew what kind of disguise Bayne was wearing now? "He's tall. Probably wearing medical garb. His hair is usually salt and pepper, but he uses disguises." He turned to the agent just coming back. "Who went into the room before Agent Donovan was brought here from recovery?"

The man frowned. "Two nurses to set up the room. I checked their IDs. And a doctor who said he wanted to make sure the room was ready. I checked his ID as well."

"No doctor should have been in there," Wenden said. "We don't check rooms to make sure things are set up correctly. The nurses do that."

"Do you remember his name?" Logan asked the agent.

"Actually, I do. Dr. Chandler. That's my wife's maiden name."

"Thank you. Please go back and watch that room."

"We don't have a Dr. Chandler," Wenden said, frowning. "Not even one with privileges. And you think he put something in Miss Donovan's IV?"

"Yes, I do. Is she going to be okay?"

"Strange, usually someone with a reaction like that doesn't recover. She wasn't breathing when I got to her room. And then suddenly she took a deep breath and smiled. I've never seen anything quite like it. Frankly, she's extremely lucky.

We're going to check out her meds immediately. We'll let you know what we find."

After he and the nurse left, Monty wheeled Logan back into Alex's room. When a nurse came to the door with new medication, Logan asked the agent outside to confirm her identity with the doctor and make sure she'd been ordered to deliver the meds. He wasn't taking any more chances. Once she'd gone, he looked at Monty.

"And now we wait," he said. "And hope we're fast enough to catch Bayne."

Alex set her phone on her coffee table, wondering why Logan insisted on coming over. She certainly didn't look her best, but she couldn't talk him out of it. She walked into the bedroom and carefully put on a clean pair of sweatpants and a sweatshirt. After only three weeks, her ribs were still healing.

She didn't really need to pick up the house since Shirley had been keeping it clean. She'd also brought over more food than any one human could possibly eat. The kids shoveled her driveway and put her trash barrels by the curb every Sunday for pickup Monday morning. She was really spoiled, and she loved it, but she was ready to get back to work. She couldn't imagine another three weeks of just sitting around.

Alex put her dishes in the kitchen sink and then sat down to wait in the living room. When she first got home, she was happy to have nothing to do. She'd spent time reading her Bible, trying to learn more about the God who had saved her—twice. And she gently played with Krypto, who loved the extra attention.

After she recovered in the hospital, Logan told Alex about his hunch that Bayne hadn't left the area and was determined to go out with a bang. Sure enough, he'd entered the hospital early that morning dressed as a doctor. He'd obviously seen an official hospital badge somewhere because his fake ID was good enough to fool everyone. When he discovered which room would be Alex's, he'd entered it and injected what turned out to be fentanyl into the lines connected to the morphine pump. When Alex activated it, the fentanyl entered her body.

She should have died. No one could explain why she didn't, but she knew God had rescued her.

After leaving Alex's room, Bayne was seen walking toward Kaely's room, probably hoping she had an IV so he could take her life too. But then the code silver went out all over the hospital. He'd headed for an exit but didn't get there fast enough. When he was stopped by an armed guard, he grabbed a gun from his waistband and tried to shoot his way out of the hospital. But the guard was faster, and Bayne was killed.

Alex was grateful to be alive. She couldn't explain the strange things she'd experienced, but they had changed her. She was convinced God was real and that He loved her. Although she still respected Kaely, she'd also realized that she didn't need to be like anyone else, not even her. Maybe she hadn't had good role models, but she had a good Father. It was her job to pattern herself after Him—and only Him. She still had fears to face, and life would certainly present other challenges, but now she was convinced that for the first time in her life she wasn't alone.

About fifteen minutes after she'd sat down, the doorbell

rang. Krypto followed her to the door, wagging his tail. You'd think after everything he'd been through, he'd be unsure of people. But he loved everyone. Visitors were fun. More people to play with.

Standing outside were Logan and Terry. She held the door open for them. "Come on in," she said. Why was Terry here? Was she going to be put on extended leave? The doctor had promised she would mend completely and get back to one hundred percent. Did Terry doubt that?

He smiled at her as he stepped inside. When he saw Krypto, he took a step back, but Krypto took that as a challenge and leaned against his leg, waiting for a rub. Terry laughed and put his hand on the large pit bull's head.

"Boy, you look scary, but you're just a big baby, aren't you?" Terry knelt and rubbed Krypto's head until the dog almost wagged his tail off.

"All right, Krypto, that's enough," Alex said. "He came to see me, not you."

Logan and Terry laughed.

Alex gestured toward the chairs next to her couch. "Sit down, please. Am I in some kind of trouble?"

"No," Terry said with another smile. "Just the opposite. You all did excellent work. Thank you. But you know, behavioral analysts aren't supposed to risk their lives in the field. I'm not sure this group understands that concept."

"Trust me," Logan said. "We're all happy to stay safe and just analyze UNSUBs. It's much easier." He eased himself into one of the chairs, wearing the special boot designed to support his ankle while it was healing.

"I'm sure it is." Terry took a deep breath as he looked at Alex. "I have two important items to discuss with you."

"Yes?" She tried to relax, but it was difficult. Her career meant so much to her.

"I hear you've talked to Kaely?"

Alex nodded. "Yes, she told me she's leaving the Bureau, decided she wants to get married, settle down, and raise kids. She's been through a lot and needs to make sure she's around for a while. I understand that."

"I'm glad. She was worried about telling you. She feels you've become good friends."

Alex smiled. "We have. She's a great agent and an even better person." She looked at Logan, who was wearing his poker face. Not that she'd ever played poker with him, but she could tell when he was trying to look innocent.

"Was that one of the items?" she asked Terry.

He nodded.

"And the other one?"

"I wanted to tell you this earlier. But after everything you'd been through, I had to make sure you were strong enough to hear what I'm going to tell you. I've already spoken to the rest of your unit. I hope you'll understand why I had to wait. We needed to be certain Bayne was no longer a threat." He took a deep breath. "I asked Logan to come with me for moral support."

Now she really was worried. "What?" She frowned at Logan. "What's going on?"

Terry hesitated. "We had no idea it was actually Cooper and Palmer, but we suspected that someone could be working with Bayne from inside the FBI. Turns out we made the right decision. If they had found out what I'm about to tell you, it would have put someone at great risk. Bayne would have done anything to destroy him. As you've seen personally, he didn't like failure. So being committed to keeping everyone safe, we decided not to take a chance by revealing the truth. I believe you'll understand."

He cleared his throat and looked at Logan, then back at her.

"Who?" Alex asked. "What are you talking about? Please tell me."

Terry took another deep breath, then said, "The night Jeff drove his car into the Potomac?"

She nodded.

"He survived, Alex. He was in bad shape for a while, but—"

"He . . . he what?"

Terry glanced at Logan.

"She's okay," Logan said. "Keep going."

Krypto jumped onto the couch next to her, and she put her hand on his head, reassuring him.

"When Jeff was pulled out of the water, the EMTs were sure he was dead," Terry said. "But in the ambulance, they detected a faint pulse and got him to the ER. We didn't think he was going to make it, but he held on. We decided we had to keep his recovery quiet, with the cooperation of not only his family but the hospital personnel. We told Logan, but only because he was acting unit chief."

"Think if Bayne had found out, Alex," Logan said. "He was determined to finish what he started. He would have tried to kill Jeff if he knew he'd survived."

She nodded. Terry was right, but she was having a hard time processing this news. "But how did Jeff stay alive after all that time underwater?"

"An air pocket in the car. But then he went into shock because of the cold water. It really was touch-and-go for a while. That's why I was genuinely emotional when I told you all he'd died. For all I knew then, he still could have."

"But he's all right now?"

Terry nodded. "He's fine. A little more time to recover physically and emotionally and he'll be back at work. He's working with some good doctors."

"Isn't it wonderful, Alex?" Logan asked.

"That's not a good enough word for it," Alex said with a smile. She realized tears were falling down her cheeks, but she didn't care. She silently thanked God for saving Jeff.

They talked for a while longer, and then when Terry left, Logan stayed behind. "I . . . I wonder if you'd like some company," he said. "I could hang around. Make dinner. Would that be okay?"

Alex dismissed all the casseroles in the fridge and smiled as Krypto barked and wagged his tail. "That would be great."

As Logan headed into the kitchen, Alex wrapped her arms around Krypto's neck and cried. She was already so grateful to God for saving her and Kaely. That Jeff was alive was almost too much for her to believe. "Thank you, God," she whispered.

The sound of a pan hitting the floor in the kitchen made her jump.

"Sorry," Logan called out. "Everything's okay."

Alex laughed, then wiped her eyes. She didn't have many visitors, but the man who was rattling around in her kitchen didn't feel like a visitor at all. He felt . . . different. As if he belonged.

She smiled to herself. This was a good day.

Acknowledgments

Thank you again to retired Supervisory Special Agent Drucilla L. Wells, Federal Bureau of Investigation, Behavioral Analysis Unit. I loved learning more about Hogan's Alley. You made it and the FBI Academy seem so real to me. You're awesome!

Thank you to Raela Schoenherr for letting me write this series and for allowing me to say good-bye to Kaely Quinn. And thanks once again to editor Jean Bloom. You made *Dead Fall* so much better.

Most of all, my thanks to the One who has allowed me to be me. I pray that something I write will touch hearts that need to know how wonderful You are. It will always be all about You. I love You so much.

Nancy Mehl is the author of more than forty books and a Christy Award and Carol Award finalist as well as the winner of an ACFW Book of the Year award. Her short story, *Chasing Shadows*, was in the *USA Today* bestselling *Summer of Suspense* anthology. Nancy writes from her home in Missouri, where she lives with her husband, Norman, and their puggle, Watson. To learn more, visit www.nancymehl.com.

Sign Up for Nancy's Newsletter

Keep up to date with Nancy's news on book releases and events by signing up for her email list at nancymehl.com.

More from Nancy Mehl

When authorities contact the FBI about bodies found on freight trains—all killed the same way—Alex Donovan is forced to confront her troubled past when she recognizes the graffiti messages the killer is leaving behind. In a race against time, Alex must decide how far she will go—and what she is willing to risk—to put a stop to the Train Man.

Night Fall • THE QUANTICO FILES #1

KAELY QUINN PROFILER
Series by Nancy Mehl

When an anonymous poem predicts a string of murders, ending with her own, FBI Behavioral Analyst Kaely Quinn is paired up with Special Agent Noah Hunter, who resents his assignment. But this brazen serial killer breaks all the normal patterns, and soon Noah and Kaely must race against time to catch the murderer before anyone else—including Kaely—is killed.

Mind Games

FBI profiler Kaely Quinn visits Nebraska to care for her ailing mother. She can't help but notice suspicious connections among a series of local fires, so she calls on her partner, Noah Hunter, to help find the arsonist. Together they unwittingly embark on a twisted path to catch a madman who is determined his last heinous act will be Kaely's death.

Fire Storm

When multiple corpses are found, their remains point to a serial killer with a familiar MO but who's been in prison for over twenty years—Special Agent Kaely Quinn's father. In order to prevent more deaths, she must come face-to-face with the man she's hated for years. In a race against time, will this case cost Kaely her identity and perhaps even her life?

Dead End

⬥ BETHANYHOUSE

More from Bethany House

When elite members of the military are murdered on the streets of Washington, DC, FBI Special Agent Bailey Ryan and NCIS Special Agent Marco Agostini must work together to bring the perpetrator to justice. As the stakes rise in a twisted conspiracy and allies turn to enemies, the biggest secret yet to be uncovered could be the end of them all.

End Game by Rachel Dylan
CAPITAL INTRIGUE #1
racheldylan.com

After Pearl Harbor, sweethearts Gordon Hooper and Dorie Armitage were broken up by their convictions. As a conscientious objector, he went west to fight fires as a smokejumper, while she joined the Army Corps. When a tragic accident raises suspicions, they're forced to work together, but the truth they uncover may lead to an impossible—and dangerous—choice.

The Lines Between Us by Amy Lynn Green
amygreenbooks.com

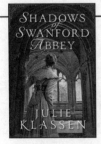

In pursuit of an author who could help get her brother published, Rebecca Lane stays at Swanford Abbey, a grand hotel rumored to be haunted. It is there she encounters Sir Frederick—the man who broke her heart. When a mysterious death occurs, Rebecca is one of the suspects, and Frederick is torn between his feelings for her and his search for the truth.

Shadows of Swanford Abbey by Julie Klassen
julieklassen.com

◈ BETHANY HOUSE